A TIME TO FLEE

UNSEEN WOMEN OF COURAGE

A COLLECTION OF FOUR TRUE ACCOUNTS OF WOMEN BEHIND THE LINES IN EUROPE DURING WORLD WAR II

ANNIE
A HUNGARIAN HOLOCAUST NARRATIVE

ISABELLE
A FRENCH RESISTANCE STORY

JOA AND ENE
AN ESTONIAN REFUGEE JOURNEY

MARGARET
A DANUBE SWABIAN FORCED OUT OF ROMANIA

By

Betty J. Iverson

First published by AuthorHouse 05/07/04

ISBN: 1-4184-5833-3 (e-book)
ISBN: 1-4184-3902-9 (Paperback)

Library of Congress Control Number: 2003097853

This book is printed on acid free paper.

Printed in the United States of America
Bloomington, IN

PREFACE

These four accounts are of women of courage behind the lines in Europe during the second world war. They face various dangers including rape, arrest, starvation and death. While their stories and countries of origin are different, they all leave their homes and become rootless and homeless. To survive, they show astounding perseverence and cleverness. Each woman eventually feels she needs a new home, and a new country for the kind of life she wants to live. Surviving the fears, dangers, deprivations and obstacles, serves them well, for each has the courage to emigrate, to leave the known and embrace the unknown.

DEDICATION

I dedicate this book to my husband, Ted, whose unwavering support and computer expertise has enabled me to complete this book. I also thank my family for their ongoing support: Adriene, Allan and Michael Ann, Mark and Wendy, and Kent and Carol, and four wonderful grandchildren.

I also dedicate this book to the women who lived the stories: Annie Gabor Aroncio, Isabelle Auerbach Armitage, Ene Bonnyay and her mother, Joa and Margret.

ACKNOWLEDGMENTS

I wish to acknowledge with thanks and gratitude the talented readers and editors who took the time to read my book and make invaluable suggestions: Carol Collier, Henry Doering, Ene Bonnyay, Sheila Bruce, and Bill and Donna Sumner. I acknowledge, too, Isabelle's daughter, Agnes, who was unfailingly helpful and supportive.

I appreciate the hours spent translating French by friends Eva Kershaw, Suzie Lescure and Marina Sportes'. I appreciate the ongoing support and help of my friend, Jean Somerset.

CONTENTS

ANNIE

ISABELLE

JOA AND ENE

MARGRET

PROLOGUE: ANNIE

We are in a reflective mode today. I feel it is very important to document what happened to us in the Second World War, so that events are not buried with the passage of time. Lily, our rescuer, and I were interviewed in Hungary, and the tape will be shown to children in school there.

When Betty asked about writing my story, I agreed. As we met together, the floodgates of my memories were opened to produce this narrative which she then crafted into words in a way I could not have done.

My daughter, Vicky recently spoke at the Bat Mitzvah of my granddaughter, Rebecca. In her speech, she commended Lily Kriszhaber, the woman who hid my mother, my sister and me in Budapest during the Second World War:

"In the Shabbat service, we are told you shall not stand idle while your neighbor bleeds." The first thing I want to say is that we would not be here without a woman in Hungary who did not stand idle. In 1944, Lily Kriszhaber risked her life to hide your

Grandma Anne, Great aunt Vali and Great Grandma Rose from the Hungarian Nazis. I want to acknowledge Lily, who is 89 years old, and still alive and well in Budapest. Although she could not travel here today, she is with us in spirit. Lily is a woman who went above and beyond the Ten Commandments in her courage to do what was right. When we look at you today, Rebecca, we are forever grateful to Lily Kriszhaber, a Righteous Gentile. That is why your Bat Mitzbah, your spiritual rite of passage is dedicated to Lily."

When I sent Vicky's Bat Mitzvah speech to Lily in Budapest, she showed it to her cardiologist, who said, "This is worth more than any monument." This story is our family's monument to Lily. I dedicate it to her.

Anne Gabor Arancio

When I first met Annie, she mentioned spending the end of the war in a wine cave in Budapest. I have had an abiding interest in World War II narratives and filed that comment away in my mind. When I contacted Annie, she agreed to tell her story. I did not know what to expect and was amazed as her powerful Holocaust experience unfolded. Her story is one you can wrap your heart around. I felt a deep admiration for Annie's spirit, her mother's wisdom, her sister's courage and Lily's compassion and bravery. Writing Annie's story was a joy.

Betty J. Iverson

ONE: Upheaval

"Christ Killers, Christ Killers," the taunt rang out. Annie felt the pelt of snow balls on her backpack. The attacks were becoming more frequent. She looked around, but did not see anyone. Annie really didn't expect to because the attackers usually hid or ran. I wonder if they are boys or girls, she mused. The taunts both hurt her and made her angry. It's just not fair, she thought.

"Hurry Vali," she called to her sister over her shoulder as she ran. "Let's head for the square." Glancing back at Valerie, Annie noticed the tears on her sister's cheeks, and spoke to reassure her. "You mustn't let them upset you. We didn't do anything wrong."

"I know, I know," said Valerie. "It's just that my leg hurts when I run."

Annie nodded. She knew that her sister had constant pain in her right leg since she'd had a bone infection two years ago. An infection that never went away. Annie was protective of her younger sister, even though Valerie was only a year younger. Vali, as everyone called her, was a pretty girl of eight with even features, blue eyes and long thick blond braids. Her hair was so curly, ringlets formed around her head, even with the tightly woven braids. Annie smiled to herself as she thought that, although Vali was pretty, and considered the brain in the family, she, Annie, was known as the beauty. Blonde, with hazel eyes and high cheek bones, Annie's beauty rested more in her precocious spirit than in her looks. She was quite slim, a fact that worried her Grandmother Ida. "You're so skinny, I could thread you through the eye of a needle," she often told her.

Annie and Vali were on their way home from school at the synagogue courtyard, a one room school where all the classes met together. They didn't mind the long walk through the village, but they hated the insults. The taunts today were frightening but not uncommon. In this village of only twenty-six thousand people, Annie and Vali knew those areas where Jews were not welcome and carefully avoided going to them. Gyula's diverse populations resided in sections such as German town, Swabian town, and Romanian town. Annie and Vali never ventured into these areas. While the Jewish people were not segregated, they were easily identified. In fact, since Annie and Vali's grandmother owned a fabric store, she was well known and thus the girls could be a visible target. The snow ball attack today was on a street they considered safe. Annie was puzzled about who might have followed them.

Gyula was the only village Annie and Vali had ever known. Their family had lived there for generations. This town, a county seat in Hungary on the Romanian border, was a commercial center for all the peasant farmers in the countryside. The tallest building in town, the city hall, was only three stories high. The Koros River wound through the town like a gurgling stream through the flat terrain. There were picnics along the banks in the summer and ice skating when it froze in the winter.

Annie and Vali stopped running once they reached the village square and collapsed on a bench next to the Reformed Church. The Catholic Church sat across the square. Resting on the bench, Annie thought about all the changes in their lives in such a short time. She and Vali lived with their Grandmother Ida and Uncle Laci, while their mother, Rose lived in the capital, Budapest. Their lives had changed dramatically when their father died two years ago.

Annie had adored her father, Emery. She was only seven at the time he died. She still thought of him every day, and images of her father tumbled constantly through her mind. Annie could see him now, the thoughtful attorney, dressed in his finest suit, standing tall in front of the hall mirror as he brushed his thinning dark hair. He looked elegant on those days when he went to court. She would never forget his look of pride when she first beat him at chess, or his encouragement as he ran alongside her bike holding onto the seat when he taught her to ride a two-wheeler. These images often brought tears to her eyes. He was never too busy for her or Vali. No one suspected then that within his chest beat a weakening heart.

When her father complained of vague chest pain, her mother had insisted that he go to Budapest to see a specialist. Tests were done, and he was told that he had angina pectoris, a heart condition related to an old war injury. He came home with pills to take when the pain returned.

Annie was troubled each time he became short of breath by just the slightest exertion. When they walked under the chestnut trees in the People's Park in Gyula, he often stopped to rest. The cane he had seldom used soon became his constant companion.

Her last picture of her father was of him standing on the bridge over the frozen river looking on proudly as Annie skated. She glanced up and waved, and he waved back. He stood there so long his feet were frostbitten by the end of the afternoon. How she loved him and longed for the way things used to be. The days when she and Vali lived with him and their mother, Rose. They would be at Grandmother Ida's house just once a week for family dinners, not all the time as they were now.

While she and Vali rested on the bench, Annie remembered her father and how quickly he was gone. That day was painfully etched in her memory. She and Vali were at school, when a boy ran into their classroom yelling, "Annie. Vali. Come home. Your father just died."

Numb with shock, Annie and her sister, tears streaming down their cheeks, rushed to the back of the room to grab their coats from the hooks on the wall. They hurried home, but were met by a neighbor, who told them they couldn't go in. Their mother came to the door then and said, "You must stay with Grandmother Ida for a few days."

"What happened to Papa? Why can't we come in?" Annie asked through her tears.

Rose calmly explained to Annie and Vali that their father had collapsed as he presented a case in court that morning. Efforts to revive him had failed. Rose's voice cracked, and she fought back tears as she murmured, "He said good bye to us this morning, like an ordinary day. Then they brought him home to me, dead."

Her shoulders shook with the sobs she could no longer contain. Annie and Vali clung to their mother. Annie asked her mother again if they could go inside, but she shook her head.

The next day, Annie and Vali were taken to their home to view their father's body laid on a bed of straw in the living room. They were ushered out before the funeral service began. Annie pleaded with her grandmother to allow them to stay.

"No," Grandmother Ida said firmly, "This is the custom. Children in our family do not go to funerals."

Three days passed before Annie and Vali were allowed to return home. Annie stared at the empty bed of straw in the living room, with the imprint of her father's body still on it. She had an eerie feeling as she saw so vividly the contours of his body.

Annie could not believe that her father was gone. She wandered into his study and sat at his desk. She waited for him to come home in the evening, and longed for the sound of his footsteps on the stairs, or the scent of soap as he bent to kiss her. Annie had seen her father's body on that bed of straw, yet she pretended that was only a bad dream. Soon he'd be back with them.

But her father's death became more real to her each day as she watched her mother observe the Jewish custom of Shiva. Rose, dressed in black, sat on a low bench, and greeted the friends and relatives who came by to express their condolences. She sat on that bench for a week. Annie's mother's tears flowed freely then, but once the Shiva had ended, she dried her eyes. Rose was no longer a teary woman, but instead one who was sad yet determined.

Rose observed the usual one year of mourning, and during this time she designed and placed the tombstone on her husband's grave. Annie recalled all the gossip about this. A woman designing a tombstone? No woman had ever done this before. Her mother was creative and artistic but nonchalant about gossip. Rose ignored the whispers. When the tombstone was placed, Annie was awestruck by the beauty of this simple marble piece inscribed with a carved replica of her father's medal of honor. She knew he had been highly decorated for bravery in World War I. Her mother's creative bent was shown in the lovely marble jardiniere with claw feet placed on the top of the marble slab. She often went with her mother to fill it with flowers.

When her year of mourning ended, Rose left for Budapest to establish herself as a dressmaker. Annie and Vali, who were now ten and nine, moved in with Grandmother Ida.

Annie's reverie was interrupted by a tug on her sleeve as Vali said, "My leg isn't hurting anymore. Can we go home now, Annie?"

"You sure you're feeling okay, Vali?"

Vali nodded. "I'm all right now." She stood up. "We don't want to be too late or grandmother will worry."

Annie stood up and helped Vali put on her backpack. As they strolled along, Annie thought of Grandmother Ida Brill, a strong, smart woman, who was stocky and big busted with light brown hair and a formidable expression, until she smiled. Grandmother Ida had been widowed in her thirties with five children to rear. She established a fabric store to support her family and proved to be a shrewd businesswoman. Ida was fiercely proud of her success and of her children.

Annie's mother, Rose, was the third child and sixteen when her father died. She had eloped with an artist at nineteen, but soon divorced him and later married Annie's father. Ida's oldest son, Emery, a university graduate, lived in Budapest with his wife and son, Gabor (Gabriel). Gabor was one of Annie's favorite cousins. The oldest daughter was Manci (Margaret), a jolly woman whom Annie adored. Manci lived in the village with her husband and two sons. The youngest daughter was Kati (Kathleen), whom Annie thought was very beautiful. Laci (Laszlo), was the last of the siblings and a bachelor who lived with his mother. He had a reputation in the village as a ladies' man.

Annie didn't mind that Laci ignored her and Vali. In fact, she and her sister found Laci rather amusing, especially when he wore an elastic hairnet at night. He looked so ridiculous. Annie had never seen anything like that hairnet, except in Italian films.

Annie loved her grandmother, but wished she wasn't so overprotective. Grandmother Ida took her responsibility to care for them quite seriously, Annie thought. Still, Annie missed her mother and longed for the day when she and Vali could join her in Budapest. Annie knew her mother would be a successful couture. She was also proud that her mother was not only smart but attractive. She could picture her slim figure, oval face, curly brown hair and sparkling brown eyes.

People often told Annie she was like her mother. While she admired her mother, she did not want to be working in a trade like her mother did. Annie's dream was to go to the university and study many subjects from people to art. She believed that Hungarian saying, "A specialist is a Barbarian." Annie wanted to know about many things. Yes, she would be an educated woman.

Although she could not visit often, Rose wrote letters to Annie and Vali. She told them about all the remarkable things she was learning from the best teacher in Budapest to her trips to Paris for the fashion shows. "I've become quite good at copying some of the outfits I've seen there," she wrote. Annie thought her mother's life sounded very exciting.

When Rose left, she had hired a governess for Annie and Vali, since Ida was busy at the store. Annie smiled as she recalled the succession of governesses. She loved the first girl from Germany, who came to teach them German, but instead learned Hungarian.

The second governess was Hungarian and she and Vali loved her, too. Unfortunately, so did Uncle Laci, and that governess left when she became pregnant. After that, Ida decided they could manage without a governess. Annie and Vali were often at the fabric store with their grandmother on Saturdays.

Annie and Vali arrived home at dusk. Much to Annie's relief, Grandmother Ida did not scold them for being late. She simply told them that dinner was on the table, adding, "Uncle Laci won't be joining us this evening."

Annie wondered why her grandmother even mentioned that. Uncle Laci rarely joined them for dinner, usually spending the evening at the Grill, a local bar in the village. Laci was called "Grill Brill" because he spent so much time there. He seldom came home before two in the morning when she and Vali were already asleep. Annie knew this because he awakened her sometimes with his loud singing, usually something from a Hungarian opera like, "I'm pining after a woman, and I can't hold myself back. Desire is pushing me." Annie would roll over and cover her head with her pillow as she dozed off, laughing, imagining that hairnet on Uncle Laci's head.

While they ate their soup, Grandmother Ida mentioned how busy she was in the store. "I'll need you there early tomorrow, Anniko and Vali. Saturday is the county market day and I expect many "paraszts" (peasants) will be coming to the village."

Annie nodded. She enjoyed working at the store. Vali went along, but usually did not help much, since her painful leg would not tolerate the brisk pace

11

and hours of standing. She often took a book along and read in the back room.

Grandmother Ida's shop, located on the bank of the river, was the most elegant in the village. More importantly, the store was on the road leading to the large plaza where the weekly markets were held. The "paraszts," who grew their crops on the lands owned by large land owners, brought their produce and wares to sell at the market. Many of them stopped at the fabric store to shop.

Annie and Vali left early the next morning with their grandmother. The day was cool and rainy, and Grandmother Ida worried that many of the peasants would stay home. "They still have their produce to sell, Grandmother," observed Annie. "Besides, the stalls are covered. If they get too cold, they'll be glad to come into the store and get warm."

"Oh Anniko," said Ida. "You're always the optimistic one. I hope you're right."

Annie loved working with all the fabrics at the store which came in large bolts and were stacked on shelves against the wall. Grandmother Ida traveled to fairs in Dresden and Vienna where she selected the best fabrics. On one of her trips, she had bought beautiful dolls for her granddaughters. Her doll was one of Annie's prized possessions because it represented travel and beautiful fabrics. One of Annie's jobs was to keep the bolts neatly stacked according to color and type of fabric. Today was no exception, and she straightened the messy shelves as soon as she saw them.

While Vali headed to the back room, Annie found the large boxes of babushkas and arranged a display of them on a table. The babushkas of blue and white were an everyday head covering for the women. Blue dye was plentiful and stylish. Babushkas woven of wool in a Turkish motif were more elegant, and customers bought these to wear on Sundays or special occasions.

Annie greeted the first customer of the day, a young paraszt woman, who asked about fabric for a dress. She knew this woman would not be interested in silks or brocades but some of the simple cottons. Chatting pleasantly, she learned the woman was pregnant and needed a wardrobe to accommodate her expanding figure. Annie reached up and took from the shelf several bolts of cotton materials in plain colors without a pattern. She took the first bolt in her hand, and unwound the light blue material, gathering the fabric in her hand to show the young woman how the material would drape on her figure. Soon Annie had made her first sale of the day. The young woman also bought a blue and white babushka. Business was brisk, and the day went quickly.

"You were right, Aniko," said her grandmother, later. "Business was good today."

Annie said, "Yes, I had fun. I love looking at all those fabrics on the shelf and imagining the kind of a dress I could make." Her grandmother was the only one who called her Aniko, a term of affection. Annie liked that.

Market day ended, and Annie strolled home with her sister and grandmother. Her grandmother's house was a large U-shaped one story corner house. Corner houses were considered the most impressive of all in the village. The house was actually divided into four apartments. Besides her grandmother's apartment, there were three others, all rented to tenants, one of whom was a judge. Annie knew how proud her grandmother was of her house, her beautiful store and the fact that she was a "Virilist," or large taxpayer.

Ida Brill's three bedroom apartment was spacious and nicely furnished, but since the building was old, there was no indoor plumbing. The bathroom was a latrine in the bed room across from the kitchen.

When Annie and Vali arrived home, they found a letter from their mother waiting for them. She wrote that now she was as well-known in Budapest as some coutures were in Paris. When she moved to Budapest in 1934, Rose felt that business there would continue as usual, despite some antisemitic laws after the World War I, including restrictions on Jewish admissions into the universities. She chose to ignore all the many exclusionary laws. Rose believed she would not be affected because she was a crafts person. "Those of us in the crafts industry have a special place in Budapest. And see, I was right. My business is going well, and no one has bothered me." Rose ended her letter with an exciting announcement, "I have arranged for you girls to go to a summer camp on the Danube River for a month.

Annie and Vali read their mother's letter over and over. Although she visited them two or three times a year, they wanted to live with her. Still, camp offered a different experience from the village.

Their two weeks at the camp passed by quickly. The camp was actually a compound of homes arranged in a circle around a large lawn, which Anna, the camp director had rented for the summer. Anna was a physical education teacher, who taught the girls all sorts of sports from volleyball to ping pong. Annie and Vali shared a bedroom in one of the homes and ate all their meals with the other girls at large tables set up on the lawn. This was the first time Annie had ever mingled with the more sophisticated upper and middle class city girls. She found it stimulating. She liked the fact that the camp not only taught sports, but encouraged intellectual pursuits such as poetry readings and singing folk songs when they hiked. Camp was Annie's first exposure to Hungarian writers and music. Anna told them that the folk songs had been collected by the great Hungarian composers, Bartok and Kodaly.

While Annie made friends easily with the city girls, she was conscious of still being a village girl. She hoped that this experience would prepare her for the day when she moved to Budapest. Perhaps she'd even go to the gymnasium with some of these girls. Going to camp became an annual summer event, and Annie and Vali looked forward to it. While Vali could not manage all the sports or the strenuous hiking, she loved the singing and the poetry reading.

When Annie was ten, she transferred to the middle school, a public school for girls. She had always gone to the synagogue with her male cousins, but now they, too, went to another school, a Catholic gymnasium. Annie walked a different route to school which wound through the town square. She often encountered a friendly Catholic priest, who always smiled a cheerful, "Good Morning." She felt accepted by him, but the Orthodox priest frightened her. He either ignored her completely or greeted her with the sign of the cross. The friendly Catholic priest, Abor, impressed Annie, and she was surprised to learn that he was a baron from a wealthy, influential family, whose brother was the ambassador to Rome. She couldn't imagine why a baron would choose to become a priest.

One day when Annie returned home from school, her grandmother greeted her with the news, "Your mother is coming for a visit. She'll be here tomorrow afternoon on the Penny Train."

"I can't wait to see her," said Annie. She had been thinking it had been a long time since her mother's last visit. She knew her mother always visited when the train fares were the lowest. "Does Vali know yet?"

"Yes she does," said Ida. "And she's as excited as you are. We'll leave early tomorrow so we can greet her when she arrives."

Annie smiled at her grandmother's words. Her mother's arrival always set off a stir of excitement through the village. Whenever people heard Rose was coming, they would line the road leading to the train station just to see her in one of her latest fashions. Rose always brought a bit of the outside world to Gyula. Who could predict what she would be wearing

16

this time? Annie could hardly contain her curiosity and excitement.

The next morning, Annie and Vali stood along the road with the other villagers. Suddenly they heard the whistle of the train and soon spied their mother walking down the road. She looked like a model in a fashion show with her slim figure and shapely legs. Rose was wearing a purple velveteen dress with a peplum, a short flounce that attached to her waist and flowed down over her hips. Her outfit was completed by a matching velveteen hat and high heels. The hat was huge, and a creation to behold with humming birds nesting in velveteen. Annie was so proud. Not only had she never seen high heeled shoes before, but she guessed that most of the people of Guyla hadn't either, nor French fashions for that matter. Her mother looked like a Paris lady. A soft murmur spread through the crowd as Rose passed by. Annie heard comments, "Look at that hat? Did you ever see such a thing? And Rose, she looks taller, don't you think?"

Annie and Vali broke away from the crowd and ran to hug their mother. "Oh my darlings, how I've missed you," Rose cried, as she bent to hug them.

Annie watched as her grandmother hugged her mother. Ida waited until they arrived home, before she began to ply her daughter with questions about the business. Rose threw her hat on the couch and sat down, looking about the familiar room she remembered so well.

She spoke about her many clients and growing business. "I've had to add two more seamstresses," she said.

Ida nodded approvingly. After a few minutes, however, Rose stood up and walked about the room and rearranged the chairs and moved the couch, as Ida and the girls watched. "The room looks better this way, mother," she said by way of explanation.

"Rose, Rose," said Ida. "Must you always rearrange my furniture the minute you get here? You're like a hurricane. I think I'll call you, "Hurricane Rose."

Annie and Vali giggled at their grandmother's words. While Ida was clearly irritated, their mother was oblivious, as if creativity granted her privileges. Rose's sense of confidence in her abilities had made her a successful designer, yet on occasions such as this her confidence annoyed her mother.

Finally, the day that Annie had been longing for, arrived. Her mother had reached a decision that would affect her and Vali. She was just fourteen and Vali, thirteen, when Rose called and talked at length with Grandmother Ida. When her grandmother handed the phone to Annie, she was elated to hear her mother say, "Your grandmother and I have discussed the matter. You and Vali are coming to live with me in Budapest because I can now support you. I'm so happy we'll be together again."

Annie had not seen her mother since she had created such a stir in the village with her new Paris outfit. She closed her eyes to recall her mother in that dress with the peplum. Annie said laughingly, "You know that outfit you wore the last time you were here?'

Rose paused and said, "You mean the purple one?"

"That's the one," said Annie. "Well the judge's wife had the dress copied. She's so fat that she looked like a sausage in a long pebble velveteen dress with a fox trimmed peplum. You would've loved to have seen her."

"I'm not so sure about that," laughed Rose. "I'll send for you as soon as I can arrange everything."

When Annie hung up the phone, she noticed the fleeting expression of sadness on her grandmother's face. She had not considered that her grandmother would miss them. She hugged her and said, "Don't worry, Grandmother, we'll visit often. And you can come to Budapest to see us. Won't that be grand?"

Ida nodded, forcing a smile. "Yes, it will, Annie. That will be grand, indeed. And remember, even though you're with your mother, I'll still buy you luxuries."

Annie smiled. She knew that she was special to Ida because she was so much like her. Vali was quiet and rather sickly, while Annie was outgoing like her grandmother. Yes, Annie understood the emptiness that lay ahead for her grandmother.

TWO: Yellow Stars

It was September 1940. Annie was excited as she and Vali followed their mother up the stairs to her second floor apartment in Pest. The apartment was in an old stone three-story building that enclosed a courtyard. On the ground floor were shops, with steps leading up to the apartments. The building had been designated as a national monument, since Jacob Marastomi, founder of the first Hungarian Art Academy, had lived here from 1846-1860. The building was near the Danube River in the downtown area of Pest, the flat spread out section of Budapest.

Annie stared at the aged stone houses of Buda rising high in the hills on the opposite side of the Danube River. She vowed to walk there soon, since she had heard that Buda was very lovely. Their particular apartment was also near the Dohany Street Synagogue, rumored to be the largest one in Europe. While Annie's family observed Jewish customs, they seldom went to services. She wondered if she'd ever have a chance to see this Reformed Synagogue, where women entered on the lower floor and sat apart from the men.

Although her mother had carefully planned how to accommodate both her daughters and her business in her two bedroom apartment, the place felt crowded to Annie. The salon, or living room, was the fitting room for Rose's clients during the day. A bedroom had been converted into a workroom. There were six seamstresses and apprentices who were kept busy sewing during the work day.

"These girls make all the dresses, including the evening dresses," Rose said. "But I send the suits and coats out to a tailor. Sometimes, I use a furrier to add the trim."

Annie was impressed with all the business activities in the apartment. "But where will Vali and I sleep?" she asked.

Rose led them to the second bedroom, where she had placed daybeds for them. Annie nodded approvingly. She and Vali then followed their mother down a wide hall to the kitchen. As they walked through the hall, Rose explained that this was where she slept, and Annie noticed a small sleeper couch, placed against one wall next to a ceramic stove.

"Now I'll introduce you girls to a very important person, our maid, Juli," Rose said as she opened the kitchen door. Juli, a tiny apple cheeked woman in her early thirties with a broad smile, came forward to welcome Annie and Vali. She had been stirring a richly fragrant stew in a soup kettle on the large iron stove. She beamed when Annie asked for a taste.

"Delicious," Annie said as she handed the spoon back to Juli. Annie looked around the kitchen, noticing the large basket of wood next to the stove. The room felt warm and cozy to her.

"Juli will need your help every day, Annie, to get the wood," said Rose." We need lots of wood for all our stoves. Besides this stove which burns wood for cooking, there is one in the bathroom to heat the water, and three ceramic stoves to heat the apartment."

Rose then pointed out the small bedroom next to the kitchen where Juli slept. Their mother had saved the best for last, the spacious bathroom with a claw footed tub. Annie had never seen such a large bath tub. Above the tub Annie saw a huge stove for heating the water. "I can't wait to have a bath in that tub with lots of hot water," Annie said, longingly. She thought to herself, that not only was the tub wonderful, but to have a bathroom indoors was perhaps the greatest luxury of all.

Rose smiled, "Hot water is precious, Annie. Most likely, a hot bath will be a Sunday treat for the three of us," she said. Annie and Vali walked around the apartment for one more look and pronounced it perfect.

The next morning at breakfast, Rose said, "We must continue your education, Vali. I've arranged for you to finish eighth grade and then continue at the gymnasium. First, however, I will take you to a doctor to see about your leg."

Annie waited expectantly for the announcement that she also would be going to the gymnasium. Instead her mother turned to her and said, "Annie, you will stay here with me and become one of my apprentices."

"What?" Annie could not believe her mother's words. "But I want to go to the gymnasium, too, like Vali. I don't know anyone who hasn't finished the gymnasium." Tears rolled down her cheeks. She realized, even at fourteen, that she was going to become a working crafts person and be pushed down to the lower class. She felt devastated as she realized her dream of advanced education was being snatched away.

"Annie, Annie," Rose said calmly. "There's an exclusionary law now. Soon, Jews will probably be excluded from the university. By the time you finished the gymnasium in another four years, you wouldn't be able to go to the university anyway." Her mother patted her hand as she said softly, "Having a trade will be good for you. You never know when it will be useful."

Annie sensed her mother had made a firm decision, and it would be useless for her to argue further. She sighed and decided to make the most of the opportunity to become involved in the fashion business with her mother.

Rose then turned to Vali, "We will see a specialist this week," she said.

Vali nodded in agreement, saying, "My leg still hurts, but not as much. Do I really need to see a doctor?"

"You've had that infection for too long. Now that you're here in Budapest, we will get treatment for it."

Vali looked scared and Annie moved closer and hugged her. "This is wonderful, Vali. Just think you will be able to run again without limping or pain."

Annie was glad her sister would finally see a specialist. Back in the village, the only doctor they knew was their uncle who had been married to Emery's sister. While he was nice enough, he lacked the knowledge of Budapest physicians.

When Rose took Vali to the doctor, Annie went along. She watched as the doctor asked questions and examined Vali. He also took an x-ray and prescribed a new medicine for Vali.

"Your daughter has osteomyelitis, and she will need to rest in bed for a year," he told Rose.

"A whole year?" Annie blurted out.

Her mother frowned at Annie, as she said to the doctor. "Of course, I'll see to it that she rests. Can she be up at all?"

"For short periods, only," the doctor replied. "That bone needs rest to heal."

Vali accepted the doctor's order without complaint. She spent most of her days in bed.

The school provided a tutor, who came to the apartment to help her with her studies. Annie was proud of her sister's patience, and knew that she would not have been so resigned if she had been the one in bed all the time. At the end of that year, Vali's leg was healed, and she was free of pain for the first time in years.

Annie proved to be an invaluable assistant to her mother. She enjoyed shopping for all the materials, accessories and fur. Her experience in her grandmother's store had given her an experienced eye for fabrics. She learned quickly, and her mother entrusted her with more responsibility. Annie took over the billing and kept a file on the clients. Most of all, she enjoyed helping her mother with the fittings. She was impressed by her mother's skill, as she watched her fit each client with a flattering style for that particular woman's figure. Many of her mother's clients were prominent women and some were also good friends. While Annie and Vali read or played games in the evening, Rose would be busy designing or bent over a sewing machine to finish a project.

As part of her training, Annie went to a school for apprentices twice a week. These classes were held in a school nearby in the late afternoon after the regular students had left. Annie felt degraded that first day when she walked into the classroom. An unpleasant odor hit her nostrils as soon as she opened the door. The room was filled with peasant girls. "These girls are here to improve themselves by learning a trade," Annie fumed to herself. Now I'm just like them. I've not only lost my dream of going to the university, but I'm a peasant, too. She swallowed hard as a wave of self pity swept over her.

Annie turned to leave when she spotted a young girl sitting alone on a bench who was dressed like she was. Annie walked over quickly and sat down next to her. As they talked and compared notes, Annie learned that this girl, Judi, was in a similar situation. Judi's mother had also told her she should learn a trade. Her father was in England, but her mother had remarried. After that first day, Annie and Judi always sat together and became close friends.

Judi lived in a penthouse apartment across the park from Annie's apartment with her mother and step-father and her grandparents. She invited Annie to a party soon after they met. Annie was very excited as she suspected boys might be invited, too. She dressed carefully in a simple blouse and plaid skirt. Her heart was pounding as she rang the bell and was admitted by a formal butler in a tuxedo. Judi came forward to greet her and then took Annie about the room, introducing her to the boys and girls, as well as her mother and stepfather. "Mother, this is my friend, Annie, I told you about from the class. Remember?" Judi said.

"Oh yes, indeed," said Judi's mother, smiling warmly. "I'm so glad Judi has a friend like you, Annie, to sit with in class."

"Oh I feel the same way about Judi," Annie replied. "I couldn't bear the classes without her."

Judi walked away to greet more arrivals and Annie looked about the spacious room, noting the elegant furnishings. Judi looked very grown up today, Annie thought, with her blue silk dress and white lace collar. Suddenly, Annie was aware of her simple blouse and skirt. I feel like Cinderella, she thought, without any party clothes.

But she did not dwell on this as she enjoyed a violin solo by a boy who had arrived with his violin tucked under his arm. He played a Beethoven sonata and a Mendelssohn piece. Annie was very impressed. She had never been exposed to social life like this and vowed she'd have a party dress for the next occasion.

After all, my mother is one of the best coutures in Budapest, she thought.

Annie became more accepting of the apprentice program after Rose's prediction that "soon no Jews would be allowed at the University at all" came true. An exclusionary clause, "numerous clausus" was put into effect, which meant that even the small number of Jews already at the university would have to leave. Jews were also barred from obtaining or renewing trade licenses. She speculated that this could affect her mother. Annie was even more alarmed when she heard that the government could take property with only minimal compensation.

A law was passed in 1920, which, for the first time in Europe, limited the number of Jewish students in higher education to 6 percent. (numerous clausus).

In 1938, the First Law on Jews stated that the proportion of Jews must be limited to twenty percent in the self-managed professions (doctors, lawyers, engineers, artists and journalists.) The law applied to the financial, commercial and industrial enterprises of a larger scale.

The Second law on Jews, passed in 1939, restricted the political and civil rights of Jews. They were forbidden to have state functions or work as artists. Teachers had to retire and their numbers were limited. This was the beginning of organized forced labor. (Special military service or conscripted.) They could not buy or sell property without permission, but had to sell at a set price if told to do so.

Grandmother Ida visited them less often in Budapest as her robust health began to fail. Annie missed her grandmother and their special shopping trips. When Ida seemed to be near death, Annie went to see her. She bathed her and massaged her feet, her way of showing her grandmother how much she loved her. When Ida died a few weeks later in 1942, Annie felt an enormous sense of loss.

Rose, Annie and Vali went back to Gyula for the funeral. All Ida's children and their families were at the funeral, except for Laci. They talked about the loss of their matriarch, who had been their strength.

Aunt Manci pulled Rose, Annie and Vali aside and explained that Laci, the fun-loving ladies' man had been sent to a forced labor camp in the Ukraine and was not allowed to return for his mother's funeral. "Not only that," continued Manci, "he just married and his new wife was too upset to come today."

Rose looked disturbed at Manci's words. "I'm so sorry to hear about Laci. I can't imagine him in a labor camp. We feel relatively secure in Budapest, but I wonder how long before there'll be more changes, even danger for us."

Manci nodded, a troubled expression clouding her usually jolly face. "Yes, I'm sure there are hard times ahead for all of us. Here in the country, we're an easy target, and I worry all the time about Martin and our two sons."

"How are things at the shop?" asked Rose. She knew that Manci had taken over the shop when their mother could no longer continue.

"Things seem to be going fairly well, although I can't travel outside Hungary to the fabric fairs. But I still manage to get enough materials here to stock the store."

A few months after the funeral, Manci called to tell Rose that because of the restrictions against Jews renewing their business license, she had gotten a strawman, a Gentile, who became the virtual owner of the business. "I had to put the agreement in writing," Manci told Rose. "And that paper gave everything away. I worry that I won't get the business back after the war. That shop has always been in our family. I'm glad mother wasn't here to see what has happened."

Rose consoled Manci, but she was more preoccupied with events in Budapest. She made a point to not only know what was happening, but also to tell Annie and Vali. Although Hungary was supposedly neutral, the country had declared war on the Soviet Union and the United States back in 1941. When she told her daughters this news, Annie asked if this meant they were partners with Germany? Rose could not answer her.

The Wannsee conference in Berlin decided upon the "final solution" of the problem: that is to exterminate the Jewish population of occupied territories. The legal equality of Jewish religion ceased to exist.

Rose had noticed more Jews escaping into Hungary from those countries that the Germans had overtaken. Since Hungary was not occupied by the

Germans, the refugees felt safe here. People passing through Budapest from Poland and Czechoslovakia talked about the atrocities in their countries, but no one mentioned extermination camps. Rose had met a wealthy Polish man, who was able to escape with his family because he was a jeweler and had the money to bribe officials.

Rose and Annie listened to the radio, but usually got news by the chain of whispers that swept through the Jewish community. Annie felt she was in the hub of things and was always on the alert for the latest information. When she stood in line at the shops, she kept her ears tuned in to the conversations around her. The more she learned, the more uneasy she felt. Where could they run if the Germans invaded Hungary?

Suddenly one day late in 1943, Rose's forewoman, Juci, who was in charge of the seamstresses, did not come to work. Rose, alarmed, made inquiries immediately because Juci had told her a few days earlier she had been called into the Hungarian Police Headquarters. Although she was Jewish, Juci hadn't been worried. She considered the call a routine check.

When Rose and Annie went to Juci's home, they learned from a neighbor that she and her husband had been taken away by the Hungarian Gendarmerie, a cruel police unit. The neighbor heard that Juci's husband was Polish and didn't have the proper citizenship papers. He told them that he had watched from his window as the Gendarmerie led Juci and her husband out of their house. He then followed along to the train station and watched them being herded into train cars along with a crowd.

"The Gendarmerie were pushing and shoving this enormous group of people into train cars. There were old people, young people, even children. Those soldiers were packing them in so tight, I doubt anyone could sit down. I saw thousands of people. I heard they were headed for the Ukraine." He shook his head as he added, "Everyone sent there is slaughtered."

Annie and Rose hurried home in a state of shock. Juci and her husband were the first Jews they knew personally who were sent to be killed. Such disappearances now were no longer rumors. They had names and faces. A bad sign.

The situation grew worse. Manci called and told them that some of Annie's and Vali's cousins, including Gabor from Budapest, had been taken to Russia as forced laborers to dig ditches for the German Army. Annie was shocked and upset as she recalled how kindly cousin Gabor had taken her under his wing when she and Vali first arrived in Budapest. He had shown her all around Budapest, even taking her up to Castle Hill in Buda. Gabor also took her to see her first opera, "William Tell."

Annie had heard that the Nazi-Hungarians had begun sending Jewish company presidents and professors to the mine-planted front lines of Russia. If the Jews survived the sub-zero winters, they'd die when they stepped on one of the explosive devices. This was part of the Nazis' program to purge the Jews of intellectuals. Now the Hungarian anti-Semitic policies were affecting her family. Annie feared for her uncles and other cousins. Everyone was in danger.

Rose handed the phone to Annie, as she sunk down into a chair. Annie's fears increased as Aunt Manci continued. "I'm so sorry to tell you this, but you see, Gabor was sent to the Ukraine, where he escaped from the Germans. When those anti-Semitic Ukrainians caught him, they sent him back to the Hungarian troops, who wasted no time in shooting him, a man of only twenty-two." She shook her head. "Most of those Hungarians fighting with the Germans in Russia are Nazis. Every week, we hear of more cousins from the villages in Transylvania or along the Bavarian border who've been taken for forced labor and sent to camps. We hear that they go, but that's all. No one knows where. At least Emery, our brother, is still safe in Budapest."

Annie cried with sadness as she imagined Gabor being shot. She handed the phone back to her mother. Rose said to Manci, "We must be very watchful now. My forewoman and her husband were herded into train cars and sent somewhere. I don't want that to happen to me and my daughters."

Rumors swirled around like a dust storm. Annie listened as her mother had long chats with her special friend, Lily. She was one of Rose's first clients, and was a Christian woman, whose husband, Akos, was Jewish. Lily had always been Annie's favorite client among her mother's customers. She was like an aunt to her and Vali, and Lily always called her Aniko.

Annie never tired of hearing how Lily and Akos met.

Lily, a middle class typist, worked for Akos, a wealthy man and a leader in the Jewish community. While she found him a pleasant boss, she was shocked when he asked her out to dinner. Soon the business relationship led to love and then marriage. Akos could not do enough for his lovely wife. He told her, "I want my wife to be a well-dressed, stylish woman."

Lily took him at his word and made the rounds of all the coutures in Budapest, interviewing each one. Rose was wearing a lovely checked blouse, cleverly stitched so the checks on the sleeves matched the bodice, on the day Lily came to see her. That blouse was the deciding factor. She chose Rose and the women formed a close friendship of mutual trust and admiration. Lily respected Rose's business and fashion sense, while Rose admired how cleverly Lily had advanced in the company until she now held a responsible position.

On her last visit, Lily had said to Annie, "Please be careful when you go shopping for your mother. I think we are heading for some difficult times."

The hard times came soon enough with a phone call one Sunday afternoon in March 1944. Annie was relaxing with her mother and sister in their large bath tub when the sharp shrill of the telephone interrupted them. Juli, the maid, brought the telephone into the bathroom. The telephone was a large black one with a long cord and mounted on a wheeled table. Since Annie was closest to the door, she picked up the phone and heard the warning, "The Germans have crossed the border from Austria." The caller hung up.

"Mother, the Germans have crossed the border. They're here in Hungary," Annie said.

Rose quickly climbed out of the tub and stood dripping wet as she grabbed the phone. She called Manci in Gyula first, and then Kati, warning, "The Germans are coming. Head for the hills and hide."

Annie and her family were apprehensive, but remained in Budapest. Annie thought that it was bad enough what the Hungarians had done to the Jews. What would the Germans do? Additional sanctions were placed against the Jews with more stringent food restrictions, especially on sugar and goose fat, a local staple. Now when Annie went shopping, she had to stand in long lines because Jews were allowed to shop only during specified hours. For the first time, Jews had to wear yellow stars stitched on their clothing. Annie and Vali hated the sight of the large yellow stars on their coats. The curfew placed on the Jews did not bother them because they were fearful of being out on the streets anyway. Next, Jews were told to bring in their silver, gold and radios, an edict which Rose ignored. She kept her radio hidden.

In 1944, Hungary was occupied by German forces by March 19th. On April 5th the wearing of yellow stars became compulsory. Laws forcing the Jews into ghettos and limiting possession of radios, use of public baths, restaurants and bars was enacted on April 26th. Jewish author's works went out of print. On April 28th, the first freight train was sent to

Auschwitz with those deported. By June 17th, the Jews of Budapest had been moved to houses marked with a star.

Rose received a frantic phone call from Lily one evening, saying that her parents home had burned. Apparently the Allies had bombed the industrial section of Budapest where they lived. "Could you take them in for a couple nights, while I arrange housing for them?"

"Of course," Rose said without hesitation, as she agreed to take them into her already crowded apartment. "Bring them to me."

Annie and Vali moved out into the hall with their mother and gave Lily's parents their bedroom. Lily's parents were very grateful and left in a couple days after Lily found housing for them.

"Come to me, Rose, when you need to," Lily said as she took them away.

On Lily's next visit, Rose asked her to stay for a cup of tea. Annie brought in the tea and began to serve. Eager for news, Annie stayed as Rose began, "Lily, we all know that the Hungarian government is fascist, and, of course, so is our Regent, Miklos Horthy. Do you think he's the coward everyone says he is and will let the Arrow Cross push him around?"

"I would expect so, Rose," replied Lily. "I've heard that his wife is Jewish, but no one knows for sure. We all know some Jewish people who have been killed or deported, but at least Horthy has refused to allow large numbers of Jews to be deported, except for the conscripted men."

Rose nodded. "I know. Most of my cousins have been conscripted, and we have no idea what has happened to them. And now, Juci and her husband have been taken along with a large group. While I'm disgusted with Horthy, I feel more anxious about the "Arrow Cross." They might call themselves The National Socialist Party, but they're really Hungarian Nazis. I think they're nothing but a bunch of bloodthirsty hoodlums. And their leader, that Szalasi? I've heard that he's worse than Hitler. If he takes over from Horthy, I shudder to think what will happen to us."

"Mother, since Hungary has an alliance with the Axis, don't you think it's inevitable that the Arrow Cross soldiers will take over?" Annie asked. "I avoid them whenever I go out. They look so fierce. I certainly don't consider them our protectors, which is what they say they are. But they're not protectors, they're persecutors."

"I don't know what will happen, but there is a strong chance the Arrow Cross will have even more power than they have now," responded Rose. "I thought that alliance would protect us, but with the Germans in our country now, anything could happen. I'm sure Horthy does whatever the Germans tell him to do."

"Akos and I have talked about what to do when matters get worse," said Lily. "When that time comes, we will leave our house and move into a villa in Buda. When Otto returned to Germany, he told me we could stay in his villa if we needed to."

This was the first time Annie had heard Lily talk about a villa in Buda or Otto. "Who is Otto?" she asked.

"Otto was a German engineer, who worked with Akos at the textile mill. Occasionally I would work for him as his housekeeper. I still keep an eye on the place even though he's gone back to Germany. The villa would be a good place to hide Akos." Lily stood up, and said, "I must go now. I enjoyed the tea. Rose, let me know if you ever need help. You know how to reach me. Remember I'm your friend, and we'll get through this together."

That last conversation with Lily was uppermost in Annie's mind when in April the Germans decided to identify where the Jews lived in Budapest. The houses or apartments of the Jews were designated with yellow stars. Those Jews who did not live in a designated house had to move to one. Rose's apartment building was designated, and Annie watched as a big yellow star was painted on the door to the courtyard.

As soon as that star was painted, Rose's business ended. Her savings were now her only means of support. Not only that, other people moved into their building. Jews either moved to the ghetto around the synagogue or into one of the designated houses. Vali no longer went to the gymnasium. Life came to a standstill.

Annie and her family took in two couples, one young and one elderly. Their maid, Juli, had left, and Rose gave the young couple Juli's room. This couple stayed only a few days before they left and went into hiding. They were agreeable people, and Annie was sorry to see them go. She had never heard of anyone going into hiding and was curious about it. The older couple, an attorney, Dr. Weber and his wife, Agi, were given the seamstress' workroom. Rose moved in with Annie and Vali. Whereas the young couple had been pleasant, the Webers were difficult and demanding. Annie felt like she was a servant in her own apartment.

She avoided the Webers as much as possible and spent her days sitting on the steps of the courtyard, chatting with some of the new residents. Annie enjoyed meeting the artists and musicians who had moved in, and she became friends with a boy her age who later became a famous violin teacher. In the midst of this uncertain time, Annie found these newcomers stimulating, and a bright spot on an otherwise dull gray canvas.

Annie's mother became wary of the Jews being clustered in clumps. "I don't like the idea of my house being labeled," she said. "They could easily throw a grenade at our apartment building and kill us all at once. It's time to make a move," she told Annie and Vali.

Rose spoke with Lily, who had moved to the villa in Buda, where Akos went into hiding. "Can you find places for my daughters and me?" Rose asked her. "I feel we would be safer if we were not all in the same dwelling."

"Of course," Lily had replied. "Could I do anything less after what you did for my parents when you took them in? Besides, I couldn't bear it if anything happened to those precious daughters of yours, Rose. Give me a week, and I will have places for all of you." Lily promised. "I'd have you come here, Rose, but my brother and another soldier went AWOL from the Hungarian army, so I'm hiding them, too."

When Rose told Annie and Vali of her conversation with Lily, they were both excited. Annie felt that going into hiding would be an adventure, while Vali was anxious. They were both careful, however, never to talk about the plan to anyone, especially not the Webers.

The week went by swiftly for Annie. Her mother had purchased three Christian birth certificates. Annie stared at the piece of paper and her new name, Maria Debrecen from a village in Eastern Hungary. She did not like giving up her name, her identity, but accepted it. Vali took her Christian birth certificate without comment. She asked often, "What's going to happen to us?"

Rose told Annie she was not concerned about leaving behind her porcelain, the oriental rugs or any valuables. "As soon as we hear from Lily," she told her, "We'll walk out of this yellow star house."

THREE: Hiding

On September 10, 1944, Annie, her mother and sister tore the yellow stars off their clothes and left early in the morning before the Webers were awake. Annie had hardly slept the night before as she wondered where she would live and what the people would be like. Would she have to stay in the house all the time? As her mother had instructed, she took with her only a few clothes along with good shoes and knee socks. Vali had done the same.

Lily had found places for each of them. Annie would stay with Rinci, a Christian woman and colleague of Lily's, who lived with her son in a lovely section of Buda. Rose would be the housekeeper for a divorced Hungarian Army Air Force Captain, who Lily said would often be gone on flights. Valerie would be sent to Lake Balaton, to live with the ex-wife of this Captain. She was a Christian woman with a large family. Rose paid both families to take her daughters.

Annie felt secure and cared for with her new family. Rinci lived in a lovely furnished apartment in a modern section of Buda. Rinci was a pleasant woman, who adored her only son, Geza, and loved to cook for him. Annie enjoyed the fantastic meals. Rinci was quite nice to Annie, while Gaza never looked at her, much less spoke to her. She thought he was an unhappy young man who was always scowling. While Rinci treated her like a daughter, Annie had the impression she was also fearful that she would seduce her beloved son. She often told Annie not to be so theatrical.

When Annie left home with her few items of clothing, she had taken one extravagant item she could not leave behind: a black silk teddy with ecru lace. The teddy made her feel sexy and when she wore it, she felt like a woman. Annie had matured into a lovely young woman of seventeen with a fine figure and an ample bosom. The dangerous times had cheated her of normal teenage activities or dating. She often tried on her teddy in front of the mirror in her room as she dreamed of romance. One day while trying on her teddy, she heard a soft knock at the door and Rinci walked in. She looked shocked and said, "Annie. What are you doing? I think maybe it's not so proper for a seventeen-year-old to have such underwear."

Annie's cheeks burned with embarrassment as she muttered, "It's only underwear. Most girls wear this kind of underwear." Rinci is so tied to her small town roots, she thought as she quickly grabbed a blouse to slip over the teddy. She is not the sophisticated city woman that my mother is. Rinci had told her that she was a mining engineer's widow and had spent most of her life in small mining towns.

Annie reflected that perhaps Rinci thought she would try to seduce her son. She vowed to keep the teddy put away and murmured a soft apology.

While Annie felt secure in her situation, she was sorry to learn from her mother that Vali had called to say she was unhappy at Lake Balaton. Vali told Rose that she was treated like a servant, often scrubbing the floors and cleaning in addition to caring for the four children.

On the other hand, Rose and the captain, Gyorgy, got along well. As Lily had predicted, the captain was often gone on missions. Annie had met him only once, since Rose was fearful about her being in the apartment. Annie found him quite interesting with his flying stories and sense of humor. He was a large, stocky man, with bold features and blonde hair. He, of course, did not talk much about his work, other than to say that he was in the Hungarian Air Force and flew under Hungarian-German command. Annie was curious to know if he knew they were Jewish, since the Hungarian Air Force was known to be anti-Semitic and German sympathizing. The main thing the captain talked about the evening she had dinner with them was how much he enjoyed her mother's cooking.

Annie was walking back to Rinci's apartment one afternoon in October, 1944, when she saw German Panzers (tanks) on the street and heard a soldier, with an Arrow Cross on his sleeve, shouting, "From now on, all the Jews will be killed."

She was frightened seeing those tanks and feared that the Arrow Cross had been given free reign to terrorize the Jews. By this time, all the Jews were gone from the countryside, and the only ones left were in Budapest. Annie felt the noose tightening around her. She had heard that Horthy had tried to pull out of the Axis Alliance. Was this why there were tanks on the street, and soldiers shouting about killing Jews? Since the Russians had invaded from the East, she felt that now the Arrow Cross would move quickly to finalize what they considered the Jewish "problem" in Budapest. To make matters worse, the Jewish Ghetto was firmly established and even the people in the designated houses had to move there.

Annie knew that the ghetto was not safe. She was glad to be on the Buda side of the Danube. Just yesterday, she had heard the rumor that people were being lined up, shot, and thrown into the Danube. How horrible and barbaric she thought. To do such a thing here in the middle of the city with shops and restaurants all around. They aren't even trying to hide the slaughter. Those Arrow Cross Nazis had found a simple way to get rid of us without having to deal with our bodies. Are we animals? Is this what a civilized society does to its people?

What's next, she asked herself. Since the Russians are approaching our borders, the Nazis won't have enough time to organize a mass deportation. She understood that the Arrow Cross soldiers were avidly hunting down Jews. Annie had heard an even worse rumor that they often stopped men on the street and made them drop their pants. Any man who had been circumcised was shot on the spot. She hurried back to the apartment to call her mother.

Rose listened as Annie told her what she had seen. She sounded worried and warned Annie to stay put in the apartment. She then added, "I have a little job that will keep you there. The Captain just got back from a trip east, and he brought home a goose. I'll bring it over to you."

"What am I supposed to do with this?" asked Annie, when Rose handed her the live goose.

"Fatten it up" commanded Rose. "We'll have a feast of roast goose and foie gras."

So Annie put the goose on the balcony. Each day she held the goose under her leg and forced its mouth open as she stuffed in soft corn and gently massaged its throat to make the bird swallow the food. After a month of fattening, the goose was ready for roasting. The roast goose and foie gras were magnificent. Annie knew that this would be their last grand meal for a long time.

One day in November, Rose called Annie and said, "Vali was homesick, so I told her she could come for a short visit. Do you want to talk to her?"

"Oh, no, I want to come over, too. I want to see Vali again. I've missed her."

"I don't know," Rose hesitated. "I don't think it's a good idea for all of us to be together. It's a terrible risk."

Annie's pleading wore down her mother's resistance. Annie felt no qualms about boarding the bus to head for the Captain's apartment. When she boarded the bus, a peasant girl sitting there looked her over carefully.

"Wait a minute," she said loudly, as Annie walked past. "You remind me of Ann Gabor. Are you Ann?"

"Oh, no," Annie said. "I'm Maria, Maria Debrecen." While Annie had gotten used to her new name, this was the first time she had been confronted and actually used the name in public. She felt scared.

The girl continued to insist that she was Ann, but Annie became quite theatrical, insisting that no, she was Maria Debrezen. She mentioned her home was in a small village in eastern Hungary, naming a village the Russians had already taken. Finally, the girl appeared convinced. Although Annie did not recognize her, she was sure the girl was one of the students from the apprentice class.

Annie quickly sat down and stared out the window, her heart pounding with fear. When Annie told her mother what had happened, a worried frown crease Rose's forehead. "Let's not dwell on it now, Annie, but you really mustn't stay long."

They put worries aside and enjoyed their reunion. Annie and Vali chatted nonstop, comparing notes. The situation in Lake Balaton sounded even worse than Vali had first complained about. Yet, they weren't bothered by soldiers in the countryside at present, so at least Vali felt safe. "We shouldn't have to live like this too much longer," predicted Annie with an optimism she didn't feel.

When the Captain arrived, he spoke to Rose in whispered tones, and Annie watched as her mother nodded frequently, listening intently.

"Annie and Vali, the Captain needs our help," said Rose.

"I have just told your mother that I'm with a Resistance Group," he explained. "I need you to do something for me in the morning."

Annie had never heard that he was in a Resistance Group, and from the look on her mother's face, she guessed that she had not known this either.

The Captain went on to share his plan. "I must leave to parachute a man from the Resistance Group behind enemy lines in the morning. I'll be leaving very early, about two or so, Rose. I want you to give this packet of important papers to the Resistance person who'll be coming here about seven or eight in the morning. He will ring the bell twice." He handed the packet to Rose.

Rose nodded, and turned to Annie, saying, "You must go home now, Annie."

"But I don't want to, Mother. I want to stay and help," Annie pleaded, even offering to iron the Captain's shirts, so she could stay. The Captain wasn't concerned one way or the other whether Annie left or stayed.

Rose sighed, saying, "Well, you have your mind made up, I see. But I still don't like the idea of the three of us being here together." The Captain left as planned. Annie slept on the couch in the living room, while her mother and Vali slept in the bedroom.

In the morning, the bell rang twice and Annie hopped up to answer. A Hungarian Nazi soldier, Arrow Cross gleaming on his sleeve, barged in, roughly pushing her aside as he closed the door. "Who are you?" he asked. "I'm here to pick up Rose Gabor. She's been denounced as a Jew in hiding. We received an anonymous letter from a loyal citizen who tipped us off."

Annie was stunned and could only mumble, "I'm Maria, Maria Debrecen."

The ominous words, "A Jew in hiding," rang in her ears. Annie pondered the probability that someone had betrayed her mother. Only her mother's friend, Lily, knew where they were and Lily would never turn them in. They had told no one at the apartment where they were going. As Annie thought about the matter further, she remembered that right before they left, one of the seamstresses, Eva, dropped by the apartment. Her mother had always trusted Eva. When Rose mentioned some valuables, Eva offered that any valuables given to her, she would take to her family in the country for safe keeping. Since there was no danger of bombing and the family wasn't Jewish, Rose felt they would be safe. As wise as her mother was, Annie felt she was foolish for allowing Eva to visit her at the apartment. At least Eva hadn't known where she and Vali were. But that didn't matter now.

The Nazi soldier pushed past Annie and found Rose and Vali in the bedroom. Rose came forward quickly, saying that she was ready to go with him, adamantly denying that the girls were her daughters. Annie and Vali each gave their new Christian names.

"I'm Maria Debrecen," Annie shouted.

The Nazi soldier was not convinced as he insisted, "Come on, you're Annie."

"No, No, I'm Maria," Annie shouted.

"Shut up, you tiresome girl and get dressed. You're all coming to headquarters with me."

Vali turned pale and said nothing, but her lower lip quivered as if she would burst into tears any moment. They dressed quickly. There was no time to take anything, just the clothes they put on. After Annie dressed, she went into the bathroom to flush the packet of resistance papers down the toilet, fearing even more trouble if they were found. As her mother put on her high top shoes, laced up to her mid calf, she hid some gold coins in one shoe. Shaking her head sadly, she said, "It's the only time we were all together."

They had just gotten their coats on when the door bell rang again. This time it was the man from the Resistance. The Nazi soldier pulled him inside and arrested him, too.

"I'm taking all of you to headquarters," the soldier muttered "Move along quickly."

The soldier then marched them up and down the hills of Buda until they finally arrived at the headquarters, a fancy hotel on a hill. Annie felt like a fish caught in the Nazis' net.

FOUR: Capture

The Nazi soldier marched the Gabors and the messenger up the stairs into the hotel lobby, a large hall with stairs winding up to a balcony. Arrow Cross soldiers were milling about, and one came over to talk to their captor. After a whispered conversation, the soldier led away the Resistance man. Annie never saw him again. Their captor then shoved Annie, Vali and Rose into a large room down the hall from the lobby. Inside the room a dozen people stood in small groups, fear written on their faces. Annie heard moans and screams in the background which only increased her uneasiness. She glanced at Vali who was biting her lips and drooling bloody sputum. She was so pale, her eyes shone like large blue balls in a white mask.

Another Nazi officer arrived. He was rude and pushy as he took everyone's valuables. Rose was amused to receive a receipt for her watch and ring. "Do you think they'll really give them back to me later?" she whispered to Annie.

The officer asked Rose her name and she responded, "Rose Gabor." There was no point in pretending.

He looked thoughtful as he asked, "Was Emery Gabor your husband? Did he serve in World War I? Was he a high ranking officer?"

Rose nodded affirmatively to each question, hoping that her husband's decorated service in World War I might save her and her daughters.

"I was his adjutant in the war," the officer said his lips tight in a grim expression.

Unfortunately this strange coincidence did nothing to improve their situation. In fact, it made matters worse. The officer appeared so angry, that Annie feared he was going to hit her mother. In the last war he was my father's servant, she thought, but now he has the upper hand. I wonder what he will do to us.

The officer then summoned a young Arrow Cross soldier. "Take these women to the clothing room," he said tersely, "and make sure they leave their clothes there."

What now, thought Annie? What was this clothing room? The soldier led them to the room next door. She glanced at Vali, who was as white as snow, and then noticed that her mother also looked scared. Her mother was a person who could always handle any situation. Seeing her mother scared caused Annie to feel even more frightened. But she was determined that she would not let that Arrow Cross soldier see that she was scared. It's all over, she thought. We'll all be dead by morning.

The young Arrow Cross soldier looked them over and muttered, "Move quickly," as he led them to the room next door. He was a pimply faced young man, whose gaze focused on Annie, making her feel uncomfortable.

"Take off all your clothes and pick out new outfits from that pile over there," he said, pointing to an enormous heap of filthy clothes. Annie looked with disdain at the pile of clothes, thinking there was nothing wearable in that miserable pile. As she hesitated, the soldier strolled over and asked if she needed help. She shook her head. He wandered away, but kept his gaze fixed on her. Annie ignored him as she slipped out of her clothes and into a pair of pants, a wrinkled shirt and an old suit jacket with loose threads around the neck where a fur collar had been ripped off. She kept her shoes on. Once dressed, she felt dirty and itchy in her outfit. Annie felt hopeless but would not let the soldier suspect that.

Rose dressed carefully in an old frayed jacket and skirt, but also did not remove her shoes. Vali chose a pair of pants, a frayed sweater and a coat with large pockets. While they were dressing, the soldier pulled Annie aside and said, "If you come with me, I can see to it that you may be saved."

"But there are three of us," said Annie. "I wouldn't leave without my mother and my sister. Unless you take all three of us, I won't go."

"Foolish girl," he said with an angry sneer. "You missed your chance."

He took them back to the room and ordered the people there to follow him. He marched the entire group down the stairs into a basement. They joined more prisoners there. The young punk, as Annie now thought of him, barked a command, "Face the wall and raise your hands above your head."

Vali whispered to Annie that someone had put papers in her pocket, which she thought were American stocks and bonds. She was afraid to be caught with them. When Annie told Rose, she suggested that Vali wiggle around so the packet of papers would fall out of her pocket, and she could kick them away. Vali wriggled about as she raised her arms, and felt the packet fall out of her pocket. She kicked it away. Doesn't that show how everyone tries to preserve themselves in a desperate situation, Annie thought. Never mind that whoever put the stocks in Vali's pocket knew he was placing her in danger. Standing there with her hands above her head, Annie sighed and looked up and noticed hot water pipes lining the wall they were facing.

"We're going to shoot you now," barked the young punk," as he poked his gun in Vali's back and then Annie's. Vali began to whimper.

"Don't worry," Annie whispered to Vali. "They're not going to shoot us down here. If they did, they'd hit the hot water pipes. Then they wouldn't be able to take hot showers." Annie tried to inject a little humor into their desperate situation. She feared the worst, but on the other hand, she could not imagine why they'd take a chance on damaging their property when they could just as easily shoot them outside. Hopelessness and resignation had set in. How could they possibly get away from this cellar?

Annie was right. Not a bullet was fired. Instead, the fifty or so prisoners were lined up and marched outside in columns, three abreast. The young punk hurried them along the cobblestone streets of Buda. We're on a death march, thought Annie. She'd heard about those marches that no one ever returned from. The sun was now low on the horizon, and Annie realized that she had lost all track of time.

The young punk was joined by another Arrow Cross soldier, who shouted constantly, "Get out of line and you'll be shot."

An elderly man stumbled and fell. He was immediately hit by the young punk with the butt of his gun. Annie looked up once and found the soldier walking next to her. He glared at her, but reached over and hit Rose in the back with the butt of his gun, shouting, "Go faster, go faster. If you stop, I'll shoot you." Rose stumbled, but recovered quickly, and resumed marching, her head held high.

Annie heard shots ring out occasionally and cries as the bullets found their mark, but she never looked back. She thought about her mother and worried that she was in pain. Did that young punk's prodding aggravate her sciatica? Rose often suffered from shooting back pains down her legs, due to the constant bending over to fit clients. What if her mother fell or didn't walk fast enough to please the trigger-happy soldiers? She could be shot to death right in front of her and Annie couldn't do anything about it.

They marched past villas and the Swiss Embassy. We must look like a ragged bunch of refugees going past these mansions, Annie thought. The further down the hill they went, the more depressed she became. She grew weary of the young punk hitting and shooting people. The situation was beyond hope. She was terrified of what the soldiers might do next.

"I can't take it anymore," Annie whispered to Rose. She felt at her lowest point, without any future. "When the next truck rolls by, I'm going to throw myself under the wheels."

"Annie, Annie, don't take yourself so seriously," Rose exhorted. "Don't be a victim. Look at the situation away from the event. From the outside. Remove yourself and it will entertain you."

Her mother's words, a quote from the "Comedy of Men," gave Annie the strength to go on. She held her head high and kept marching. The soldiers marched them to the outskirts of old Buda, into a huge abandoned brick factory. This warehouse was apparently a gathering place for the Jews found in hiding. There were already hundreds of prisoners inside who had been placed twenty to thirty to a section. Annie could hardly breathe because of the strong stench of human waste. Not only were they shoved into a section with a clay floor and heaps of bricks piled against the walls, but there were no bathrooms. Instead, one corner of the section had obviously been designated for this purpose. She was tired and hungry, but food and water were nowhere in sight.

Annie sank down and leaned against a stack of bricks. As her eyes adjusted to the darkness, she glanced around and noticed with dismay that not only was there no privacy or comfort, but men and women were lying about on the floor together. They had not been placed separately as if the Nazis were bound to destroy any civility. Everyone in Budapest had seen the Russians' large guns on the hills about the city, and knew the troops were closing in. The Nazis are in a hurry to get rid of us, she thought, so it doesn't matter to them.

As soon as Rose and Vali sat down, Rose looked at her two daughters and said, "I'm proud of you both for your bravery. I wanted to spare you all this. I promise I'll do whatever I can to get us out of this."

"Mother, I don't know what you can do," said Annie. "It's obvious that we're going to be on some sort of a death march, probably to the border. They haven't fed us tonight and probably won't in the next few days. Perhaps they mean to starve us to death. Or worse yet, they will shoot us at the border"

Rose shook her head, "I don't know. But each one of us must look after herself. You, Annie, should have gone with that young boy. He might have saved you."

"Oh no, mother, I couldn't leave you and Vali. Besides, he was obnoxious," said Annie.

Rose and Vali laughed. "Did you ever see so many pimples?" said Vali. Annie was relieved to hear Vali laugh. At least for the moment, her anxiety was abated. Rose looked thoughtful, as she whispered very quietly, "We must each try to escape tomorrow. Grab any opportunity and seize it. Then make your way to Lily's villa. Remember the directions I gave you?"

Vali and Annie nodded. Their mother's plan was their only hope. They shivered in the cold night and sat close together to keep warm. Annie longed for morning to come.

In the morning, a different Arrow Cross soldier came in and said brusquely, "Get up and line up in the courtyard. Raoul Wallenberg is waiting".

Once they were lined up in the courtyard, the soldier said, "All of you with Swedish protective papers step forward."

Annie longed to be in that group but without Swedish papers she could only stand there and watch passively. She knew that Wallenberg was a Swedish diplomat on a mission to save Jews by offering Swedish "free passes."(Schutzpass) A handful of prisoners stepped forward. Wallenberg took them with him and left. The soldier then ordered the rest of the prisoners to line up again. "We will march you west to Austria," he said.

One of the male prisoners leaving with Wallenberg was a casual acquaintance of Rose's. As he passed by her, he asked quietly if she had any money. When she shook her head, he handed her some coins, saying, "You can use this for bus fare." Rose slipped some coins to each of her daughters as they took their place in line, three abreast in the column, ready to march.

Annie was tired and hungry, but those few coins gave her a boost as if escape was a possibility.

As the column of prisoners rounded the corner of the warehouse, Vali quickly stepped away and ducked behind a column of bricks. Rose saw this and whispered to the man marching behind, "Please step forward." Without a question or change in his stride, he quickly moved up and marched beside Annie.

As she marched down the hills of Buda, heading for the river, Annie looked for her opportunity. She wondered about Vali. Would she make it to Lily's? She hoped the Nazis hadn't seen her leave the column. Actually, Vali was rather clever to leave the march right away, she thought.

Annie noticed that they were headed toward the Margit Bridge, which had been bombed and replaced with a pontoon bridge connected to the island. Margit Island was a park with many chestnut trees in the wide section of the Danube River. The only obvious way on or off the island was the pontoon bridge. The island was like a prison surrounded by water. Why are we being marched onto the island, Annie puzzled.

Suddenly an air raid siren shrieked. Everyone ran in different directions. It was pandemonium. Annie and Rose were marching parallel to the river just steps away from where they should turn and head over the pontoon bridge. "Now is the time," Rose whispered to Annie.

The soldiers were shouting, "If you run away, we'll shoot you."

Annie and Rose ran in the direction of the pontoons, but veered away at the last moment and faded into a large crowd surging toward an air raid shelter. As they sat in the shelter, they looked at each other and asked, "Do you think Vali made it to Lily's? Where is she?" Their relief at escaping was overshadowed by worry about Vali.

FIVE: Escape

After the air raid was over, Annie and her mother left the shelter and boarded a bus. A second air raid interrupted their trip. Finally, Rose nudged Annie to get off the bus. They walked up many hills, at last arriving at the villa, a fairly new house in an old section of Buda. The house sat high on a hill above the Danube River, just below the Citadel monument. Annie noticed there was not a garden around the stone house, and the massive front door was just a few steps up from the street. Before they could ring the bell the door sprang open, and there stood Vali.

"Vali, you were so clever," Annie cried as she hugged her.

Vali shrugged, saying, "I saw that huge stack of bricks and felt I could hide there for awhile. I watched until I couldn't see the soldiers and marchers anymore. Then I listened for any sound. When I didn't see anyone around, I ran fast and caught the first bus I saw. Here I am."

Lily came in just then and hugged them all "All of you made it. I can hardly believe it." She wiped away the tears streaming down her cheeks, as she said, "I didn't want to interrupt your happy reunion, but we must not take the risk of any of you answering the door bell again. I'm really the only one here who the Nazis are not looking for."

Lily then went on to explain about their living situation. "You see, after Akos and I moved in here, my brother, Laszlo, went AWOL from the Hungarian army along with his friend, Lev, who was a judge. They felt it was useless fighting the Russians alongside the Arrow Cross and the Germans. Then just yesterday, a Jewish engineer who had worked with Akos came by and asked if I could hide him, too. He told me that his son in the underground had just been apprehended and was sentenced to death by hanging. He didn't know, of course, about all the others, but no matter. What could we do but take him in? He was quite good at forging documents in the ghetto, he told us."

"Lily, Lily," interrupted Rose. "With all these men here, how could you possibly take us in?"

"Don't give it another thought. Anyway, where would you go? Food is scarce everywhere, but we'll manage. My brother has already proven he is good at stealing food." Pointing the way upstairs, Lily said, "Come, I'll show you around and introduce you to the others."

Annie looked around the spacious villa, and noticed the staircase leading upstairs that Lily was already climbing. "Up here, we have three bedrooms. Akos and I will keep ours, and we'll have to move two of the men into the hall on mattresses. Rose, you and your girls will have one of the other bedrooms."

They heard the scurrying of feet as they followed Lily upstairs. Suddenly, four men appeared. Lily hastily introduced the men. Akos was quick to greet them, but Lily's brother and the other soldier hung back, briefly nodding and averting their eyes. In times like this, personal contacts are kept to a minimum. The less one knew about someone else was all the better in case of capture. The forger, however, greeted them and said slyly, "You girls can call me "Mr. Police Document." Annie and Vali laughed and said they would.

"And you can call me Annie," said Annie.

Lily led the way downstairs, and she pointed out a trap door under the stair case. "This is your hiding place. Whenever the door bell rings, I want you to hide here. If you're upstairs, you must stay there and not make any noise."

"Will we all fit in there?" asked Annie, peering inside. "The space looks very small."

"Yes, it is small and you will be cramped, but you must find a way to fit. If we're eating when the door bell rings, you must move quickly and take your plate with you."

As they walked through the living room, Annie noticed that the furniture was modest, square furniture. A couch and three chairs were placed at one end of the room. At the other end was a large dining table. Lily told them that Otto had left all his furniture in the villa. Lily led the way into the kitchen where she found some bread and jam for the hungry women.

That night, as Annie crawled onto the mattress which she shared with her sister and mother, she could not believe all that had happened to her in the last two days. She had been captured, the worst fear of any Jew, but she had escaped. And more importantly, she was with her mother and her sister who had also escaped. In spite of all the people in the villa, she felt safe at Lily's. She wondered if Rinci was worried about her or knew what had happened. And the Captain? Was he in trouble, too? She doubted she'd ever know.

The next morning, Lily told them she would be going to work. She had found a temporary office job, which not only brought in a little money, but enabled her to kept abreast of what was happening and to buy food whenever she found it.

"Can we go out for walks?" Annie asked.

"You must be very careful," Lily replied. There are German soldiers swarming all over the neighborhood. Oh, I almost forgot the most important thing. The Russians have started bombing the Citadel. When you hear the air raid siren, go across the street to the wine cave. See it over there?" Lily asked as she led Annie to the window, and pointed out the cave.

"Oh yes. Could Vali and I go over there this morning and just see what it's like?"

"Be very careful," warned Lily. "The family that owns that estate and vineyard are living in the large house above the cave you see there across the street. This wine cave is actually their basement. They never come down to the cave, however, unless there's an air raid. The cave is a good shelter because the walls are very thick and extend into the hillside." Lily left for work, promising to be home by early afternoon.

Rose had some misgivings about the girls going across the street. Annie told her mother that it would be a good idea to at least see their air raid shelter before they actually had to go there. Reluctantly, Rose allowed them to go.

Annie and Vali crossed the cobblestone street to the cave. The estate was planted with grape vines, now untended and weed choked. There was a large three-story stucco house, Annie observed, with a wing extending off one side and a cellar beneath it. That must be the wine cellar, she concluded. The house appeared to have been carved out of the hillside. As they pushed open the door and walked into the cave, Annie and Vali shivered with the cold. The floors were dirt, and there were wine barrels lining the walls.

"It's pretty big, don't you think, Annie?" asked Vali.

"Yes, it is big, all right, but it certainly is damp. I hope we don't have too many air raids. I wouldn't want to spend a lot of time in here. I noticed that this house is on a hill under the Citadel. Let's hope there aren't any battles or more bombings there."

"I know," Vali agreed. "Staying in here for very long would be miserable. This cellar is so dark and damp."

Lily was able to bring home only a few staples that evening. Her brother, Laszlo, had gone out in his uniform. Since he had been a high ranking officer, no one asked for his papers. He had found a nearby army camp and was able to steal some food. "This is appropriated for the army," he told them. "He looked around at Annie and Vali and added, "You are the army I appropriated this food for," he said with a twinkle in his eyes.

One day, Mr. Police Document appeared very sad, and by evening he was sobbing. Annie and Vali sat on either side of him on the couch, comforting him and asking why he was so upset. Finally he said, "This is the day and the time when they hang my son." He murmured this over and over again. Annie patted his hand, in an effort to console him, but he continued to sob. The next morning, he left without a word.

The bombings continued night and day, and Lily decided that it was no longer safe to remain in the villa. "We will have to move into the wine cellar", she said. "Take your mattresses over to sleep on."

The thought of living in that cave was distasteful to Annie, but the thought of being bombed was worse. The move meant that they would have to come back to the villa for food or to use the bathroom. They could not do any cooking in the cave. Two days before Christmas, they took their mattresses and moved into the cave. Laszlo's friend, Lev, left. Lily's fears were realized when the villa was bombed a few days after they had moved into the cave. Amazingly, the kitchen at the villa was left nearly intact.

Laszlo continued to steal food from the army and scoured the neighborhood for apples that had been left on the trees. Lily worked each day and brought home whatever food she could find. Many days she came home empty handed. "The shelves in the stores are now completely bare."

Living in a damp wine cellar was not Annie's only problem. She had begun to itch all over and scratched constantly. When Rose looked over Annie's body, she concluded that Annie had gotten lice from her jacket. Annie shed the jacket, and Lily found another jacket for her to wear. That evening, Annie went back to the villa and rubbed some of the fine dust from the bombed out walls on her skin to kill the lice. As she dashed back across the street, she shuddered. A dog lay there mutilated by a bomb. That could have been any one of us, she thought.

Food became even more scarce. Lily told them the store shelves remained empty. Laszlo mentioned that the Hungarian army was retreating and they were killing their horses as they went. That piece of news gave Annie an idea. She put on her brightest smile and went to the nearby Hungarian army camp, which was in disarray. No one paid much attention to her. She walked about until she came across a butcher who was chopping up chunks of horse meat. She struck up a conversation with him, and soon they were laughing together. When she observed that her family was very hungry, he gave her a few chunks. After that, Annie simply wandered through the camp and looked for an opportunity to steal horse meat.

One afternoon, Rose wanted to bake and looked about the kitchen at the bombed out villa. She found some flour and walnuts, and even poppy seeds and butter. She decided to make "beigli, "a tasty roll made with just those ingredients. Annie watched as her mother carefully formed the long beigli roll and placed it in the oven. Since the gas was still turned on at the villa, they were able to cook the horse meat and could now bake. "What would we do if the kitchen walls weren't still standing?" Annie said.

After her beigli roll was in the oven, Rose asked Annie to stay and watch it. She headed across the street. Soon Annie became nauseous and started to vomit, so she quickly ran across the street to the cave. "You'd better lie down for a little while," advised her mother.

Rose then took Vali across the street to watch the beigli, but she, too, vomited. Rose became suspicious and looked about and discovered a gas leak. Fortunately, by then the beigli was baked. That was the last of the cooking.

The beigli became the staple of their diet. Rose cut pieces from this long roll every day for each of them. Annie and Vali were also given chewable vitamin pills to take with the beigli. Rose had bought the vitamins when they went into hiding as preparation for the times when they might be starving. Annie found the taste of the pill obnoxious, but often the beigli and the vitamin were all she and Vali had to eat for the day.

Thus far, the Hungarian Nazis had left them alone in the hills of Buda, but this peace did not last. They knew that the Russians had taken Pest in a bitter house to house fight by January 1945 and felt sure the same thing would soon happen in Buda.

The neigh of horses and the clank of knives brought Annie and the others to the doorway of the wine cave. They watched a fierce fight between German S.S. officers and Russian Cossacks. The Cossacks stabbed the Germans with large knives. When the battle ended and all the soldiers had gone, a dead German soldier was left lying on the road. A Cossack soldier looked up and saw them watching. "Bury him," he ordered and rode off on his horse.

Akos and Laszlo went outside and rolled the dead man over. They took off his dog tag and threw it down. Annie ran outside and hung the dog tag on the fence. Burying the soldier was not easy since the ground was frozen solid and the day was bitter and cold as every day had been lately. They could easily believe the rumors that this was one of the most severe winters in Budapest. Akos and Laszlo managed to bury that soldier, using shovels and picks they found outside the wine cave, to dig a hole. They worked for hours. Annie noticed the Cossack's dead horse lying on the road, too. "What are we going to do with the horse?" she asked.

"What should we do? Eat the horse or bury it?" asked Akos.

Annie pointed out that cutting up the horse and cooking it was impossible since by now the villa had been completely leveled. They all nodded thoughtfully. "But that ground is so hard. We could barely get a hole deep enough for a man, let alone a horse," said Akos.

"Why don't we just drag the horse off the street and into a ditch," suggested Laszlo. Akos nodded. And that is what they did.

That evening, a Russian soldier, clutching a machine gun, pushed open the door and came staggering into the wine cave. "Give me wine and women," he said, his speech slurred.

Annie and Vali were already in bed with their mother on a mattress near the front of the cave. Laszlo, Akos and Lily lay on mattresses further back in the cave. Rose quickly sat up, pushing the girls under the covers and said, "No girls. No wine. The barrels are empty."

The Russian squinted at her and staggered over. As he felt around under the blanket, he grasped Vali's hair, and a surprised look crossed his face as if to say, "What a lot of pubic hair this woman has." He began to unbutton his pants when he suddenly fell on top of Rose on the mattress and went sound asleep. He was very drunk, and snored noisily.

"Please, someone get this man off me," Rose called out. "Take him away."

Not a person moved. No one could come to her rescue, because the Russian still had a tight grip on his machine gun. The men were afraid to challenge him and possibly all of them would be killed. Rose tried to move away, but each time she did, the soldier snorted and mumbled as if he would awaken. She lay very still, and Annie and Vali also lay frozen on the mattress all night long. Amazingly, the soldier got up in the morning and left without a word.

"Since the Russians have liberated us," Laszlo announced in the morning. "I don't have to hide anymore. They're not looking for men like me, just women. I'm going to head down the hill and check out my apartment. It would be safer and more comfortable than this cave. I'll be back," he promised as he left.

Lazlo returned in a couple hours and invited all of them to move in with him. "We'll be crowded," he said, "but it will be better than this cave."

Laszlo's apartment was like paradise to Annie after the damp cave. She didn't even mind that she, her mother and sister were given the maid's room, which was furnished with only a single bed. Laszlo was in his bedroom, and Lily and Akos in the other bedroom. Annie felt squished, as she and Vali took turns sleeping at the foot of the bed, but she didn't mind. After all, she was in an apartment which provided some security and comfort. The bombing had stopped since the Germans were gone. Her only fear now was the Russian liberators.

The safety of the women was uppermost in everyone's minds. They had heard the rumors of women being brought in to peel potatoes who were then gang raped by the Russians. Annie and Vali dreaded the frightening nights with Russian soldiers roaming the streets, poking guns through windows and shattering glass. In fact, there was no glass left in the windows in Laszlo's ground floor apartment. There were piles of rubble under every window.

Early one morning, Annie was awakened by a strange noise. She looked up and saw a Russian soldier peering in the window at them. She expected him to climb into the window, but he didn't. Instead, she heard him coming in the front door, and then walking around. By this time, everyone was awake and gathering in the living room. The soldier was rummaging through drawers and asking for shoes. Lily had brought along a box of her shoes, which she brought out from the bedroom. He grinned impishly as he took one shoe from each pair. He then wandered about the apartment haphazardly grabbing things and putting them in a bag he carried. He gazed at an Oriental carpet. He took it outside and put it on his horse which was tethered in front of the building. He came back inside and they heard him rummaging around in the small bedroom. Soon he came out with an ocelot jacket that Lily had given Annie. He went outside and put that on his horse, too. "My horse's name is Konya." he said to no one in particular. His speech was beginning to slur.

A second soldier strolled in, who was obviously drunk. In fact, Annie could see that both men were drunk. The second soldier pulled out a World War I sword and pierced the couch and chairs with it. Annie watched in amazement as he poked his sword in the furniture. She'd never seen such a huge sword before. Annie couldn't imagine why he slashed the furniture. What was the point in that?

The first soldier staggered down the hall, and Annie followed to see what he would do next. He went into the bathroom, pulled a live fish out of his pocket and put it in the toilet. Annie watched as he pulled the chain and his fish flushed down the drain. He was furious and uttered a string of words. He denounced the toilet as a "stealing machine." Annie quickly rejoined the others in the living room, but she laughed to herself imagining that the soldier probably came from a poor Russian village and had never seen a toilet before.

"Davaj chasi." Give me your watch, shouted the second soldier. Like many of the Russian soldiers, he wore watches from his elbow to his wrist. "Give it to me," he added impatiently. Only Lily and Laszlo had watches left. The soldier took them and went out the door.

"What was there left to steal?" asked Annie.

Rose took the girls into the bedroom and said, "It's time for us to go home and see if our apartment is still there. Once we get to the river, we'll have to find a way to cross. What do you think?"

"The Germans are gone and the Russians are everywhere. We can't avoid them. There's no point in staying here. I'd love to see our apartment, see if it's still there. Let's go home," said Annie.

Vali agreed, adding, "Then there would be only three of us to feed." A frown creased her forehead. "Do you really think our apartment will be there? What if someone is living there?"

"I don't know," said Rose, "but we must go and see."

They went back into the living room. Rose said to Lily, "We've imposed on your kindness long enough, Lily and Akos. You, too, Laszlo. But now we're going to head across the river and check on our apartment."

"Oh Rose, do you think it's safe?" asked Lily.

"Pest is already liberated, and Buda appears to be, too. I feel we have to take a chance. Besides, if any of my family survived the war, they'd come to our apartment. I hope it's still there," she said, shaking her head.

"Of course, Rose. You must go. Please come back if your apartment is gone. You'll always be welcome here with us."

After a tearful good bye, the Gabors left. It was February 15, 1945

By January 18, 1945, Pest had been liberated, and Buda was liberated by February 13th.

In 1941, 725,000 Jews lived in Hungary, including the reattached territories. 600,000 of them died in the Holocaust.

SIX: Home

Annie led the way down the hill to the Danube River, with Vali and Rose following. They came to the tunnel that led to the Chain Bridge. The passageway smelled terrible and was filled with heaps of rubble and stacks of dead people. Annie stood aside as Russian soldiers marched a column of captured German soldiers through the tunnel to the shore. She speculated that these were the German soldiers who had held the Citadel long after everyone else had surrendered. Hitler had ordered them to "hold out" even after they were surrounded by the Russians.

The Chain bridge, the first suspension bridge in Budapest, had been destroyed. In fact, Annie didn't see any bridges left connecting Buda with Pest because the Germans had destroyed every one. Annie stood on the shore, watching large chunks of ice floating by. Rose and Vali walked up and joined Annie on the shore.

"The bridges are all gone, Mother. How can we get across?" asked Annie.

Just then a young university student rowed up in his skiff and offered to take them across for a price.

Rose struck a bargain with him and then turned to her daughters. She had given each of them a roll of paper bills to place in their bosoms for safekeeping. Vali was so flat chested, she promptly lost hers, but Annie's bills were snugly tucked in her ample ones. Annie handed over her money, and the young man invited them into his boat.

Vali climbed into the boat, but Annie hesitated. She was terrified by the ice floes (Zajlik) rumbling by in the river. She was sure they'd be hit by the swirling floes. A firm push by her mother ended Annie's indecision, and she sat down warily in the tippy boat. The young man skillfully rowed around the ice floes and landed them safely on the opposite shore in Pest.

Annie breathed a sigh of relief as she stepped out of the boat. The journey across had not been as bad as the anticipation. She hurried up the street, anxious to see if there was still an apartment waiting for them.

"Annie, Annie, we're not in a race," gasped Rose as she attempted to keep up with her daughter.

"I'm sorry, Mother. It's just that I'm so eager to see if our apartment building is still standing."

As they rounded the corner, they saw that the apartment building across the street had been leveled, but their building stood tall, the walls intact. The only damage they noticed were a few deep holes in the courtyard.

"It's those thick 1846 walls," said Rose. "Not even a bomb could knock them down." Warily, they went in the door and up the stairs to their old apartment. When their knock on the door went unanswered, they opened the door, which was unlocked. Once inside, they saw new furniture, but Rose's 19th century Killim rug was there as well as her Oriental runner in the hall. They wandered about the apartment, but found no one there. While the apartment had obviously been occupied, no one was there now. Rose guessed that Germans had probably lived there and bought the furniture.

"Isn't this amazing?" said Annie. "I can't believe we're here. The apartment looks like it was waiting for us. I'm astounded that there's no one around. And see, no broken windows."

Rose shed a few tears as they all hugged and settled in. Unfortunately, their privacy did not last. A few days later, a Russian soldier appeared and asked for a room. He was an officer from the Ukraine, and communicated with them in German. Rose allowed him to stay, feeling she couldn't refuse him.

Annie was wary of him from the outset. He not only looked at her in a way that made her feel uncomfortable but often tried to force his attentions on her. She turned down his frequent offers of jeep rides, and made sure she was never alone in a room with him. The officer, whose name was Constantine, was around more than he was gone. Annie couldn't imagine that he didn't have more duties. After all, she speculated, he was an officer and must have soldiers under his command. Constantine was polite enough, but his gaze followed Annie whenever she walked by. Her uneasiness increased.

One evening, Rose, who had found a head of cabbage in a small store, boiled the cabbage and was preparing a pasta to serve with it. The stove was cooling down and she asked Annie to go down to the basement and bring up some wood.

"Let me help you," said Constantine, rising from his chair.

Annie shook her head, but Constantine persisted until Rose said in Hungarian, "Stay seated. You stay glued to that chair."

Annie started to get up from her chair, when Constantine said to her, "If you get up from that chair, I'll shoot you in the leg."

Annie stayed seated. There was no wood brought up from the basement that night. Not long after that, the Russian officer moved out. Fortunately, no other Russian soldiers came by to ask for a room.

As the war neared to an end in the spring, Annie, Rose and Vali speculated about the rest of the family. Would anyone come? Who had survived? They were sure that everyone had been deported. Annie felt that the waiting and worrying were almost as stressful as hiding. They had heard about Emery, Rose's brother. His girlfriend told them that he had been one of those who was shot into the Danube.

"Who will come back to us in Budapest?" Rose asked often. "Who's left in our family?"

They were on an emotional roller coaster, and left a note on the apartment door each time they went out. The Jewish Joint Distribution Committee (JJDC) had been set up to reunite families. Annie went to the JJDC office every day for news, but thus far there were no lists of survivors. While she was frustrated, she would not give up.

One afternoon the doorbell rang, and Annie opened the door. To her astonishment, Aunt Manci was standing there. Annie screamed with delight and hugged her. Rose and Vali came running in to see that the commotion was about. Rose hugged her sister and said, tears streaming down her face, "I wondered if I'd ever see you again. Let me have a look at you? Where did they send you?" She stepped back and looked at her sister as if she were seeing a ghost.

Manci came inside and set down her backpack. She was thin, but not gaunt. "Rose, they sent all of us to Auschwitz, that death camp. Fortunately, I was heathy and useful to them, so I survived. There are many others who didn't, I can tell you."

"And the others?" Rose asked anxiously.

Manci shook her head. "All of our family in the village was sent to Auschwitz. There were other camps that some of our cousins were sent to, but I don't know where. They herded us up so quickly. I don't even know where they took Martin or our sons." She shook her head sadly.

"Enough of that sadness. Manci, come and sit." Rose led her by the hand to the couch. "Vali would you make some tea?"

Manci sunk down gratefully on the couch. "I've been walking a long time. When the war was over, I felt grateful just to be alive. Look, I've brought you some gifts."

She opened her backpack and pulled out two Nazi flags. Annie drew in a large breath, a horrified expression stealing over her face.

Manci laughed at Annie's distaste. "Don't worry, I haven't become a Nazi. But I'm a practical woman. The material in these flags is a fine Egyptian cotton. We have lots of red and a little black and white to work with. What do you say, Rose? Do you think you can make some dresses for your daughters?"

"Of course," said Rose. I'll start right away."

Rose carefully removed the white circle and black swastika, and used the large piece of red cotton to make a lovely low cut dress for Annie with a square neckline. Annie covered the buttons in the back with the white material, and added a white sash. Rose took into account Vali's figure and stitched for her a high necked red dress with a large pocket bodice and white buttons down the back. Vali embroidered a bird on the bodice.

Annie could not remember the last time she had a new dress, or even any clothing that was decent. She viewed this red dress as a symbol of returning to normalcy, a time when a woman could think about how she looked and how to make herself attractive.

The first time Annie wore the red dress she walked down the street as if she were going to a special occasion. The event was made all the more special because she chanced to meet her friend, Judi, from the apprentice school. The two friends chatted and promised to meet soon. Judi's parting words were, "Annie, you're a knockout in that red dress."

Chaos was gradually replaced with a semblance of order. Rose reestablished her dressmaking trade, often sewing skirts from men's suit material. Manci was determined to reclaim her business and find her family. After a week, she left for Gyula. Annie reassured her that she would keep checking at the JJDC office.

Two weeks later, Manci's husband, Martin, came to their apartment. He was astounded to learn his wife was still alive. He quickly headed to the country to join her. The only other relative who survived was Dr. Friedman, whose wife had been Emery's sister. Dr. Friedman returned to his village and reestablished his medical practice.

Manci kept Rose informed of life in the village and who had returned. Sadly, there was no news about the Gabors. Manci was heartbroken when she eventually learned that both her sons had been killed She was able to reclaim her store and struggled to get her business going again.

Many relatives did not return and their fate was unknown. Occasionally, Annie would get a name or two at the JJCD office, but always the notification was of a death. The conscripted men had simply disappeared. Annie assumed that they had been killed, like cousin Gabor. The rest of the family, the lovely Katie, all of the Gabors were gone. Her mother assumed they had been gassed at Auschwitz. They heard from Laci's wife, that he had been killed in the Ukraine. A fellow prisoner told her that Laci had been hung up and sprayed with water. He froze to death. Annie wondered why the man had to be so graphic with Laci's wife. Wasn't it enough that he died in the camp?

May 1st, May Day, was memorable for Annie that year. What a beautiful holiday set aside to honor workers, Annie thought. She watched the parade of Communist workers proudly march by and sensed the hope and optimism they embodied. The war was over. She and her family had survived, thanks in a large part to Lily and her mother's resourcefulness. I'm a woman of nineteen, she thought. I know I can meet any challenge the future will bring. After all, I've had the best of teachers.

EPILOGUE I

Annie left for a summer session in Lyden in the Netherlands, along with a girlfriend and her two brothers in 1948. Although Annie was not a student as they were, she was able to get a student visa. This was the only way anyone could leave the country in those years.

The euphoria and optimism Annie had felt at the end of the war quickly faded. As she thought about past events, she realized she no longer felt any attachment for her country which had treated people in such an inhumane manner. Early on it was not the Germans killing and mistreating Jews, but fellow Hungarians, Nazis sympathizers. She was disillusioned even more when she worked on the election board in her neighborhood and saw the cheating of the Communists who put in extra ballots for their candidates so they would have a majority.

Annie watched as the Communist government slowly took away companies. People had just regained their companies in 1945 only to have them nationalized in 1948. Her mother was taxed more heavily, because her business was a private enterprise. Rose was considered an exploiter because she hired employees. Her business, too, was taken over by the state.

Annie decided to leave the country at her first opportunity. Her mother assumed she would be in Holland for only two weeks. Indeed this is what Annie had initially planned. Once the summer session was over, however, Annie stayed. When she could not get a work permit there, she went to Brussels, Belgium to establish a couture business. Her mother's prophetic words about the value of having a trade came true. Annie became known as a talented and stylish couture. Clients often remarked that they couldn't have Rose in Budapest, but at least they could have her daughter in Brussels.

Annie married an American soldier in Brussels and came to the United States in 1950. They settled in California. Their son, Tom, was born in 1951 and their daughter, Vicky, was born in 1953. Annie was stricken with tuberculosis and was hospitalized for eighteen months. During that time, her husband took care of the children. Shortly after her recovery, they divorced. Annie then enrolled at University of California at Berkeley and earned Bachelor of Science degrees in Anthropology and Political Science. She worked as a social worker for 17 years. Annie has been married to her current husband, Remo, for a number of years. Annie's children and three granddaughters live nearby.

Annie did keep in contact with Lily, her benefactor. She returned to Hungary in 1968 to see her.

After years of working for the state, Rose established her own business again. One of her clients was Mrs. Andropov, the wife of the Russian ambassador to Hungary. Rose came to the United States in 1956.

Vali lived with her mother in Budapest and finished her university degree in chemistry. She married her boss, who was a brilliant chemist. Rose convinced them to emigrate, and they, too, came to the United States in 1956.

Rose never spent those gold coins in her shoe. Annie still has them and fashioned them into a necklace which she proudly wears.

EPILOGUE II

Annie and her sister, Vali visited Hungary in 2002. They went to Gyula and were surprised to find that the village had become a spa town and a vacation destination. There are no Jews left in Gyula now. The synagogue is now a music school, named after Erkel, a composer who was born in Gyula.

They visited the Jewish cemetery, which was overgrown, and Annie cleared the ivy away and finally found her father's grave. A memorial had been erected in the cemetery honoring those Jews killed at Auschwitz.

In Budapest, the street in front of their apartment is now a shopping mall. While the visit brought back memories to Annie, Vali had little to say about the past. Lily is now deceased. Annie had several visits with Lily through the years. She and Lily were featured in a video about the war which was shown to middle-school children in Hungary.

PROLOGUE: ISABELLE

Isabelle was born Jewish, but converted to Catholicism. She was a French Resistance fighter, who died at the Hospice in Monterey of breast cancer on March 17, 2000. Monks came to comfort her prior to her death and to conduct her funeral mass.

Isabelle once told a reporter, who wrote a feature article about her French Resistance experience, that she had lived many lives. This story is about her experiences during the Second World War. Her years in the Resistance network were the epitome of her love and devotion to France. I met Isabelle just a few months before she died. On the day I interviewed her, I sensed that she was weary after a few hours. I asked if she was tired and would she like me to come back another day. She shook her head and said softly with a glint in her eye, "We're just getting to the good part." She then continued with the story of her escape from the Gestapo. At another point when she was coughing, she said with her wry sense of humor that she might be dying, but that was nothing compared with what she was telling me.

Isabelle was a complex woman, as was the Resistance organization. Yet her courage and commitment were straightforward in the face of impending arrest or danger. Marriage, pregnancy, a baby to care for, nothing would keep her from Resistance activities. She was an amazing woman with a powerful story to tell. I regret that I did not meet her sooner and have the opportunity to know her better.

I also want to acknowledge her daughter, Agnes who met with me and added dimension to the story. Isabelle's Uncle Georges, who also served in the Resistance, wrote a book about the Marco Polo Network. Some information from his book enlarged and clarified the organization and events.

This is Isabelle's story, a compelling personal experience during the "War of the Century." This tale is written so that we might remember this courageous woman. Isabelle, herself, said she had lived many lives, and this story is about just one of those lives. The Resistance touched her deeply and was filled with adventure and challenges. She never avoided the challenges. Perhaps from her, we may learn how to meet the challenges in our lives.

Betty J. Iverson

ONE: Drawn into War

The exciting times of the Thirties in Paris ended abruptly for me in 1939 when the Germans entered Poland on September 1st, so swiftly and with so much power that the battle was over before it began. This invasion, known as the Blitzkrieg, was a terrifying air and ground attack. France, as well as England, would soon be drawn into the war, since these countries were bound to defend Poland in the event of German aggression. Poland was divided by Germany's invasion from the west and Russia's from the east.

Thus my beloved France was drawn into the maelstrom of World War II on that day, even though the formal declaration of war was not made until September 3.rd Hitler continued to seize other areas, such as the Czech provinces of Bohemia and Moravia, on the pretext that he was only interested in restoring to Germany what was rightfully hers. France and Britain now began to rearm. But when Hitler demanded the return of the free city of Danzig, and transit rights through the Polish corridor to East

Prussia, France and England announced they would back Poland against Hitler's demands.

I had been absorbed in my life as a student, and paid little attention to the outside world until now. All the news that I used to ignore, I now read eagerly. Gone were my carefree days when I attended classes at the Lycee during the day and often spent the nights studying or singing in the cafes and meeting my friends. I was ambitious and planned to attend university to fulfill my dream of becoming a doctor. Soon, everything I did was subject to the uncertainty and craziness of war. We had blackouts at night and alerts with sirens blaring. Everyone wore a gas mask, or at least had one ready at all times. Our French soldiers were on alert, but thus far they were experiencing a lull. People referred to the phony war or "Sitzkreig". (Sit down war) Now that I had some idea of what was going on, I lived in dread of the future. Even my mother Lucie, who had always been the pillar of our family, appeared uneasy.

Life in our family had been changed dramatically by the last war. My father, Charles Heymann, was gassed during World War I at Verdun and never fully recovered. He died in 1924 when I was just two years old. His father had also been killed in the war. In fact, both my grandfathers had lost their lives in that "war to end all wars." Although my American Grandmother, Rose, had lost both her only son and her husband in the war, she never once considered going back to her wealthy and prominent family in San Francisco. She thought of herself as

French, not American. Like all of us, she feared what another war might bring.

Thus I was raised by women, because we were a family of women, except for Georges, my uncle, who was only eleven years older than me. Georges was a small, skinny man, not much taller than me. After father died, my mother and I moved in with my Grandmother Camille and her son, Georges. Even though we lived in the same house, I never got to know Georges very well. He was studious and interested in literary studies. We lived on the Left Bank or the intellectual side of Paris, while my Granny Rose lived in a residential hotel on the Right Bank, the place of power and wealth. I shifted often between these two households. Granny Rose enjoyed being taken care of by her many friends and rarely cooked a meal. I remember the charming restaurants she took me to each week when I visited her as a child. Her maid would bathe me and dress me in one of Granny Rose's lovely dresses. I sensed that Granny Rose was very proud of me, her only grandchild. These memories were precious now as I was preoccupied with my studies and couldn't visit her as often. Was she speculating as I was about the invasion of our country? I had begun to think that it was not a question of if, but when. How would this affect my education and future plans?

In the spring of 1940, the German armies swept across the low countries of Belgium and the Netherlands and into northern France along the Channel coast. The German army quickly established a 150 mile front. The French and Belgian armies were overwhelmed by the Germans' huge tank formations and their combined air and ground tactics. Soon they headed southward across France toward Paris.

One day my mother told me that she feared the Germans would soon be entering Paris, and she decided that we should leave. "I think we will go to Chartres, Isabelle." This town, in the corn belt of France in the Eure Valley, would likely not be of interest to the Germans. Mother was a strong-willed woman, who would make decisions quickly and influence others to follow. I guessed that she had to be decisive in our family of women.

I understood why she was resolute, not only because of the Germans coming, but also because our family was Jewish on both sides and this put us in danger. My ancestors had fled from Alsace after the war of 1870 and came to Paris because they wanted to remain French and not live under the Germans. Even though I understood why Mother wanted to flee from Paris, I reacted strongly to her plan to move us to Chartres. "I'm in the middle of my studies at the Lycee. I don't want to leave." I said. "If I stop my classes, how can I continue at the university to get a medical degree?"

"There's a Lycee in Chartres, too, Isabelle, where you can enroll," Mother replied confidently. "I've heard of a job in accounting at a factory there. I expect that the Germans will be on our streets soon. I don't think that we are safe in Paris any longer."

And that was the end of the discussion. After a hurried good-bye to Granny Rose who had decided to move to Nice with her friends, Mother, Grandmother

Camille and I left for Chartres. My Grandmother Camille had no objection to the move. A sweet, amiable woman, she was agreeable as always. We bid Georges a quick adieu. Georges lived nearby in an apartment with his wife, Gyp. They were also planning to leave Paris. We vowed to keep in touch.

As she had mentioned, my mother took the accounting job. To my relief, I had no trouble enrolling at the Lycee to complete my studies in Latin, Greek and Philosophy. I was sure I could then enter the university without a problem.

At this time, Mother changed her name to Lucie Charles, dropping the surname of Heymann in an attempt to hide her Jewishness. Many people took aliases at this time, but I chose to keep my name and identity. After all, I felt I looked Jewish with my prominent nose, and I was proud of my heritage. Mother always minimized the size of my nose, saying that I was lovely with my oval face and curly black hair. She, on the other hand, had wavy brown hair that softly framed her face, a small even nose and high arched eye brows.

I found Chartres a quiet, rather dull place compared to Paris. This town of twisted streets and half timbered villas was dominated by the huge Cathedral of Our Lady. No matter where I walked, the cathedral towered high above me on that hill. But I never set foot inside it during the time we lived there. I had turned my back on the church, and I will explain why.

Strange as this seems, my mother and I were both baptized Catholics, but no one in the family knew this, except for Grandmother Camille. One of my father's friends, Jacques, and his sister had befriended Mother and often took her to mass with them. Mother was touched by the caring of Christ for His people, especially the story of His care for the lilies of the field and the sparrows. She was instructed, baptized and became a devout Catholic.

When I was ten, Mother asked me if I would also like to become a Catholic. I knew nothing about the Jewish religion, the Catholic religion or any religion for that matter, but I was curious. Each day when I passed by the orphanage next to our house in Paris, I read a sign on the wall, "Who has Jesus, has everything." I wondered what this "Jesus" word meant. Not only that, but all my peers were Catholic, and I wanted to be part of the crowd. So I agreed to be baptized. The very next year, my Mother and Grandmother Camille took me to Rome for my first communion. One of my mother's friends in Rome had arranged this and also offered to be my godmother. Mother told the family that we were on a holiday in Rome. So I was a Catholic Jew, who until now, had never felt alienated from the church.

Now I found it difficult to remain a Catholic. Once Adolph Hitler rose to power in Germany, many Jews were ostracized and fled to our country in fear. As a Christian, I could not understand what those German Christians were doing to the Jews. What did this mean? I could not reconcile the treatment of the Jews with the crucifixion of Christ and the love He preached. When I could no longer celebrate Easter, I left the church. However, I didn't renounce my faith in God. I absorbed myself in my studies and worked feverishly to finish my degree before the war could interfere.

TWO: Move to Vichy

The Germans did indeed interfere. After the May 6th invasion, the Germans headed for Paris, as we expected. I realized now the wisdom of my mother moving us out of Paris. By June 10,[th] the German troops were approaching Paris, and our Prime minister, Paul Reynaud, resigned and left for Tours with a large group of refugees. He wanted to leave the city deserted when the Germans arrived. We heard that people in Paris wept openly as the German soldiers marched through the Arc de Triomphe. They had entered without firing a shot. When an armistice was signed with the Germans eight days later, Reynaud resigned and left for England. He was replaced by Henri Petain, the Vice Premier.

I was in a turmoil, as was my country. The date to take our Lycee examinations was advanced by one month, and I found it difficult to concentrate. Here I am a baptized Catholic, I thought, yet I am a Jew in terrible danger. I knew that if I tried to go on to the university, I might not be accepted, because there was now a quota on Jews. This was not the future I had anticipated. On the other hand, how could I think of my career when my country was being overrun by Germans? In the last war, my grandfathers had died to keep France free, and my father had been gassed. I vowed that I, too, would find a way to serve my country in this war.

The morning after I completed the examinations, Mother, Grandmother Camille, and I climbed into my tiny two-seated car with our gas masks on. I was just eighteen with a new driver's license. We joined the mass exodus of people heading for the city of Vichy in the unoccupied territory of Vichy. Since German troops had swept across Belgium and northern France, the roads were packed with refugees from those areas and from Chartres as well. The clogged roads hindered the movement of the troops. Chaos and confusion reigned. I tried to be patient and not let Mother see my frustration, but I was discouraged by the crawling traffic. I had hoped to reach Vichy before dark.

As I sat in my car on that packed road, I thought of the many things that had happened in rapid succession since our country was split in two. Paris, now occupied by the Germans, was no longer an open city. A new government was formed by Marshal Henri Petain, who signed armistice agreements with Germany and Italy on June 10,[th] and agreed to Hitler's terms. This Franco-German agreement allowed for the German military occupation of the northern half of France and the entire French Atlantic seaboard. The French navy was demobilized. Italy would control an area along the Franco-Italian border. French deputies and senators who opposed the capitulation of France and the exceptional powers given to Petain were either deported or arrested.

Petain was now the Chief of State of the Vichy government, in control of a temporarily unoccupied zone in the south. The French empire was under the control of the Vichy government. I questioned whether this Vichy regime was set up in order to save what could be saved of France, or was it just a puppet government run by the Nazis? Nevertheless, Mother had once more decided that we should flee, this time to Vichy, the unoccupied zone. She felt that this was preferable to living under the Germans. On the other hand, I felt we were just one step ahead of them.

General Charles De Gaulle, former undersecretary of war, denounced the armistice and fled to London, where he established a French National Committee. He pledged to continue to fight the war from there. On June 18,[th] he told us in a radio broadcast, "France has lost a battle, but not the war." And another time, he said, "Nothing is lost for France, because France is never alone." I felt that he was reminding all of us that even though he was in England, he was still a part of France and representing France there. In fact, General de Gaulle was recognized as the French leader by Britain. Later in London, he organized the Free French Forces. The French military units that escaped to Britain became the nucleus of this. I speculated about what they would actually be able to do.

But for those of us who remained in France, our country was now split by a demarcation zone that separated the occupied (roughly from Bordeaux and Tours north) and the unoccupied zone in the south. Family and the homeland were now subject to the new politics of collaboration. The remnants of the French parliament met in Vichy on July 10, 1940 and gave Petain dictatorial powers, which allowed him to establish a totalitarian government. He immediately began to transform unoccupied France into a regime, similar to that of Nazi Germany. We had heard that anti-Semitic regulations were enforced in Vichy just like in the occupied zone. Still we went, hoping for the best.

We arrived at dusk, and my resourceful Mother found a small apartment for us. Once we were settled in the lovely spa city of Vichy, my Granny Rose came from Nice to join us. The four of us were very crowded in the apartment, but managed. Mother found work as a tutor, while I volunteered with the Committee de la Reconnaissance Fracas. I also took a nursing course and volunteered for the Red Cross. Besides being committed to serve in this war effort, I also felt, that as the youngest in the family, it was my responsibility to volunteer.

I watched this beautiful city change under Petain as he set up his government. He chose Pierre Laval, a French politician and staunch anti-Communist, as his prime minister. Laval sought to align France with Mussolini's fascist Italy. The lovely spa hotels in Vichy became embassies or government ministries. People around us grumbled about the situation but always ended their complaint with, "What can we do?"

Mother observed all this with growing uneasiness. After six months in Vichy, she decided once more that we should move. This time, she told me that we would head for Marseilles on the Mediterranean coast and away from the seat of Petain's government. Even though I was engrossed with my volunteer duties, I went along with her decision. Before we left, however, we were faced with a critical decision.

We had received an offer from Granny Rose's nephew, James Hart, a professor at the University of California at Berkeley, to bring Granny Rose, my Mother and me to California. He and another nephew, Joseph Bronstein, even sent us emigration visas and tickets on a Pan American flight from Portugal. They had also arranged for my admission to University of California at Berkeley. Our Granny Rose was Tante Rose to her American nephews.

Granny Rose refused to leave. "I am French," she declared. "I have a son and husband buried in this soil, and I will not leave them. Being an American makes me feel safe, but I am first and foremost French. Does that make sense?" she asked me. I hugged Granny Rose and assured her that I understood exactly how she felt, and she did make sense. I told her that I was overcome by her nephews' offer; however, it was unthinkable for me to leave France when our country was in such a terrible state. Mother agreed with us, saying she couldn't leave either.

So we all stayed. Granny Rose left to rejoin her friends at the residential hotel in Nice. "I miss my Jewish friends," she said. "I will always be French, and I will not accept special privileges nor hide like a deer in the woods." This would prove to be an unwise decision.

Uncle Georges contacted us to tell us that he and his wife, Gyp, had rented an apartment in the Dordogne. When we told him that we were heading on to Marseilles, he offered to take Camille in with them. We left for Marseilles, and Grandmother Camille joined Georges and Gyp in Dordogne. Grandmother Camille told me that she did not want to live in Marseilles. Apparently she feared Mother and I would be moving often.

THREE: Marriage in Marseilles

Mother and I headed to Marseilles in our small car in December 1940. Marseilles was a large city on the Mediterranean coast and the most important port. Soon after we arrived, we were introduced to an established community of Jewish people, and were reunited with some friends from Paris. We were fortunate to find a large apartment to rent, one which was spacious enough to entertain our friends often. I looked forward to picnics on the beach or rowing boats on the Mediterranean. Whenever Jews arrived from Paris, they were added to our group, and enjoyed our frequent social outings. Sometimes I could even pretend there was no war. Then bad news would reach our ears, the latest being that the Vichy government had ordered a census of all the Jews. Even worse was the word that 12,000 Jews had been interned at a camp in France before being sent on to Auschwitz.

Mother and I both felt a measure of security, albeit temporary, here. She volunteered with an organization, the Emergency Rescue Committee. This group of intellectual New Yorkers, headed by Varian

Fry, came here on a mission to save Jewish artists and other anti-Nazi intellectuals hunted by the Nazis in the Vichy zone. I was at loose ends and also volunteered to work alongside her. Mother spoke a little English, while I was fluent. Both the French and American governments were less than enthusiastic about this organization and gave them only three weeks to get these artists out of the country. (In reality, the organization functioned for thirteen months.)

Many of these creative people had been persecuted in their own countries and sought refuge in France. I felt I was doing something worthwhile by being involved in an activity that saved Jewish people. This was my first experience with clandestine activities. I was very impressed by Varian Fry, an American professor and a deeply committed man. He appeared to be a man who would not let anything stop him from achieving his goals. He often used his own fortune to get these artists out of the country and to the United States.

Over the course of months, aided by some American expatriates and French volunteers, like Mother and me, about four thousand people were evacuated from French territory. The committee provided them with false passports and undercover passage through Spain. Varian Fry often commented that even though his country maintained diplomatic relations with Vichy, they never helped with the emigration of these artists. One day, he told me about some of the artists they had managed to save: artists like Max Ernst, Marcel Duchamp, Marc Chagall, and the sculptor, Jacques Lipschitz. The writers included

Andre Breton, Hans Habe and Franz Werfel. He also saved some scientists and philosophers. Without Fry's group, the talent of these people would have been lost to the world.

I was impressed with his organization, and told him that what he was doing was a valiant thing. "You have placed yourself in danger for these creative people," I said. Varian shrugged modestly, and told me that he never worried about himself. His main concern was the limited amount of time he'd been given to get them out. He knew that not only was the government not helping their effort, it was actually working against them.

Because of these activities, Fry was pursued by the Vichy authorities and eventually arrested. The American consular representatives refused to renew his passport. He was expelled from France in September 1941 and forced to return to the United States. The American Rescue Committee, however, continued the work. In 13 months they rescued thousands of refugees. I managed a fast good bye to Varian Fry before he left.

My days flew by quickly and my life was so full that I had little time to think about myself. Thoughts of romance were out of the question, until one evening. Mother and I were invited to an engagement party for Jacqueline, a woman in our social group. Apparently her fiancé had come from Paris, and she wanted all of us to meet him. I was excited about going to a party.

Jacqueline was the center of attention as we walked in the door. She soon swept over to greet us, waving her hand and showing off her lovely ring. The diamond sparkled brilliantly and looked immense. I murmured polite congratulations as I thought to myself that she must have snared a rich man indeed. "And who is the lucky fellow?" I asked.

Jacqueline told me that I must meet him, and that I would find he was very charming. Without waiting for a reply, she took my arm and guided me across the room to a group of men, who were chatting loudly. She touched the arm of a handsome fellow, saying, "Pierre, I'd like you to meet another of my friends, Isabelle."

A young man with dark curly hair and flashing brown eyes turned to me and smiled. "Isabelle? What a lovely name. Why don't we get to know each other better," he said as he led me out to the balcony.

I was surprised by such solicitous attention and apprehensive about Jacqueline's reaction. For some strange reason, I allowed myself to be guided along by this intriguing man. My heart was fluttering. As soon as we reached the balcony railing, Pierre said that he wanted to know all about me. I was taken aback and mentioned that there was really not much to tell. I recounted our journey from Paris to Marseilles and my volunteer duties for Varian Fry's Emergency Rescue Committee. My words sounded so mundane to me. Then I asked him if he had heard of Varian Fry.

He admitted he hadn't, but then he had only just arrived. Pierre seemed interested in this committee and soon I was telling him all about it, and mentioning some of the artists we had managed to get out of the country. As we chatted, I discovered that he shared the same deep patriotic feelings for France that I did. Suddenly I realized we'd been talking for over an hour. I told him we'd been on the balcony such a long time that we must return to the party.

Pierre was reluctant, but I persisted, saying that surely his fiancee would be missing him. "On one condition," he said, "And that is that you give me your address. I'd like to talk with you again soon." I was stunned and told him that since he was engaged to Jacqueline, I wasn't sure that she would understand. Pierre very nonchalantly said, "Of course she will, since we will meet for a chat, and nothing more."

I shook my head and hurried back into the room. I found Mother looking for me. She had been puzzled by my absence. I was embarrassed and could not look at Jacqueline. I murmured something vague about being tired. Mother and I left quickly.

I spent a sleepless night. I couldn't understand the attraction I felt for this man. Not only had I just met him, but he was engaged to another woman. I vowed to put him out of my mind and plunge even more deeply into my duties for the Emergency Rescue Committee. But the very next afternoon when I rounded the street corner by our apartment, I found Pierre standing there, leaning on a lamp post. "What are you doing here?" I cried. "How on earth did you find our apartment?"

"It was not hard to find out where you lived. I just couldn't figure out when you'd show up. Are you ready for coffee and a chat?" Pierre asked, as if all this had been arranged. I shook my head and opened my mouth to object, but before I could get the words out, he took my elbow and guided me down the street. I let him guide me along like an obedient child. He had swept me off my feet. I had never felt this way before.

This chat led to many more, and soon we had fallen in love. Mother did not approve of all the hours I spent with Pierre, and told me I was being very foolish. "Not only is it wartime, Isabelle, but you don't know anything about him. More than that, he is engaged to Jacqueline. I think you should end this now before things go any further." Her usual sunny face was clouded with disapproval.

"I know, I know, Mother. You're right. I can hardly believe what's happening, myself," I said. "But we love each other. He told me today that he's going to break his engagement with Jacqueline. He wants to marry me."

"What? Isabelle, have you lost your mind? What about his family? Surely, they would have something to say about this." Mother urged me to think the matter over and not act hastily.

"Pierre and I have made up our minds. This is not a decision we came to lightly, Mother. Since there is now a curfew for the Jews, if we want to have any time together, the only sensible thing to do is to get married." I saw that Mother was upset, but I was as firm as she was and did not back down. And so Pierre and I were married in a civil ceremony. There was no big engagement ring for me. I was twenty and very naive.

Pierre told his family of our marriage, but he never shared their reaction with me. I assumed they weren't pleased. After all, he had been engaged to

Jacqueline, whom they had known for years. He told me that his father, Henri, was Jewish, but his mother, Marguerite, was not. Therefore by Jewish law, Pierre was not technically a Jew, but he liked to think of himself as one. Perhaps that was part of my appeal to him. He said his family lived in a mansion in Paris that covered an entire block. His father owned the Imperial Hotel in Carlsbad, Czechoslovakia, and also held interests in gambling casinos. Pierre mentioned that he had spent a lot of his early years in residential hotels.

I was surprised to learn of his family's wealth and power, and told him I hoped to meet his family one day. I hoped the war would be over soon, and we could do ordinary things again. I asked him if he had any brothers or sisters. I felt as if I'd married a man without a family. He spoke of his sister, Madeline, and his half-sister, Luciene, who lived with her husband in a suburb of Paris. He assured me that I would like them. He spoke about them casually as if we would be meeting soon.

Life in Marseilles became increasingly onerous for us. I also found it difficult to keep track of just who was running the Vichy government. Admiral Jean Darlan had been made commander of the French navy, but hated the British so much that he joined the Vichy government, after the fall of France in 1940. Darlan was made Petain's successor, and was known as a collaborator with the Germans. Pierre Laval, Petain's prime minister, also promoted collaboration with the Germans. French Underground Resistance to the German occupation grew. Clandestine newspapers passed from hand to hand and helped combat Nazi propaganda and gave us hope. The Resistance printed tracts and leaflets, targeted to young men, to counteract the Nazi propaganda. The Nazis urged our young men to go to work camps in Germany to be educated.

The Nazis searched for any signs of the printing presses. They often hunted them down in the middle of the night. Whenever they found agents printing leaflets or underground newspapers, the agents were arrested and tortured.

Pierre and I learned all we could about Resistance activities. We had heard that Civil Resistance Societies rose up spontaneously, and people acted in groups or alone. I admired these men and women who took up the fight, often without weapons, to stop the collaboration with the enemy. One Resistance agent, a woman who owned a bookstore, was a courier. Messages were frequently left at her book store. She was eventually arrested and executed.

I read about violent acts, bombings, arson and attacks on those Frenchmen who were pro-Nazi. In retaliation, the Germans arrested thousands of French Communists and Jews. Then in November of 1942, the Allies landed in North Africa, and the line of demarcation in France disappeared. France was now totally occupied by the Germans, except for the Rhone River and Corsica areas, which was occupied by the Italians. The Germans pushed Darlan for closer collaboration in the war against Britain, and he consented in secret negotiations. Germany had invaded the Soviet Union in June 1941, and the Vichy and Nazi governments drew closer then, which caused

France to sever relations with the Soviets. After this, the French Underground Resistance to German occupation had increased even more. In reprisal, the Germans accelerated their arrests of French Communists, Jews and others. They were often shot at the ratio of 20-100 for each German death.

Petain, whose role in the government was unclear to me at this time, denounced the Resistance movement. The Vichy government set up special courts to deal with hostile elements, but the Resistance activities continued. In fact, a student, acting on the order of the Resistance, assassinated Darlan for his treachery, on December 24, 1942. (By 1943, Petain had lost favor with the Nazis, and Laval assumed the reins of power. Petain became little more than a figurehead.)

We no longer felt safe in Marseilles. Food rations were insufficient as were many of the usual necessities of shoes, soap and clothing. To complicate our lives even more, I discovered that I was pregnant. Pierre and I were delighted, but Mother was clearly worried because of the war. We decided to move north near the Swiss border, and chose Aix-Les-Bains, a resort town in the Savoy on Lake Bourget in the Alps. All I knew about this area was that it was known for the therapeutic baths, lovely hotels and spas. I hoped that this village would be a safe haven for us. I could not anticipate then how much more deeply we would be drawn into the war.

FOUR: Joining the Resistance

Pierre, Mother and I left for Aix-Les-Bains early one morning in August 1942. Mother had been in contact with Uncle Georges, who also planned to bring Gyp and his Mother Camille, to Aix- Les- Bains. Georges had hinted about some important work he was doing for France. Mother and I were puzzled, as this was the first we'd heard about that.

Pierre and I settled into a cozy apartment on the second floor of a small building. There were four apartments in all. Mother and Georges had no trouble finding apartments, since there were few tourists here at this time of year, and the war made travel difficult. Mother promptly found a tutoring position.

Pierre was restless and eager to serve France. He had already been in contact with Resistance Organizations. My Uncle Georges, who was involved with a network, invited Pierre and me to join the Reseau Marco Polo, which was regularly in contact with London. The Reseau (Network) Resistance Army, consisted of eleven different units, each operating independently. The Marco Polo was set up in London by par le Commandment "S" an officer of the Free French Forces, in November 1942. Georges told us that the main purpose of Marco Polo was to pass along messages. Georges added that Commandment "S" was a code name.

Pierre and I didn't hesitate to join. I was eager to do what I could for my country, but I knew I could not be as active as Pierre because of my pregnancy. Overnight, our apartment became a center for resistance activities. We frequently housed refugees leaving France for Switzerland. We had boxes of forms in our apartment which we used to forge essential identity papers. When people left the country, they needed visas and passports. Without these, they would have to get off the train at the border, and go over the Pyrenees Mountains on foot.

I quickly learned more facts about this particular Resistance group. Besides providing false papers to establish identities, we were primarily message transmitters. We used liaisons or agents to communicate between groups and agents. Each agent had two contacts: one who sent the message and one who received it. This was a very dangerous occupation in occupied France. Nevertheless, there were a number of women agents, who were often more successful than men. One of these women was my cousin, Francoise. Apparently, Uncle Georges had recruited her for the Marco Polo Reseau as well. At this time, I had no idea where she was. I only knew that she carried messages.

Since I assumed the role of typist, I had to learn about the transmission procedures. I would sit in bed with a cover over my head, to muffle the noise of the typewriter, as I transcribed the messages. Often messages were very specific with sketches or maps or details of troop movement. Since many messages were sent in code, I had to memorize many codes, as well as learn to type well.

Pierre did most of the forging of identity papers, and he worked diligently to make them appear genuine. He often copied papers of people who had actually existed. In addition to the visas and passports, he forged birth and baptismal certificates and food identity cards. The police departments were zealous in verifying any and all information, but Pierre's looked so authentic that we never heard of anyone being caught who had been given documents forged by him.

The movement of the messages was a difficult process. The radio was completely controlled by the government and mail was censored. There was no gas for cars, very few trains were running, and those that were in service were always packed. Phones were scarce. In spite of these obstacles, our network functioned. Pierre and I no longer had a car. Our only transportation now was by bicycle.

I'm not sure when Uncle Georges joined the Marco Polo Reseau, but he told me that when this network was set up in November 1942, by par le Commandant "S," he was the first Chef (Chief) and the contact person with the Free French Forces in London. Commandant "S" then established this incredible network of person to person. If an agent was lost, the chain was broken. The second Chef was Agent "F." Uncle Georges had met him once and described him as a tall and aristocratic man. (I wondered if Uncle Georges was impressed by that since he was short.)

The current Chef was Gaston, who kept the network functioning well. Uncle Georges felt Marco Polo was organized differently than the other networks, because each agent appeared to have more mobility in movement. I observed that Uncle Georges was more deeply involved and given increasing responsibility. He passed on orders to us, and also asked Pierre to help set up a communication and escape route to Switzerland. I was quite impressed with my Uncle Georges. I had not had much contact with him in recent years, and now it appeared I would be seeing quite a lot of him. He was very dedicated to the Resistance cause.

As I learned the details of the communication system with the British Embassy in Switzerland, I thought it was quite clever. French actors with good memories would come to Aix-Les-Bains and stay with us. They were told important information which they memorized. Then, they'd go over the border at night to the British Embassy in Switzerland, and recite their valuable facts. I remember particularly Claude Dauphin and his brother, Franc-Nohain Jaboune, as two of these skillful and brave actors.

Pierre became even more valuable when he learned photography. He got a job with a local photographer, who often sent him to take pictures of the German officers at the luxurious hotels and spas in town. Germans liked to have their pictures taken, and

Pierre gladly accommodated them. He made extra copies to pass along to the organization.

Thus Aix-Les Bains was a major center for the Resistance activities. This tourist city was not only strategically located near the border, but the spas and hotels were frequently filled with Gestapo and German officers on a holiday from the stress of their jobs in Grenoble. In fact, the head of the Gestapo, who was proud of the excellent French he spoke, often brought in his film to be developed at the photography studio. Pierre was friendly, and this Gestapo officer often talked to him about the events in these pictures.

Pierre's latest challenge was to devise a means to pass these pictures along to agents, who could then route them appropriately. He often talked to me about a better way to send the photos, rather than through the mail, or hidden in the clothing of the agents. There, the pictures were easily found if an agent was arrested. Pierre wondered if he could put the pictures on tiny rolls of film. I knew my husband well enough by now to believe that he would not give up, until he had solved the problem.

My priorities soon changed, from that of Resistance activities to my soon-to-be motherhood. I felt so young and ill equipped. I could not simply go to a shop and buy all the things my baby would need. I spent many hours knitting little sweaters and outfits. I tried to eat well, but food was always scarce, especially meat. We ate whatever fruit or vegetables we could find. Diet was important, since I wanted to nurse my baby. The realities of war were ever before us.

FIVE: A Child is Born

On March 31, 1943, our son, Marc was born. Fortunately I had found a very competent doctor, and experienced no problems with the birth. Pierre was so excited to have a son. Marc was our delight. Mother's misgivings faded away when she visited often to see her grandson. She was a great help to me, since I now divided my time between being a mother, and typing the messages, which now came in ever greater numbers. Pierre and I were careful to maintain confidentiality. We got to know the manager of our apartment building, but he only knew that Pierre worked for a photographer. A woman with a new baby was above suspicion.

The war ground on. The British were fighting hard in the West while the Russians fought on the Eastern Front. The United States was now involved. The trains were packed with people. We were told that the Germans frequently demanded papers of the passengers, along the way between stations. Network agents told Pierre that blank identification papers were needed in Northern France. Pierre regretted that, at this time, he had no way of getting the papers there. I became anxious about our situation. I heard that more Jews had been arrested and sent to concentration camps. I didn't know where the camps were located. We all had heard of Auschwitz. I imagined that people were being tortured and killed no matter where they had been taken. Pierre and I often talked about our precarious situation of being both Jewish and also in the Resistance.

During the summer, I received a coupon for sugar, because I was a new mother and nursing my son. I used the sugar to make jam since there was an abundance of fruit in the countryside around Aix-Les-Bains. I felt the jam would provide fruit in the winter for us. With the scarcity of food continuing, I planned, as best I could, for our uncertain future.

Late in 1943, Georges came by one day, very upset. "The most awful thing has happened," he said. "There's been a catastrophe at the network center in Lyon. Our Chef, Gaston, and his wife, have been arrested and deported. I just got word this morning that they were betrayed by French citizens, who were collaborating with the police. Some may have even been in the Resistance. We'll have to set up another headquarters, since the police arrested them in Lyon." Pierre appeared shaken by this terrible news, and asked what we could do.

"For now, we'll continue on, but obviously we're in greater danger," Georges said. "These arrests are decimating our army of volunteers. Three agents were arrested this summer. I heard that one of them was sent to Buchenwald. Now this." I knew that arrested agents were usually tortured to coerce information out of them. We had been learning more all the time about enemy positions on our western coast. I hoped none of these facts were passed on.

I stood and listened, holding Marc, who was content, having just finished nursing. My curiosity was aroused, as I heard things I hadn't thought about before. I questioned how people got back and forth from England and asked Georges how our bureau Chef got to England when he was called back. Fortunately, he was in an expansive mood and eager to answer my questions.

"Well my dear, one reason you have been told very little is for your protection. As you can see from what I mentioned, dangerous events are happening. I feel I can now tell you this much. We've always had close communication with London. We have a regular courier, and when weather permits and there's a full moon, a small biplane lands in a field of string beans near Lyon. Our courier gets on the plane to give the French news, and their courier gets off with the English news. That is how our bureau Chef often went to London, but I'm not sure how or where our Chef left this time, since he was deported. I would guess he wants to come back, but he may not be allowed back in the country. I'll know more about that soon. I understand the French authorities don't want him back.

Georges left, and Pierre and I looked at each other. I was conscious of my son, and worried that I might be placing him in danger. Pierre must have read my thoughts, because he said, "Perhaps you and Marc should go to my sister, who lives near Paris."

I shook my head. "No Pierre, my place is with you. I may be in danger, but is Paris any less dangerous? I want to be with you, and continue to work for France. In Paris, I'd be at loose ends, not knowing what you were doing. Besides, who'd type the messages? Whatever happens, we'll be together."

Pierre walked over and took Marc and me in his arms. "You're a brave woman, and I love you for it. But if things ever appear imminently dangerous, you have to go to safety. Promise?" I nodded, but felt things would have to be terribly bad for me to leave him.

Pierre and I continued our work, and received even more messages than before. I became very adept at crawling under the bed sheets and typing. Pierre was now a peg, part of the network with pegs, or agents, here and there. Our work was escalating, reflecting the growing intensity of the war.

Individuals and small groups, necessarily ignorant of each other, worked against the enemy. The British Special Operations Executive, SOE, trained and supplied agents to carry out sabotage and relay vital information. By 1943, Resistance networks had helped thousands to escape.

SIX: Threat of Arrest

A few months later, early in 1944, Georges came with exciting news. "We have a new Chef. This man, Rene Pellet, is a teacher, as is his wife. Rene was the director of a school for the deaf and blind children at Aveugler de Villeuerbanne, a suburb of Lyon. No one knows where Gaston is since he was deported, but this Pellet is our new Chef. His school has become a seat of the resistance and agents often meet there. His code name is Jacques Octave and he has already been sent to London to be approved as our new Chef. He was given full power to be the leader of the Marco Polo Reseau"

Georges continued, "This man appears to be a young peaceful teacher, but he barely got back here before he started organizing sabotage and a coup against the Germans. Jacques told them in London that his work was here in Lyon and he was eager to get started. Some of his friends wanted him to return to London for his safety, since the police were already watching him. Jacques chose to stay here."

Georges paused for a moment and mentioned that he had gone to a welcome meeting which Jacques had called. The meeting was held in a room at the school. "We were packed in that room like herring in a barrel. All of us were eager to meet him and hear what he had to say. He told us that London had given him authority and also money to buy a farm outside Lyon. He had looked around and bought a 30 hectacre Domaine (farm) in Chaponost (a suburb) outside Lyon. Since he was well known to the police, he knew he would have to change his identity. He planned to assume the identity of Mr. M. Dumont, an engineer and a refugee from a town in northern France. All the archives concerning Mr. Dumont had been destroyed, so nothing could be proven about him. Therefore he had no papers to show, and he would have his office in the country. Since the police knew his wife, she would remain as a teacher at the school, but their two children would come to the farm with their father. Rene Pellet was now Jacques Octave, but known as M. Dumont to the community."

Georges said he was shocked at his appearance. Jacques had grown a mustache and flattened his hair. He wore a torn cap and the coarse blue clothes of a peasant. He told us he would play the role of a gentleman farmer. We were surprised. He said the headquarters of the Reseau Marco Polo would now be at the farm at Chomponost. He also brought the news that a French Committee for National Liberation (FCNL) had been formed, and General De Gaulle was appointed as the President.

Pierre nodded thoughtfully and wondered if the arrival of this new Chef meant that we would carry on as usual. Georges nodded and indicated that Octave had plans which would involve him.

"Since the network has regrouped at this farm, Octave wants to establish a photo lab and put the documents collected by the agents on film. This will be much easier to transport than on paper. He also wants to photograph the instructions from London for all the agents," Georges explained all this quite rapidly, but I suspected his intent was to involve Pierre.

His next words validated my hunch. "I immediately thought of you and all your experience. I told him you were the man for the job." Georges paused and looked expectantly at Pierre. "Will you do it?"

Pierre nodded, and said without hesitation, "Of course I will. This is an idea that I have been mulling over for a long time. I can probably get the necessary equipment from the photography store where I work." He glanced at me as he added, "Isabelle and I will need to talk about the details. I'll let you know in the morning."

I stood there in a quandary. I knew Pierre was the man for the job, but I was concerned about going to the farm with Marc. What sort of quarters would be there for us? Marc was barely a year old and just beginning to take a few steps.

After Georges left, Pierre said, "Isabelle, I feel the best thing for you to do now is to go to my sister, Lucienne in Paris. She has a large apartment and my parents are there, too. You will have a chance to get to know them, and they will get to know our wonderful little son."

"I know you're right, Pierre. But I want to join you just as soon as I can. I will feel so lost not knowing where you are or how to contact you."

"Of course, I'll get in touch with you just as soon as I can." he said. Then with a boyish twinkle of excitement in his eye, he headed out the door, saying, "I'd better go check on the equipment I'll need to set up a lab."

I smiled to myself. My husband was like a little boy who loved to play war and be a part of intrigue. I thought back to the time when we joined the Marco Polo Reseau. Very soon we became members of the French Forces of the Interior when it was formed to coordinate Resistance groups. Neither of us fully comprehended how much this decision would change our lives. In our youthful idealism, we would do anything to help our country. This zealous commitment bound us together.

Like everyone else in our Reseau, we had our special password and a sentence, cut in two. One half was kept at headquarters in London and the other half on our person. (My code name was Elizabeth and Pierre's was Jules.) Gradually we learned about our attachment with the London Central Bureau of Action and Information. Now Pierre was a peg for le Reseau Marco Polo and was presented with this new important challenge.

My thoughts strayed to all the important things that Resistance Groups had accomplished. Because of the agents' diligence, they had discovered the site of the Nazi's V1 and V2 rockets launching pad on our east coast which were aimed for England. These rockets, along with the German Luftwaffe, were responsible for some of the blitz raids on London. The destruction of these launching pads was a coup that made us all proud. We had also heard about the Norwegian resistance group destroying the heavy water factory at Venmark. The Germans had planned to use this heavy water in the manufacture of a new, powerful weapon. All the orders we carried out in our Resistance Groups: sabotage, assassination, intelligence gathering, the constant flow of vital information to the Allies and more. All this, we hoped would shorten the war.

We had been fortunate. Even when plans went astray, we survived. We had laughed with relief when a mail carrier was arrested and the mail sent to the Gestapo headquarters in Lyon. During the night that Gestapo headquarters was bombed and the mail destroyed. A stroke of good luck for our Free French Forces of the Interior.

I resolved to do what was best for us and make the most of the situation. I was just about to take Marc for a walk, when there was a light tap at my door. I opened the door and found Mother standing there, tears streaming down her cheeks. This was so unlike her, that I pulled her inside immediately and asked, "Mother, what's wrong?"

"I've just gotten word from a French couple passing through from Nice that Granny Rose has been arrested, along with the other Jewish guests at her hotel. This couple was staying there, too, and had gotten acquainted with Rose. She had taken them under her wing and shown them around. They were very upset by the horrible scene of Nazi soldiers storming into the hotel and rounding up all the Jewish guests. Rose managed to give this couple my address before they left and begged them to let me know what happened to her. They watched her go with the Nazis, her head held high. They asked around and heard that the group was being taken to Auschwitz. As you and I both know, that camp appears to be the usual destination for Jews these days."

I sank down in the nearest chair. Visions of my beautiful grandmother with all her refined ways and lovely clothes being crammed into a dirty train car filled me with horror. I could not stem the flow of tears. "Oh no, no—surely there must be some mistake. Did she tell them she was an American?" I asked.

Mother hugged me. "Isabelle, you know Rose would never do that. Remember? She thought of herself as French. Anyway, what difference would that have made to those animals?"

"Somehow I had known this could happen, Mother. I wonder if Granny Rose ever realized that she, an American, could suffer the same fate as a French Jew or a German Jew? What she chose to ignore was that to the Nazis all Jews are bad." I paused for a moment. "Oh Mother, there is so much happening. Not only is Granny Rose captured, but we may have to leave here."

Mother asked what I meant by that, and I quickly explained. "Pierre has been chosen to go to

130

the network headquarters on a farm outside Lyon to set up a photography lab. He wants me to go to his sister's home outside Paris, until he can send for me. Will you come, too?"

Without a moment's hesitation, Mother said she would. She added that she had a friend she could stay with, who lived near Paris. "That way I will be nearby whenever you need me." I told her we'd probably leave in a week or so. Pierre needed time to get his equipment together, and to contact his sister.

After Mother left, I sat quietly for awhile and let the profound sense of loss I felt for Granny Rose sweep over me. She was not unaware of the danger, but I guessed she didn't realize the full extent of risk until it was too late. I swallowed my grief and considered the task at hand of packing and preparing to leave. Marc toddled over to me and uttered a few cooing sounds as if to ask if I was all right. I hugged him tightly as tears streamed down my cheeks. The memories of my visits with her and eating in grand restaurants flowed through my mind. She was always so gracious. Those scenes seemed like a world away from my life today. Saddest of all, Granny Rose would never see her great-grandson. She would have been so proud of him.

Pierre came in, eyes bright with excitement, and arms loaded with packages. "Look Isabelle, at what I have managed to get at the shop. A used, but very good, Leica camera, and all the equipment I will need to set up the dark room and photo lab. Isn't that great?"

I nodded numbly, but didn't trust myself to speak. Pierre looked up and noticed my tears and asked what had happened. I cried again when I told him about Granny Rose. He had never met her but knew about her from my stories. He put his arms around me, and I wanted to stay there forever. But I knew I could not stop my life to grieve. I must prepare for the move.

The next evening we had just gone to bed, when we were suddenly awakened by a loud boom, boom knocking sound on the front door downstairs. I heard Paul, the manager, call out from his first floor apartment, "Who is it?" I could not hear the muffled reply, but I heard Paul say next in a very loud voice, "Oh, the Gestapo. Just a minute, I'll get the key."

With that, we jumped out of bed and scurried around the apartment, getting rid of all the incriminating materials. Pierre grabbed a box of blank identification cards and threw them out the window to the court below. I put the typewriter in the closet and threw a heap of dirty clothes over it. We knew the Gestapo had come for us.

Soon we heard a rap on our door. I had just finished nursing Marc and went to the door, with a sleepy, stupid look pasted on my face. I opened the door and said in a low voice. "Please don't make any noise. My baby has just gone to sleep."

Two soldiers came inside. They were large, officious men, who looked around as if they were sizing up the situation. They did not divulge any reason for their visit. I wandered around aimlessly, keeping that dumb expression pasted on my face, belying the anxiety I felt inside.

Pierre had quickly dressed in his robe and came forward now, his knees shaking, as he extended his hand and spoke to the German officers in their language. "What do you want of us?" he asked. "We're just a young couple with a baby."

The soldiers appeared surprised to be addressed in German. "We will visit with you for a while," one of them said.

Pierre invited them to sit down and chatted casually with them. The officers continued to be non-committal about the reason for their visit. Not only that, they appeared in no hurry to either search the apartment or leave. As Pierre chatted with them, the officers relaxed, but I could see that Pierre was far from relaxed. Finally, after two hours, they left, but it seemed like an eternity to me. They had not searched the apartment or threatened us. Nor did they enlighten us about the reason for their visit.

After the Gestapo officers left, and we had shut the door behind them, Pierre and I looked at each other, feeling the danger of their visit more than our exhaustion. "What do we do now?" asked Pierre. "We can't stay here."

He paced the floor, frowning in deep thought. "I'll go on to Lyon tomorrow, but I can't leave you here. You'll have to go to my sister, Lucienne's now. She has a baby, too, just a few weeks younger than Marc. The cousins will get acquainted."

I had many questions, but Pierre seemed to anticipate them all. "Of course I will accompany you.

Unfortunately, we don't have time to let my sister know we're coming. I know her apartment is quite large, and she'll be happy to have you stay with them. Her husband is not Jewish, so you should be safe with them.

SEVEN: On the Move Again

I waited until morning, before calling Mother and telling her to get ready to leave. Pierre and I quickly got all our belongings together. He packed his photography equipment neatly in a box, while I struggled to sort and pack all Marc's things and his carriage. I'm not sure how, but Pierre managed to get train tickets to Paris for all of us. I was not as apprehensive about the trip as I was about meeting his parents and his sister and her family.

We managed the train trip in spite of the crowds and the abundance of things I had packed for my baby. Mother came with us to Paris but headed for the apartment of her friend. Since her friend lived in a small town nearby, she promised to visit me every week.

As we stood at the door at Pierre's sister's apartment, my hands were clammy with fear. I didn't know what to expect. Would she turn us away? Would she be cold and distant? I had not met any of Pierre's family and felt so inadequate. This was certainly not a time when I looked my best. Fortunately, Marc lay content in my arms.

Pierre rang the bell and a lovely young woman with dark hair and flashing eyes like Pierre's, opened the door. She stared at the two of us in disbelief. "Pierre, Pierre, I'm so happy to see you. We were just talking about you the other day. Mother worries about you constantly." Then she turned to me and said, "And you must be Isabelle. Pierre has told us all about you, and I'm glad to finally meet you."

She invited us inside, and Pierre told Lucienne our plight. He kept the details of his destination vague, but hinted at some danger and difficult circumstances. Lucienne nodded, her eyes focused on Pierre as he talked. Then she turned to me and said, "Of course, you can stay here, Isabelle, and we'll love having little Marc." She looked at our son as she said, "Perhaps the two cousins can play together. Little Beatrice is a fussy baby and takes all my time. Perhaps with Marc here, she'll be more content."

Pierre's parents came in just then, saying that they'd heard our voices and wanted to see who had come They were overcome with joy to see Pierre, and hugged him. They greeted Marc and me warmly. Still, I did not feel they were overjoyed to see us. I smiled wanly and determined I would make the best of things. After all, this was an opportunity to get to know the family into which I had married. Lucienne made me feel welcome, and not like an unwanted stranger. I was grateful for that. She indicated that there was a spare bedroom for Marc and me.

Pierre stayed just long enough to get us settled, and then left for the central network headquarters. I did not know exactly where he would be or when I'd see him again, even though he assured me that he'd be back in six weeks. I only knew that he was in danger. After he left, I was very lonely. The thought that Mother was nearby was comforting, but I knew I would not see her often. I hugged Marc and went to our room to settle in.

The days crawled by at an interminable pace. Instead of feeling grateful for the sanctuary Lucienne and her husband offered me and my child, I felt bored. Lucienne and her husband had no interest in the war, and could never have understood the zeal Pierre and I felt about our Resistance efforts. Lucienne was a devoted mother and, true to her word, little Beatrice did occupy all her time. Marc, just over a year old, was beginning to take a few steps. He was a friendly toddler with dimpled cheeks and curly, brown hair. My son was a lively child and a delight to me. I was disappointed that Pierre's parents paid little attention to him. They often told me how cute they thought Marc was, but they did not play with him or cuddle him.

What separated me from Pierre's family, more than anything else, was our differing politics. I considered myself a patriotic woman, who would gladly do anything to help her country. Since Lucienne's husband was not Jewish, she seldom thought about her situation. She was totally absorbed in little Beatrice.

Pierre's father, Henri, often remarked that he felt his son was wasting his time and risking his life needlessly. He did not conceal the fact that he was not interested in the Jewish problem, and, even less in underground activities. I tried to avoid the subject, not only because Pierre's father had firm opinions, but I also suspected that they felt I was responsible for Pierre's involvement in the Resistance Organization. I looked forward to those rare occasions when Mother visited. We usually took Marc for a walk, so we could talk freely. While Pierre's parents were pleasant to Mother, they did not appear interested in getting to know her, either.

The weeks dragged on. While I was safe, I felt useless. I wanted to be part of the Resistance movement again and do something for the liberation of my country. Never mind the danger. I'd prefer danger to sitting out the war in boredom. I longed for Pierre.

Lately, I had noticed that I was nauseated in the morning. I guessed I was probably still grieving over Granny Rose or just bored. When the nausea continued, I realized that I was pregnant again. I was shocked. Since I had been nursing Marc, I assumed I would not get pregnant. I supposed I was the exception to the rule. I worried about Pierre's reaction.

Clothing was scarce and I knew a maternity dress would be out of the question. I had difficulty obtaining even the simplest items. There were no silk stockings for women. I didn't have a coat, but managed to find a few rabbit pelts, which I draped around my shoulders for a wrap. I constantly wore my only pair of shoes, a pair of Rafia sandals. I was delighted when I was given a coupon for shoes, because I was pregnant. I sent the maid to pick up the shoes, but she never returned. So I lost that pair of shoes, before I ever got them.

When the weather grew warmer, I began to expand, and I knew I'd have to create a maternity dress. I fashioned a loose tent style dress out of one of my old dresses. I now wore that tent dress most of the time. If the situation were not so sad, I would have laughed at this hilarious outfit. If the girls from the lycee could only see me now, I thought.

One day as I was crossing the hall, I heard a light tap at the door. When I opened the door, I saw a strange man standing there, a felt hat pulled over his eyes. When he stepped inside, I was delighted to find Pierre in one of his disguises. When he hugged me, I whispered softly, "I can't continue like this. I love you and miss you terribly. While your sister has been good to us, I cannot stay out of the action. I must join you, no matter how dangerous."

Pierre listened to me and then replied, "I'd rather have you stay here for your safety, but it's obvious you don't want to do that. I'll see what I can do." I nodded gratefully and then told him that I was sure he'd want to be around when his second child was born.

"My second child?" he said as he backed away to get a better look at my expanding figure. "Isabelle, Isabelle," he said, shaking his head. When I asked if he was happy, he responded quickly that of course he was. "It's just that this isn't the most opportune time."

I had to admit that he was right about that. "But I don't feel the situation is impossible. We'll make the most of it. What else can we do? Tell me all about the place. What have you been doing?"

"Well, Georges and Gyp have come," he said. "The farm itself is an odd assortment of buildings, some rather primitive. There are two large two story houses, fairly new, connected by a glass gallery, a hallway actually, built around a little park with large trees. I'm afraid these houses are rather primitive, my dear, with the bathroom and kitchen in the pavilion next door. The pavilion is actually about 50 meters from the houses. The former owners still occupy the pavilion, but should be gone soon. In the meantime we have to go to the dairy building for running water or simple cooking. Things are rather sparse."

My hopes sank. The living conditions did, indeed, sound crude. I asked if there would be room for Marc and me. Pierre shrugged as he said, "You and Marc will share my bedroom. The room is small with few furnishings, but that's all everyone else has. Georges and Gyp are next door to me. The place really is rather a mess. Are you still sure you want to come?"

"Oh yes," I said. "I can manage most anything as long as I'm with you." Pierre hugged me and told me how much he had missed me, but he was still worried about the danger I might be in. I put my fingers on his lips and said, "We'll face it together."

Pierre's parents came in just then, having heard our voices, and were surprised to see their son. They asked many questions, and Pierre told them quite a different story about the farm, than the one he had told me. He made light of his experiences, focusing on his photography duties. They urged him to stay, but he left quickly, saying he had arrangements to make so I could join him soon.

EIGHT: Le Domaine de Chaponost

True to his word, Pierre sent for me, and Mother as well, for whom he had received special permission, to come by train to Lyon. He planned to meet us at the train station. When Mother came to help me pack, she looked at my now pregnant shape with surprise, and asked where this child would be born. "Well, Mother," I murmured, "There was a child born in a stable."

Mother and I bid hasty adieus to Lucienne and Pierre's parents. While they encouraged me to stay, I sensed they were relieved that I was leaving. Mother managed our luggage while I carried Marc when we boarded the Metro to the train station. There were four stations in Paris, and in our turmoil, we got off at the wrong one. But Mother, in her determined way, led me along as we backtracked to the right train station, where we boarded the train to Lyon. Once on board, the conductor gave us a compartment with a couchette. I gratefully stretched out on the small couch. Marc was excited and seemed to realize that we were going on a trip. Fortunately, we had no problem with the passport control, and arrived at Lyon at dusk.

Pierre was there waiting for us on the train platform in Lyon. He gathered me into his arms, and little Marc ran up to be included in the hugs. Mother stood a short distance away. I turned to her and asked, "Where will you go, now?"

"Don't worry about me, Isabelle. I will find a position, and let you know where I am."

I nodded. On the trip, Mother and I had discussed at length how to keep in touch once we were in Lyon. Since I would be at the headquarters, I knew I would not be allowed to contact anyone outside. Pierre had been very firm that this was a strict rule, and would include my Mother. But we had decided that at least she could communicate her whereabouts to me. She planned to find a spot at the station, where she could leave a note for me.

Mother gave Marc and me a goodbye kiss, and then walked ahead through the station, with Pierre and me trailing behind. I watched as she stopped by the posting board, which listed the arrivals and departures of the trains, on the weathered front wall of the station. Pausing just a moment, she slid her hand behind the board and looked at me, signaling that the left lower corner would be the spot.

As Mother walked away, I noticed a scruffy man standing by a horse drawn wagon. I assumed he was a peasant farmer, since he was wearing the usual blue jeans with a knitted cap pulled low over his forehead. He approached us and nodded to Pierre, but said nothing as he helped Pierre load my luggage into the back of the wagon. Pierre helped me into the wagon, and then settled Marc on my lap. The peasant climbed up to the driver's seat and proceeded to drive the horses down the road. We sat in the back of the wagon, which bounced along on the rutted dirt roads. This old cart and the bumpy roads were primitive compared to cars and paved highways. I felt as if I had gone back in time.

Strangely enough, the peasant sitting in front struck up a casual conversation with me that soon became rather personal. Questions like, "Where was I from? What was my education? What did I think of the war?" I couldn't imagine why a peasant would ask me so many questions. I answered his questions with as few words as possible. I was puzzled by his behavior. Strangely, Pierre said nothing to enlighten me.

Darkness had fallen by the time we had arrived at the farm. The peasant got out of the cart and opened a pair of metal gates fastened to cement pillars and drove the horses on through, their hooves clattering on the circular drive. Soon I saw dimly in the darkness the connected houses with the pavilion nearby that Pierre had told me about. He helped me out of the wagon, and we followed the peasant into a house and up the stairs to the second floor. Our bedroom was near the end of a long hall. Although Pierre had told me about the sparse accommodations, I was not prepared for the reality. I was appalled to find only a single bed and table in the room, a small sink with a water faucet and a closet. Somehow Pierre had managed to unearth a crib for Marc. I knew the bathroom and kitchen were next door, but this was small comfort for a pregnant woman.

The peasant placed my luggage in the room and left quickly. I sat down on the bed and looked over the room. "I know this is the bedroom you occupied before we came. While it is adequate for one man, it hardly seems suitable for a couple with a baby."

Pierre shrugged and said, "No one has it much better here. Actually, things were worse at first. There were many broken windows and the birds flew in and built their nests in all the openings. We finally got the windows fixed. I warned you, Isabelle, that living here wouldn't be easy. Most of us consider our situation to be a sacrifice for our country."

In the morning, Pierre showed me around. "The farm is on thirty acres with three main houses and some smaller houses for the workers. See, Isabelle," he pointed out, "there is another two story house, just like the one we are in. The houses were recently constructed around a little park with large trees and are connected by a glass gallery or hallway." He pointed to a circular driveway. "That's where we came in last night."

I was especially interested in the pavilion, which was completely separate from the other two buildings, with an open balcony and bedrooms upstairs. Pierre showed me the bathroom and the kitchen and a dining room. All these rooms appeared to be adequate. He mentioned that Octave's quarters were upstairs. On the other side of our complex were the small houses of the farmers, the barn for the animals, which included five cows, three horses and four pigs. There was also a shed for grain storage, the dairy building and a chicken coop for a flock of chickens. Pierre pointed out two cars and some farm machinery.

Then Pierre took me to meet the Chef, Jacques Octave. The Chef rose from the table in the dining room where he'd been eating breakfast with some other agents and came forward to greet me warmly. I was both surprised and embarrassed to find that the scruffy man, I assumed to be a peasant, was actually the Chef. Obviously, he had been looking me over last night. We all laughed about the situation. My Uncle Georges and his wife, Gyp, were there, too, and came forward to greet me. "We're right next door to you," Georges said, "and will be around to help you any way we can. Where's my sister, Lucie?" he asked.

"She's somewhere in the village, I assume. She came with me on the train and plans to find a teaching position," I responded. I knew that Georges would be concerned about Mother, but I wasn't going to tell him that I would eventually know her whereabouts.

When we got back to our room, I railed at Pierre for not warning me, but he put a finger on my lips to stop me. "Now, now, Isabelle. I had the same sort of initiation, if you can call it that. When I arrived at the station in Lyon, Octave was dressed in the outfit of a gentleman farmer and met me along with the agent, Margot. I had never met the Chef, and I was disappointed that he had not bothered to come to meet me, but had instead sent this servant, who did not bother to greet me but said only, "Mr. Jules, get into my carriage." I turned to Margot and observed to her that the old chauffeur was very unfriendly and rude.

"But the ruse continued even after my arrival. Each time I saw Octave, he would be attired in his vest, hat and boots, still playing the role of a gentleman farmer. I was beginning to wonder where the Chef was, or if he even existed. After what seemed like a long time, they ended the charade. One evening, this gentleman farmer appeared at our dinner table, which was unusual. After dinner, Georges stood up, turned to me, and said very solemnly that he would like me to meet our Chef, Jacques Octave. The gentleman farmer stood up and came over and hugged me. I was astounded and didn't know whether to be angry or amused. I soon knew when everyone at the table, some ten people or so, burst into laughter. Your uncle laughed the loudest of all, and I suspect he had a lot to do with this little game. Anyway, we all had a good laugh and enjoyed champagne that night. That is also when I learned that the agent Margot is your cousin, Francoise."

I smiled at Pierre's story and felt better. I could sense the camaraderie he enjoyed here. I was surprised that Pierre mentioned Francoise. I had forgotten that my cousin was involved, too. I never knew her very well and hadn't seen her in a long time. I asked if she was at the farm all the time.

Pierre explained that Margot traveled around a lot and was only at the farm now and again. Apparently Octave trusted her and sent her out on important missions. Pierre frowned as he said that sometimes he was puzzled about her. He went on to tell me that Octave was not at the farm all the time, either. He was often away, and then his two children, four and seven years old, were looked after by Francoise or a young agent, Sophie.

"Pierre," I began hesitantly. "I know we can't tell our whereabouts, but Mother wanted to tell me hers. She planned to leave a note at the departure board at the station in the lower left hand corner—back side. Could you pick it up when you go to the village for supplies? I'm afraid if I went, I would arouse suspicion." Pierre nodded but warned me that we had to be very careful. He agreed that I should know where she was, and assured me that he would check the board tomorrow.

"Come along now, I want to show you my lab and all the equipment," he said eagerly. Pierre then led the way to the end of the hall where he had assembled a dark room complete with Leica lab equipment, and all the necessary chemicals. "These industrial chemical products are rare and difficult to get, but we've been able to purchase small quantities at a time. I've been busy reproducing thousands of leaflets, which represents our mail. I work six days, usually at night when the electricity is on. Georges often helps me. The results weren't very good at first, but now the pictures are quite excellent. Look," he said as he picked up a photocopy. "Now they are clear on all sides and small, the size of a playing card, yet big enough to read without a magnifying glass. We can put these in a small box that can be placed in a jacket or overcoat pocket, instead of a briefcase."

I was impressed and proud of my husband. He had achieved what he set out to do What a difference this would make in passing messages. All my misgivings about our sparse accommodations faded away, as I thought of getting started and being part of the network again. I knew I was only a small part of something very big, yet what I did was important. The network continued to piece together bits of information gathered by the agents roaming the country.

The next day as he had promised, Pierre swung by the station when he went into town on his bicycle to buy supplies. He told me he had looked around very carefully before he slipped his hand behind the board and came out with a folded piece of paper which he quickly placed inside his shirt. He told me to read it carefully and then destroy it.

I sat on the bed next to Marc, who was napping, and quickly scanned Mother's letter: She wrote, "My daughter, I hope you are all settled in your new place. I have done better than I thought possible. Once I left you, I walked into the village, looking for a room to rent. I knocked on the door of the first house I came to that had a "Room for Rent" sign in the window. A woman answered my knock, and I told her I would like to rent a room. The woman asked me what sort of work I did. When I told her that I tutored children with learning problems, she called to her husband and said, "I think God has descended upon us." Then she told me, with tears in her eyes, that her young son had learning problems. She was overjoyed to have a tutor under her roof. I will receive room and board in exchange for taking care of and tutoring this boy. There is no fuel, so the house is not heated, but I have a room and food. I'll wear my heavy sweater. What more could I ask for? Take care, my dear."

Wisely, Mother had mentioned no names and had not signed her letter. She had included an address and a phone number, which was dangerous, but necessary. I quickly memorized the numbers and destroyed the letter. I glanced at my sleeping son, and realized he would not be able to see much of his Grandmother now.

His Great Aunt Gyp, just next door, was already a granny substitute and often took Marc for walks about the farm. Sometimes I would join them. If it were not for the war, I could not have imagined a more peaceful place to live.

NINE: The Farm

I gradually adjusted to life on the farm with its few comforts, communal living and a fluctuating number of people. The farm was just outside Lyon near the small village of Chaponost. Jacques Octave had obviously organized the farm well to serve as the network headquarters. Agents came and went, and we always used first names, our code names.

De Gaulle had sent Jean Moulin to organize all the Resistance groups, including the Communists and Socialists, into the Free French Forces of the Interior. The Resistance re-formed and grew. Each region had a military delegate in liaison with London. (Unfortunately, Moulin was captured and executed in June 1943).

I grew accustomed to being called Elizabeth. Often there were a dozen of us at the table for meals in the pavilion, which we referred to as "Jacques' House." To prepare meals for so many people was challenging due to very little money and a short supply of food. Since the network center was on a farm with cows, we had milk, which we boiled, since it was not pasteurized. I was still nursing Marc, so I used some of the milk to make soups and puddings for him. I had brought along a small trunk of the jams I'd made in Aix Les Bains, which supplemented his diet. I had considered this my most precious possession when I carried it with me on the train.

We planted a vegetable garden including potatoes and snap peas. Our staples were dried beans and spaghetti, which we bought in large sacks. We varied our menu by having pasta at noon and beans in the evening on one day, and on the next we'd reverse the order. I made cheese from the milk, but unfortunately the worms ate the cheese faster than we did. One of the puddings I had made for Marc and left on the table overnight to cool, was eaten by a rat.

Occasionally, one of the farm hands would kill a pig, but the meat was reserved for the men. We women got very little of it. I often wondered about that, but no reason was ever given. Perhaps this was the farm custom. Did men in the Resistance work harder than the women? But at least, we could use a ham bone to flavor the beans. The smell of the beans and ham bone cooking in the kitchen was tempting. I helped with cooking as often as I could, but I was busy taking care of Marc and typing the messages for Pierre to photograph.

Besides Pierre's well equipped laboratory, there were also transmitters, guns and the network archives. These and other items of importance could be placed in underground cylinders (or silos) in an emergency. The previous owner had planted wheat which he stored in these. Thus the grain was hidden from the Germans, who would have sold it on the black market. Now the underground cylinders were a useful storage place for us.

Managing a baby still in diapers was a problem. To wash Marc's diapers, I found a large basin but had no soap and only cold water. During the day he walked around with a small apron to cover his bare bottom, since I saved the precious diapers for night. I hoped that he would use the potty I had placed in the middle of the bedroom to inspire him; however, I spent more time cleaning the floor than potty training my son. I lamented to Pierre one day that I tried to teach him to be kind and sit on the potty, but he wouldn't do it very often. Pierre was unconcerned, and told me that I couldn't rush things like that. I knew he was right, but I wanted to be rid of the diapers.

Pierre was quite busy in his lab, working at night when the electricity was on. I noticed that the messages now contained warnings to beware of this or that. The photographed messages were then dried on a small electric dryer, eight at a time. Thus far this unobtrusive, yet close to Lyon, location for the network headquarters had worked well. The Nazis hadn't noticed us, and we were able to carry on the business of passing information. My Aunt Gyp often transmitted the messages and was in charge of the kitchen as well. At other times, an agent would come to take the messages and pass them on. Uncle Georges often helped Pierre at night in the lab, and I would hear them singing, "We stand or fall, and each for all and all for each, until we reach the journey's end." Uncle Georges appeared to be very close to Octave and involved in special projects. My cousin, Francoise, also appeared to have a special relationship with Jacques Octave. Could she be having an affair with him, or were they just good friends?

Our days were turned upside down when Marc developed whooping cough. He was even more miserable, since he was teething as well. One day as he sat in his crib, he leaned over, grabbed the curtain on the window, and chewed on it so hard, he literally ripped it to pieces. I was astounded to find that he had eaten half the curtain in the short time that I was gone from the room. Every time I fed him, he coughed and particles of food flew everywhere. To make matters worse, Pierre and I also caught whooping cough. Somehow, we managed to keep the lab functioning and messages moving.

Once we recovered, Pierre and I decided to go to Lyon and find a doctor for my pregnancy check up. The doctor could give me a pregnancy card which would entitle me to certain benefits. I begged Pierre to allow Mother to meet us in Lyon. He relented, and left a message for her. Gyp agreed to take care of Marc for the day.

I was excited to see Mother again. For this special occasion, I wore my one good dress, which I had made from an old dressing gown with snap buttons down the front. Mother looked me over after giving me a big hug. Although she didn't comment, I knew what she was thinking. She looked well, and said she was happy with the family. The boy she tutored was quite agreeable. This family had taken in another boarder, a young woman, she told me, who had become her good friend.

I felt uneasy as we strolled along the streets of Lyon because there were many German soldiers milling about. When I asked Pierre about it, he nodded and said that there were more in evidence now then when he had last been in the city. I knew there was no obvious sign that we were in the Resistance, yet I felt uncomfortable each time a group of soldiers passed us.

Finding a doctor was an adventure in itself. Since we did not know anyone, we simply looked for a street with lots of doctors' offices and strolled along. Pierre read all the brass plates on the walls, which listed the physicians' names and their specialties. We quickly eliminated the surgeons and psychiatrists, and finally found a "doctor for women," who sounded promising.

The doctor was very kind, and said he could see me right away. He told me I was in good health and that the baby would be born the 12th of October. He advised me to continue wearing my maternity corset, as I had done every day. My corset was a cumbersome cloth contraption with sewn in metal rods to support my growing abdomen, and laced in the middle. He then gave me a small cup, in which to give him a urine sample. This was quite an embarrassing task since there was no toilet in his office. The doctor then gave me a pregnancy card which granted me a seat on public transportation, and entitled me to more food. I took the card gratefully, thinking this would not only help me, but everyone on the farm as well.

We left the office and headed down the street, when I noticed a small coiffure shop. I stopped and stared in the window. I told Pierre that I was so tired of looking like a rag. I begged him to let me get my hair washed. Pierre readily agreed. He and Mother then went their separate ways.

As I walked into the shop, I had a sudden urge to color my black hair red. And so I did. When I left the shop an hour later, I felt elegant in my good dress and new hairdo: purplish-red hair swooped up high and held in place by big combs. I stared at my reflection in the shop windows and was astounded. Oh my, I look like a tart, I thought.

I went into the café next door and sat down at a table to wait for Pierre and Mother. A German soldier walked by and not only gave me a second glance, but looked at me flirtatiously, smiling invitingly. At that moment Pierre walked in and I stood up, my pregnancy no longer obscured. The soldier appeared stunned and quickly looked away.

"See that soldier over there?" I asked Pierre. "He's been flirting with me, but look at him now." The soldier had turned crimson red and was staring intently at the menu. Pierre did not seem offended. On the contrary, he smiled, and appeared pleased that his pregnant wife could still turn a few heads.

Then he looked me over carefully, saying, "Oh my god, Isabelle, what have you done to your hair?" I glanced down and told him that I had been so disgusted with myself and felt so ugly, that I decided to be daring and do something different. I asked what he thought. "I don't know. It'll take some getting used to a red-headed wife. I rather liked the black hair. But on the other hand, you haven't gone unnoticed," he said impishly.

Just then, Mother walked up and added her opinion to my transformation. "I like it. You look daring and sexy. Perhaps just what you need in your present condition."

We bid Mother a hasty farewell, and headed off to find our bus. Since we had ridden our bicycle to the train station, we needed a bus to get us back there. I was quite used to riding perched on the back of the bicycle while Pierre pedaled.

There was no bus at the bus station which threw us into a panic, because we had to be in before curfew and the hour was fast approaching. A truck driver drove up and offered to drive us to the train station for a fee. Pierre negotiated with him, and the driver told us to hop into the back of his truck.

The truck was a large flatbed truck. When Pierre helped me up, I was astonished to find the truck already full of people. Pierre and I stood in the front section. I guessed that since the bus was not operating, this clever truck driver had taken advantage of the situation by offering everybody rides in his truck.

We started down the road, and the ride was bumpy and swaying. I had a hard time remaining standing. When the truck chugged up a very steep hill, the engine overheated and streams of hot water spewed out all over those of us standing in the front of the truck. I was drenched. "Oh my beautiful dress," I cried as I looked at my soaked dress. Strands of red hair hung in clumps around by face. "And my lovely hairdo is ruined." My combs had been knocked off by the force of the water.

Pierre and I arrived back at the farm late. Octave greeted us sternly. "I take my position as leader seriously, and I will not tolerate any breach of security." When he found out that we had not only been in contact with Mother, but had actually met her today in Lyon, he literally put us on trial. Uncle Georges was also present and looked just as stern as Octave.

"Jules and Elizabeth," Octave began, "You are both second lieutenants in the Free French Forces of the Interior. As such, you know that you are not to have contact with anyone outside the organization. I am not a strict military man, but I must keep the network center safe. This was a serious infraction of the rules, one which deserves punishment."

I glanced at Uncle Georges, but he did not look at me or give me any indication of support. He continued to stand with a stern expression on his face, nodding in agreement to all that Octave said.

My thoughts drifted off as Octave continued to speculate about an appropriate punishment. What a day, I thought. I get my hair dyed red and am nearly propositioned by a German soldier. Next, my new hair-do is ruined, my one good dress is soaked with rusty water, and I'm about to face court martial. What else can happen?

My reverie was interrupted by Octave, who asked, "And do you also agree, Elizabeth?" He looked at me expectantly. I took a moment or two to collect my thoughts and then told him that I was sorry. I was so tired, that I hadn't heard what he had asked me.

"I asked if you would promise never to see your mother again or anyone else, for that matter, who is not one of us." I assured him that I would obey this command, and I promised never to contact anyone outside the farm again.

There were sighs of relief all around, and we shook hands. Pierre and I went back to our room and tumbled quickly into bed. Gyp had put Marc down in his crib earlier, and he was sleeping soundly. You were almost the son of criminals, I thought. What could they do to us, anyway? Pierre and I were a vital part of sending messages. They could replace me, but no one knew what Pierre did about the photography and film development.

Pierre and I kept our promise and did not contact Mother. Life continued on as before with my typed messages being put on film and taken by agents, who passed them on to other agents throughout our region. While we were isolated on the farm, we could send messages from the transmitter in Tours in western France for transmission to England. Usually an agent delivered the message. I had heard that my cousin, Francoise, had left for Tours. I saw so little of her, that I never knew if she was at the farm, or gone on a mission.

TEN: Arrests. Flight

On June 6, 1944, the news of the debarkation of Allied troops on the shores of Normandy filled us with joy. Unfortunately our joy was short lived. Pierre was so excited about D-Day that he ran about hugging people and jumping up and down like a crazy man. "This is it! This is it! The liberation has begun." He grabbed Marc and danced about with him, and then ran next door and gave Georges a big hug. Georges did not look pleased about being awakened so early.

Pierre then went to the wine cellar in the pavilion and grabbed a few bottles of champagne to celebrate. Soon we were all saluting one another with a glass of champagne. "This is a day incontestable, one that can't be beat," Pierre led the toast. "We'll save some champagne for the first American jeeps that appear." He said this as if he expected them to arrive any moment.

Jacques Octave was very skeptical. "There are Germans swarming all over Lyon, and the Allies are a long way from here. We'll have to be on guard more than ever. When the Germans realize that defeat is near, they will be zealous to arrest anyone involved in subversive activities before the Allies arrive."

We continued passing vital information to the Allies about German defenses and troop movements in Normandy as agents brought the news to us. We heard that the coordination of a railroad and telephone sabotage campaign during the Normandy invasion by a Resistance group had been quite successful. Another of these groups was the Maquis, young men who had gone underground to escape forced labor. They moved to Normandy and delayed German reinforcements from arriving.

In just a few weeks, Octave's prediction came true. Early one morning as we were finishing breakfast, one of the agents, Marc (Sarigue) came riding up on a bicycle. He was terribly upset and nearly gray with fear. "The Gestapo came to our house very early before the sun was up and arrested everyone there, including my parents and my sister, who is pregnant. My family was unaware that I was working for the Resistance. I chose not to tell them, because I did not want to put them in any danger. But now look what's happened. I'm the only one who got away. I ran out while the soldiers were occupied and jumped over the hedges," he shook his head sadly. "I found a neighbor's bicycle and hopped on, pedaling here as fast as I could The agent was nearly hysterical and took a moment to compose himself before continuing his story. Looking at Octave, he said, "I came to warn you. The Gestapo is on your trail."

Octave looked grim and troubled This was not Octave's only problem. We all knew his personal liaisons were catching up with him. When he became Chef in 1943 and moved the headquarters to the farm, his wife had stayed behind at the school. Cherie, his mistress of long standing, had been arrested and released. The organization later took Cherie back again as an agent, which proved unwise. She was allowed to work for the Resistance as a letter-box, or receiving agent for passing messages.

Cherie, also known as "the Duchess", and her sixteen year old daughter had shown up at the farm the previous month seeking refuge. She begged Octave to allow them to remain as they had nowhere else to go, and she felt her life was in danger. She was unaware that Octave had a new love interest: Sophie, the young agent, who was rather free with her affections. To resolve his dilemma, Octave sent Sophie on a mission rather than sending a more experienced agent. (Cherie and her daughter often took care of Octave's children.)

Sending Sophie proved to be a fatal mistake. Not only was she known by the Gestapo and often watched, but she was also careless. We learned that Sophie had gone to Chaponost to shop for us and purchased some bottled water. She shoved the ticket for bottle redemption in her pocket and forgot about it. While on the mission, she was arrested at a friend's house where she had gone, instead of going to a designated safe place as she had been instructed. The Gestapo searched her and found the ticket in her pocket. Thus the Gestapo knew where she came from, and her trail led back to the farm. (Octave had shared this with us earlier to increase our diligence, to be on guard.)

Octave called Georges over and the two men conferred. Their voices were low, but they frequently gestured and nodded. Octave looked worried. Finally he announced, "We'll have to leave and abandon our headquarters here, since we don't know for sure who's been arrested and what information has been tortured out of them. We know Sophie has been arrested, and Margot (Francoise) is late in returning from Tours. Sarigue (Marc) has warned us that the Gestapo is on our trail."

He paused for a moment and then continued, "We obviously won't be able to take everything with us. At present, we don't know where we can go. Georges will take Jules and the two of them will scour the countryside on bicycles and see what they can find to rent." Looking at Jules (Pierre,) he said, "I'm sorry, but the photography equipment will have to be left here as well as the typewriter. I know you'll be starting all over again, but agents are more important than equipment."

We quickly banded together and placed the archives and other incriminating and valuable items in the cylinder underneath the greenhouse. We gathered the guns, the transmitter, the photographs and the contents of the lab. We destroyed as much of the incriminating materials as possible. The darkroom now looked like an empty bedroom.

Pierre and Georges took off on bicycles to begin their search. I watched them ride off, feeling as if I were sitting on top of a volcano that could blow at any moment. I spent the day in my room with Marc and Gyp. The air was hot and humid, almost stifling, even though the windows were open. A sudden noise drew me to the window and I looked out and saw Francoise walking about under the trees in the courtyard. What was she doing? I considered running downstairs to greet her, but then saw a man following her who I did not recognize. The situation was not only puzzling, but scary. She was casually strolling about the courtyard, gesturing and pointing. One of our agents appeared, but rather than greeting him, she smiled, placed her fingers on her lips to indicate he should keep quiet. Then she left. I told all this to Gyp and she was as puzzled as I was. What did this mean? Did Octave know she was back? My throat was dry with anticipation.

Pierre and Georges appeared at dusk, empty-handed. Although they had ridden all over the countryside, they found nothing to rent, not even with an offer of gold. They told us that the surrounding area of Lyon had been heavily bombed and was devastated. We talked about the situation with Octave and he decided that there was nothing we could do but wait for morning. Octave appeared quite worried about the sudden appearance of Margot, (Francoise) especially since she had not come to see him.

Early the next morning, July 31, 1944, around 6:00 a.m., we were awakened by a noise in the courtyard. I got up quickly, peered through the blinds, and saw a German soldier pointing a gun at the window. He gestured to another soldier, while he walked stealthily toward the door of our building, his rifle slung under his arm. I struggled to get dressed, which was no mean feat since I had to get my corset around my large abdomen prior to pulling on my tent dress. Before I could even arouse Pierre, a German soldier burst into our room, his gun drawn. He walked over to Pierre and ordered him to get dressed. "Macht schnell," he said grimly.

Marc started to cry and I picked him up and held him in my arms. As Pierre got up and reached for his pants, I noticed his shoes on the floor and quickly kicked them under the bed. The soldier demanded that Pierre hurry and come with him. "But he doesn't have any shoes," I said.

"Where are they?" demanded the soldier. I told him the shoes were in the closet at the end of the corridor. I spoke innocently, vying for time.

I knew that Pierre and I must get rid of the most incriminating item of all: our half sentences with our identification numbers for the Free French Forces of the Interior. (When we were accepted in the Free French Forces, we sent our sentences to London. One was kept there, while the other was sent back along with a number. Mine also had "La Catholique," my nickname, written on it.) I kept mine in a book, which I noticed lying on the table. While the soldier was preoccupied with Pierre pulling on his pants, I backed up to the table, with Marc in my arms, and felt around for the book. I quickly snatched the piece of paper, crumpled it up and turned my back to the soldier as I shoved that paper in my mouth and swallowed it. To swallow a piece of paper with a dry mouth at 6:00 in the morning was an awful task. Then I put on my stupid look and said, "I'll see about those shoes." I opened the door and headed down the hall to the closet.

The soldier came with me, prodding me in my ribs with his gun. As we passed the room where Pierre dried his negatives on the wires strung about, the soldier asked what those wires were for. "Oh, those are the wires for drying my son's diapers," I said calmly, hoping he didn't notice my quaking voice.

When we passed the darkroom, my pulse raced as my anxiety rose higher. Even with everything removed, the space was obviously a darkroom with the windows totally covered. Fortunately, the soldier marched me past the room, without giving it a second glance. I shuffled along to the closet at the end of the hall and found Pierre's other pair of shoes and an old brush. I reached in, brought out the shoes, taking my time, brushing the shoes while balancing Marc on my hip. He clung to me, his eyes wide with fear. "What are you doing?" demanded the soldier. Playing the idiot, I very calmly told him that I was cleaning the shoes because they were dirty.

"Enough of this," the soldier grunted as he again prodded me in my ribs with his gun and marched me back to the bedroom. I hoped that Pierre had enough time to dispose of his paper. As we walked by Uncle Georges and Aunt Gyp's room, I saw they were receiving similar treatment. I suppressed a grin when I noticed that Uncle Georges had left his bottles of paints open and had a half finished landscape painting up on an easel. He loved to give the impression that he was an artist living in the country. He had obviously planned this charade last night. Another Gestapo soldier was not fooled and was prodding him in the ribs and marching him out the door.

Back in our room, I handed the shoes to Pierre, and he gave me a meaningful look which I assumed meant that he'd gotten rid of his incriminating paper. The soldier then took Pierre with him, but left me and Marc in the room. As I stood there waiting for my summons, which I felt would be any moment, my glance fell upon the table. I remembered that we had carelessly left an undeveloped film with pictures of agents in the drawer.

Last week, Uncle Georges had arranged a party for all the agents in the area. He suggested a fantasy wedding charade, a social evening to relieve the tension and pressure we felt. Rarely did so many of the agents gather in one place as they did that night. They came from all around in wedding finery for the party and we celebrated the Allied invasion again. Pierre had taken a number of pictures, and then tossed the film in the drawer and forgot about it. I opened the drawer now and quickly exposed the film, tossing it back in. At least that danger had been eliminated.

I heard shouting and footsteps all about and imagined that the farm was literally swarming with soldiers by now. The next thing I heard was the clunk of a heavy boot in the hall, and a soldier walked in and ordered me to come with him. At least this one did not feel the need to poke his gun in my ribs. I picked up Marc and went with the soldier to the dining room in the pavilion. There was quite a crowd assembled, and I guessed that the soldiers had gathered all the people who lived on the farm, as well as any delivery people who happened to show up at the farm this morning. There was even a neighbor who had picked this inopportune moment to come by. All of us stood around uncertainly. I wanted to sit down, but the young soldier kept all of us standing.

We heard moans and shouts from upstairs where Jacques Octave shared his bedroom with his mistress, Cherie. I noticed she was standing in the dining room with the rest us, her face ashen with fear. I trembled as I heard the sound of water running and muffled screams of pain from our leader, who was apparently in the bath tub, being interrogated. Between shouted questions, I imagined that the soldiers were pushing hot or cold rods down his throat, a frequent interrogation torture. Another well-known method was to plunge the prisoner's head under water and then hit his head with a stick to bring him back to consciousness. If the Gestapo did not get the answers they wanted, they hit the prisoner over and over again. Next I heard loud slaps and the sound of blows to his head. Octave's moans became fainter and fainter, and then I heard nothing for awhile. I felt faint and began to sway. Pierre moved closer and supported me on his chest. His expression was grim. I had never seen him look so afraid.

The young soldier guarding us was a Frenchman in a German uniform. He was part of a legion of volunteers who had offered to work with the Germans. (This police military organization was created in 1943 for those Frenchmen who chose to work with the Gestapo.) He was pacing back and forth between the table and the fireplace. As he paced, he grabbed apricots from the large basket on the table where they had been placed to dry, chewed them up and spit the pits into the fireplace. I was aggravated and glared at him. I thought his behavior was rude and condescending, at the very least.

Next, the soldier commanded us put our hands over our heads, except for me because I was pregnant. A farmer's wife fainted, and the soldier relented and allowed us to sit on chairs or on the floor, against the wall. I sank gratefully into a chair, and settled Marc on my lap. He did not whimper, which was surprising to me since he had not had any breakfast. His eyes were still wide with fear, and he clung to me.

A well-dressed man, obviously one of the lieutenants of the Lyon Gestapo, came in and began asking questions, while the young Gestapo Frenchman looked on. "Where is Marc?" he asked, as he came to each of us in turn. Everyone shook their heads or said they had no idea who he was talking about.

I knew he was referring to Marc (Sarigue) the agent who had come to warn us yesterday, but I decided to play my dumb role when he came to me. "Marc? "I said. "Why he's right here sitting on my lap." In that moment I felt that I could defend myself in any situation either by being arrogant or stupid, whatever the situation warranted. I was no longer paralyzed by fear. I could change my demeanor in an instant. By now, I had had enough of these traitorous Frenchmen and wanted to give them a hard time.

My interrogator was not amused. His response was to glare at me and tell all of us to stand up again with our hands above our heads, facing the wall. This time he included me. I gently stood Marc on the floor in front of me and he wrapped his arms about my knees. I moved a little in an effort to see what was happening. Marc peeked through my legs and appeared to be fascinated by the soldier's shiny guns on his belt. I stood quietly, vowing to avoid encouraging the rage of this man again. I whispered to Pierre, "Before they leave, do you think they'll shoot us as we stand here, facing the wall?"

The lieutenant remarked that we had entirely too much liberty and he would put our noses to the wall. He then walked around the room and chose a person at random and made accusations. When that person didn't react, he moved on to the next one. When he came to Gyp, she also didn't react, even though he grabbed her glasses off her nose and ground them under his foot.

Suddenly, Francoise walked into the dining room and sat down. She was accompanied by another soldier. "Why are you interrogating these people," she asked. "They don't know anything. They're all refugees from Paris, who came to the country so they could have food and live a little better. See that young woman over there," she said pointing at me. "She's pregnant, and she was starving in Paris."

Her intercession helped our situation. Yet, I suspected that Francoise had led them to the farm, a traitorous thing to do. Why had she done it? Was she angry with Octave? When the Nazis arrested her, had she traded us for her freedom? Yet I was grateful that at the last moment, she tried to save us. But her betrayal had harmed Octave most of all, and no last-minute intervention could save him.

I had the distinct impression that they didn't know what to do with us. The lieutenant then told us to turn around, and allowed us to drop our arms to our sides. He next commanded all the men to drop their pants and expose their genitals. They were obviously looking for signs of circumcision. Fortunately neither Pierre nor Uncle Georges had been circumcised. (My grandfather was an artist who chose to defy traditions). The soldiers appeared disappointed that they had not found any Jews among us.

Around noon, Jacques Octave staggered down the stairs, supported by two of his torturers. His wrists were tied behind his back and he was wearing only a pair of shorts. His face was expressionless and a mass of bruises. He did not look up or speak. Apparently he had not had time to swallow the cyanide capsule he always kept in his pocket, because they had hauled him out of bed before he was awake. I noticed his seven year old son look at him and murmur, "I won't see my Daddy again."

The whole troop of thirty Gestapo soldiers, French, German and Italian, suddenly appeared outside the dining room. Several of them came inside and headed down to the wine cellar. I watched as they came upstairs with armfuls of bottles. The precious champagne that we had saved to celebrate the anticipated liberation went out the door with the Gestapo. With expressions of glee, they headed outside and piled into eight black Citroen cars.

Octave was firmly held by two soldiers. They said they were taking him to Fort de Montluc, an infamous prison in Lyon. Many of those from the Resistance who were arrested were sent there. The lieutenant told us not to move until 8:00 p.m. The parting word from the lieutenant in German was, "If we're not back by 8:00 this evening, you can consider yourselves free. If anyone leaves before 8:00, the others left will pay for it." I noticed he wore alligator shoes. I did not want to look at him, so I kept my gaze fastened on those shoes.

As soon as the last car had pulled out with the soldiers and Octave, the farmers and the delivery people left without a backward glance. The Gestapo was not interested in them. The farmers went back to their chores. They obviously did not understand what was going on and appeared frightened.

One by one the other agents also quickly exited until there were only Georges, Gyp, Pierre, Marc and me left. Cherie and her daughter took Octave's children with them. We sat there mulling over what we should do. Although the Gestapo had left, their threat to return remained. Now I knew what fear really was. My bravado crumbled as I mulled over the choices: Leave? Stay and see if they return?

"If we leave, it will be one more proof against our leader," I said. "I think we should just stay here." The others nodded in agreement, and so we stayed. The time between noon and eight felt like an eternity.

Pierre and Georges finally left on bicycles to tell Mother what had happened. Gyp and I looked about at the damage and saw that the cellar was now totally empty of any wine. Even worse was the sight of our rooms with all the drawers emptied and the contents thrown on the floor. Anything of value had been taken. Fortunately for me, they were not interested in baby things or a pregnant woman's items.

As I thought about our situation, I realized that if they returned, we would also be marched to prison. I knew that when a woman was arrested, her child was taken away from her and my blood ran cold at the thought. Uppermost in my mind was the survival of my son and my unborn child. I also knew that pregnant women in prison often suffered miscarriages because they were packed so tightly in cells that they couldn't sit down.

Pierre and Georges came back shortly before 8:00. Pierre breathlessly told me the plan. Mother was adamant that Pierre should take us and leave the farm immediately. She gave him the address of a friend in Lyon, whom she felt would provide us with a safe place to stay. Pierre had mulled over her advice, not wanting to back down, but ultimately concluded that she was right. He told her that he had exposed his pregnant wife and young son to danger long enough. Now was the time when he must protect us. He promised her we would leave.

Georges, on the other hand, decided that he and Gyp would stay on the farm and take their chances. He would cover for Pierre and me, should there be any questions. Pierre then told me that he had arranged transportation for us to the train station. "Now it is not elegant, Isabelle, but reliable and above suspicion." Pierre began. "I found a vegetable farmer with a charcoal powered truck, who will take us to the train station early in the morning. He will be here at 4:00 a.m."

I quickly agreed with Pierre's plan and began throwing together the few things we could manage to bring with us. I thought that with each move, I found less and less essentials to take along. I packed boxes of dry milk for Marc, but decided to give his carriage, bath tub and potty to the truck driver for his pregnant wife. Pierre had gotten to know all about the truck driver and his struggles. In the midst of packing, I had to lie down a few times because of cramps. No, no, I said to myself, I can't go into labor now. No, no. The cramps passed. I got up and finished packing.

In spite of the fact that we had not eaten for 24 hours, we had no appetite because we were so afraid. Even Marc threw up anything I tried to feed him. We rested quietly until the truck driver arrived promptly at 4:00 in the morning. I had dressed Marc in his best outfit of a little white coat and white gloves. I wore my best maternity dress with the snap buttons.

Pierre loaded our possessions into the back of the truck, which included our indispensable radio (to listen to London) and the bicycle. He helped me climb into the back of the truck and then handed up Marc. I settled among the carrots and cabbages. Pierre climbed up then and took Marc on his lap. The trip took over an hour and a half, even though we only went fifteen kilometers. The truck driver dropped us off at the train station and helped Pierre unload our belongings. Streaks of pink light appeared across the sky, ushering in the dawn.

ELEVEN: Liberation in Lyon

Pierre pulled out the scrap of paper on which Mother had written the address of her friend. In spite of the fact that rain was falling softly, we were able to find the apartment. I did not know if Mother had time to let them know we were coming, but she must have felt certain they would take us in. A maid answered the door and invited us in. Although she appeared surprised, she led the way to a small salon, where we sat down on comfortable chairs. Marc must have sensed that this was a safe place, because he ran about, chattering happily.

The maid said she would inform Monsieur and Madam that we had arrived. She asked if I was the daughter of Lucie Heymann, a friend of Madam's. I nodded as I looked about at my new surroundings. Mother had told Pierre that her friend, Maria, from school days, was married to a doctor with a prosperous practice in Lyon.

The salon was beautifully furnished with several paintings of landscapes on the walls. I had the impression of wealth from the spacious, comfortable apartment. I could not believe that I was seated in a lovely room, when only a few hours ago I had been facing the Gestapo.

Soon the doctor and his wife came in and introduced themselves: Paul and Maria Le Bec. Then they told us that Mother had called and was on her way. I was astounded that they had welcomed us so warmly, especially since they'd never met us before. The doctor also indicated that they were friends of the Resistance movement. They appeared to be charmed with Marc, who nodded to their invitation to have "petit dejeuner."

Mother arrived in a couple of hours, and I was much relieved to see her again. She scooped up Marc in her arms, and told him how much she had missed her precious little boy. Are we near the end of this War, I thought. How soon will families be able to visit and live together without fear?

The Le Becs held a whispered conference with Mother and then met with us. They told us that it would be too dangerous for Pierre and me to stay with them. The Gestapo was all around Lyon and often searched homes at the slightest provocation. Dr. Le Bec said he would find us a place in the suburbs, but Mother and Marc could stay with them in their apartment. Pierre and I nodded in agreement. We both felt that the Le Becs had already taken a great personal risk having us under their roof. We knew this was a dangerous time. While the Allies were in France and we hoped for victory soon, the Germans were still very much in control of Lyon. We had to be cautious.

Dr. Le Bec secured a room for us at a small pension in the suburbs. I was heartbroken to leave my son, but at the same time was relieved that he would be safe and well cared-for by his Grandmother who adored him. Marc was so sleepy, he hardly knew what was happening. I ached with the uncertainty of not knowing when and if I would see him again. But safety was paramount. Pierre and I left quickly with Dr. Le Bec for the pension.

We settled into our tiny room, which was tucked under the eaves. Pierre could only stand up in the middle of the room because of the sloped ceiling. We shared the one bed, a single bed, which was a tight squeeze, especially as I grew larger every day. The August nights were hot and stifling, so we usually left the windows open for air. Unfortunately the mosquitoes flew into our room in droves. I spent my nights slapping at these pesky creatures and my days, scratching the red welts. This pension was a boarding house so we were fed. While the rations were meager, they were adequate. I was relieved that I did not have to bother about meals.

I focused instead on my unborn child. I purchased some yarn in a small shop and spent most of my days knitting baby clothes. Pierre was not one to be idle or out of action, and he quickly established contact with the Resistance network.

A few evenings later, an agent who had been at the farm showed up with a bulky package in his hands. He had gone back to the farm one night and retrieved the archives from the cylinder. He asked Pierre to hide them, and he readily agreed. Pierre placed this

181

package of incriminating information under our bed. I was uneasy sleeping over the archives. If we were discovered with them, we'd surely be arrested. "Pierre, don't you think it is risky for us to have the archives?" I asked. Pierre shrugged nonchalantly and told me that this was an unlikely place for the Gestapo to be looking for us. While it was a risk, Pierre didn't think we were in any danger. I was not reassured.

A few days later, Uncle Georges and Aunt Gyp showed up and moved into a room down the hall from us. Dr. Le Bec had arranged a room for them, too. Georges told us that the Gestapo never came back. Since virtually all our transmission activities had stopped and everyone was gone from the farm, except for the farmhands, he and Gyp decided to head for Lyon and wait out the end of the war. They went to see my Mother and ended up at our pension. He smiled at me as he said, "Your Mother told me to tell you that Marc is doing fine. He asks for you, but seems content with his Grandmother." He sighed, "Let's hope this will be over soon when the Allies arrive. Meanwhile, we must keep a low profile."

Pierre then told Georges about the agent delivering the archives to us. He asked Georges if he had heard anything about Jacques Octave. Georges shook his head sadly and told us that the news was not good. "Octave was sent from Fort de Montluc to St. Geneis Laval, where he expected to be executed. Surprisingly, he was not killed and instead sent back to Fort de Montluc. An agent told me that Octave was allowed to see his children on August 15th. The Germans told the children that soon they would have their daddy back. I was surprised to hear that. Then on August 20th, he was taken again to St. Genies Laval with a lot of other prisoners they planned to eliminate. But at the last moment, he was saved from the slaughter. Then on August 22,nd a group of killers took him out of the prison. At the Pastain Bridge, Jacques was taken out of the car and shot, his body thrown into the river. His body was found a week later, 35 miles downstream. The agent who told me this, was not convinced Octave was dead, and said he hoped to find him alive at the end of the war."

I shook my head sadly, and Pierre's eyes were blazing with anger. "Those swine," he muttered. "I'm sure they killed him." Georges went on to say that there was more bad news. He reminded us that the pregnant sister of Marc (Sarigue) was sent to prison. Apparently they forgot all about her and just left her in a cell. She couldn't sit down and suffered a miscarriage. Then they let her go. Sarigue was consumed with rage.

Pierre was restless that night, tossing and turning. I lay awake next to him, distressed about the news. We were so close to liberation and yet still in the thick of danger. In the morning, Pierre appeared preoccupied and said little. Then he left without a word. I didn't speculate about it, because I knew he was upset. When he didn't return home in the evening, I was concerned. By the end of two days, I was frantic but could not go to the police. I was about to tell Georges about Pierre's disappearance, when he showed up.

Pierre stood in the doorway of our room, looking the picture of a fighter with a revolver tucked into his belt. I was absolutely furious with him, but grudgingly had to admit he looked rather elegant in his brown shorts and a custom made pink and white striped shirt with his initials stitched on the pocket. When I looked at his feet, I saw that he was wearing my old stretched sandals.

"Pierre, where have you been?" I cried. "And what are you doing with a gun?" Not pausing for breath, or giving him time to answer, I said, "We have those archives under our bed. We're both still secret agents. If you get caught with a gun, and are arrested, the Gestapo will be here in a minute and search the place. What on earth were you thinking? And what have you been up to?" I was so scared and angry, my words tumbled out furiously. He had not only left me without a word, but now he had returned with a gun.

"Oh Isabelle, I have been a busy man. I'm sorry, I should have let you know, but to tell you the truth, I wasn't sure what I would do when I left here. But I have organized a group of people here in our suburbs to fight the Germans."

"What?" I was shocked. "You're going to fight the Germans, and you're running around with that gun stuck in your belt? You haven't even bothered to hide it. Do you want to be hauled before the Gestapo?" By now, I was trembling.

Pierre looked chagrined, and his hero stance wilted. He insisted that he must go back and meet with the group. "I can't let them down without a word, and I must return the gun." I soon realized that since Pierre

184

had no way of concealing the weapon, I would have to go with him, since I had a large purse in which to hide the gun.

Georges came to our room to find out what the ruckus was all about. Pierre spilled out his story, and Georges could hardly contain his fury. "Irresponsible!" he said. "The sooner that gun is gone, the better. We are supposed to be keeping a low profile. Even the agents aren't communicating much these days, because we aren't sure what information was tortured out of Octave."

Pierre and I left to meet with the group of fighters. He returned the gun to them and we left quickly. As we walked down the street, a car suddenly appeared and drove by slowly. Pierre reacted with fear and shoved me into a doorway while he took off running. This was a large coach doorway with a small pedestrian door on the side. When he pushed me, I tripped and fell against the door, which burst open. I fell inside, landing on the lap of a man. As if that wasn't embarrassing enough, all the snap buttons on my dress pulled apart revealing my infamous corset to a group of about fifty men. A couple of the men were very kind and helped me up and cleaned away the smudges on my dress. I had no idea what kind of meeting I had inadvertently burst into. But I was grateful that they were pleasant Frenchmen and not Germans.

Once outside the meeting room, I looked about but saw no sign of Pierre. What else could I do but walk back to the pension? My main problem was that I had never been outside the neighborhood of the pension. I had no idea where I was in relation to the boarding house. The streets were empty and the sun shone brightly. Suddenly a bullet whizzed over my head, and I fell again. I cautiously looked around but didn't see anyone. I got up quickly and took off at a fast pace, determined to keep walking in what I hoped was the direction of the pension. Amazingly, I found my way back without having the slightest notion of how I got there.

Pierre arrived an hour later. I told him about my adventures and said that I felt we needed to get out of our situation immediately. He was hesitant, but after a couple of days he agreed with me. The liberation of Lyon had begun and the city was in a turmoil. The Nazis were enraged, and the jails were crowded.

We handed over the archives to Georges and Gyp, who were going to stay put. We left with our radio and bicycle. A man stopped us and suggested that we hide the bicycle as the Germans were sure to take it. "The Germans are in such a state of confusion that they are stealing everything in sight, especially bicycles," he warned us.

We took this kind man's advice and went into a café. We asked the proprietor if we could leave our bicycle with him for a few days. "Oui, oui." he replied without hesitation. We continued on foot as a soft rain began to fall. I trudged along, keeping up with Pierre as best I could until I became exhausted. When I told Pierre that I needed to rest on as bench for a little while, he insisted that we continue going on since we were almost at the Le Bec's apartment. Pierre had a good sense of direction and I trusted him. The rain was a downpour and my red hair was hanging in strands all about my face.

We arrived at the apartment at dusk, and Mother opened the door. She was overjoyed to see us and told us that the Le Becs had gone to stay at their home in the country. "There's just Marc and me here, so there is plenty of room," she said.

I grabbed my little son and twirled around with him, in spite of my tiredness. He squealed with delight. I was so happy to see them again, but Pierre was strangely quiet. When I asked what was wrong, he told me he didn't think he could stay here, but that I should. When I pressed him for a reason he made flimsy excuses. I wondered if he wanted to connect again with a group and fight. I couldn't understand him. No amount of pleading would change his mind, and he left to find a room to rent, but promised to come by every day.

Mother and I waited out the liberation in that apartment, and Pierre continued to float about the city. I was never sure where. Apparently he had found a room in the center of Lyon. On one of his visits, I remembered those archives that had caused me some uneasy times. "Have you heard anything about the archives," I asked. "I know Georges intended to pass them along to an agent when we handed them over to him." Pierre insisted that he hadn't seen Georges or heard anything. He told me that the agents had scattered, and he rarely saw any of them. "We may never know what happened to those archives," I concluded.

I knew we were still in danger, and longed more than ever for the Gestapo to be driven out of Lyon. When we heard that the American Allied Forces and French soldiers had landed on the coast between Cannes and Toulon and were moving northward, we were sure that they would reach Lyon soon.

Once in Lyon, the French and the U.S. armies pushed the Germans out in a matter of days. Two rivers, the Rhone and the Saone, flowed through the city forming an island between them, which was the center of Lyon. There were twenty-two bridges connecting the center with the rest of the city. These bridges had all been bombed by the Germans by placing an airplane bomb on each bridge and then methodically blowing them up, one by one, every ten minutes. The French managed to defend one bridge, so it was not destroyed.

When he saw that the Germans were on their way out, Pierre felt safe and went back to the café to retrieve his bicycle. Surprisingly it was still there waiting for him. I looked forward to his visits to us every day at the apartment, as did Marc, but I still never knew where he was or what he was doing. I felt secure in the apartment with Marc and Mother and wasn't eager to leave until I was certain the Germans were gone.

After the Americans had finished the liberation of Lyon, they quickly set about the task of restoring the city. They constructed pontoon bridges to connect the island to the shores. One afternoon I realized I would need diapers for the new baby. I walked into the city center across one of those bridges. The streets were crowded. I was able to purchase some diapers, and then I headed back to the apartment. The crowd had swelled just as I began to walk over the pontoon bridge. We were packed solid on that swaying bridge. Suddenly I felt a woman's arms close around my large abdomen as she pulled me close to her to shield me from being crushed. When I exited the bridge, I turned to my rescuer and thanked her profusely. She shrugged as if she had done nothing, but I was deeply touched by this kindness from a stranger.

As the date for my delivery drew closer, Pierre and I decided we should return to Aix-Les-Bains for the birth of our second child. Marc had been born there, and we knew the hospital. I had seen the doctor in Lyon only once, so I did not know him well. Besides, there was no longer any reason to stay in Lyon. When I heard that the hospitals were full, that was an additional incentive to leave.

We hoped the war was nearly over. On August 25, 1944, the U.S. and Free French Forces had made a triumphal entry into Paris. General Charles de Gaulle led the triumphal precession down the Champs Elysees. Our baby would be born in freedom.

TWELVE: To Paris

We realized we would need a car for the trip, as well as petrol. This was one time when Pierre's rash action earned him my admiration instead of my aggravation. Pierre contacted a man who he knew had collaborated with the Germans and said firmly, "I need your car." The man let him take it. Pierre generously added, "You'll get it back when I'm finished with it." Collaborators were not liked by those who had suffered under the Germans, and they were well aware of this. When demands were made of them by fellow French citizens, they usually acquiesced.

Then, in his own charming way, Pierre managed to obtain petrol from the American troops. Before I had time to comprehend all the arrangements, we were headed to Aix-Les-Bains in a black Citroen. Marc and I in the backseat, and Pierre at the wheel, humming as we rode along. I glanced admiringly at Pierre, for he was not only a good driver, and a clever fellow but at ease in the midst of uncertainties. "You're so enterprising," I said. "I don't know how you did it. I wouldn't be surprised if you come up with a place for us to stay when we arrive."

Pierre grinned his charming smile and told me to leave everything to him. True to his word, Pierre found an apartment for us immediately. The apartment had been occupied by a Frenchman who had collaborated with the Germans. When he attempted to escape during his arrest, he was killed. We settled into the apartment and, on October 13, 1944, our daughter, Agnes, was born. She was a darling baby and such a joy, that I nearly forgot all the hardships.

After a month, we headed to the Auerbach family estate in Normandy. The Auerbach's hired a nanny for the children. Pierre was now in business with his father, so we went to the Auerbach mansion in Paris in 1946, now a family of four with a nanny, to join Pierre's parents there. The mansion covered an entire block, with sixty bedrooms, but half of this home was closed. Pierre's father, Henri, had suffered financial losses from the war, including the famous Imperial Hotel. Mother rented an apartment in Paris, and my Grandmother Camille, settled in with her again.

Pierre and I resumed contact with the Resistance groups, but sadly, there were few members left of the Free French Forces of the Interior. While we were a small group, our casualties had been considerable, and our contributions to Allied victory in France significant. Of our 26 leaders, only 2 survived. Most died in concentration camps or were killed by the Gestapo, as was Octave. My cousin Francoise (Margot) became known as "the girl who betrayed the Chef of the network." She one of the few arrested by the Gestapo, who was released from Fort de Mont Luc.

And what became of those Nazi collaborators? I learned that Petain was tried by a French court and sentenced to death. This was later commuted to life imprisonment. Laval was condemned to death for treason by the French High Court of Justice. He took poison, but was resuscitated and then hung on October 9,[th] 1945. I thought the sentences were well deserved.

The memory of the constant danger we had lived in under difficult, even primitive circumstances, was an experience that sat in the forefront of my mind. I loved France and had gladly sacrificed for my country. I was puzzled, even angered, by those French citizens returning from London, where they had lived in exile during the war, who now touted themselves as the big liberators. There were also the turncoats, who had cooperated with the Germans, but were now suddenly patriotic. Some of them even found positions in the new government, which Charles De Gaulle had come back from London to head. He had been recognized as the ruler of France on October 23, 1944. The Jews in France had been decimated. In our family, we had lost our lovely Granny Rose, who had died in the train on the way to Auschwitz.

During the German occupation, Pierre and I had felt a tremendous amount of hope and vitality. But after the German surrender on May 7,[th] 1945 and then Victory Europe Day on May 8,[th] the enormity of all that had happened began to be told and to take its emotional toll on some of us. Pierre took all this in stride, but I was disillusioned. I couldn't reconcile my feelings now with the love and devotion I had once felt for my country.

On the day I was honored in a ceremony for my bravery and courage as a second lieutenant in the Free French Forces of the Interior from 1942-1944, I experienced mixed emotions. When the Croix de Guerre with a silver star was pinned on my jacket, I felt proud, yet sad.

The post-war time was one of upheaval all about me, and inside me as well. Without our youthful idealism and our staunch patriotism to bind us together, Pierre and I found our marriage crumbling. Did our romance end when the war ended? Could our marriage not survive the routines of an ordinary life? He grew distant and usually ignored me, until I felt as if I had no marriage left. What could I do? I had no profession and no income.

I knew that not only would I be facing these problems, but many changes as well. My life would be difficult. Yet I felt prepared to meet the challenges that lay ahead. After all, I had faced the Gestapo twice and eluded arrest. I had managed a child and a pregnancy in a war under difficult and dangerous circumstances. Through all this, I had discovered my own courage and sense of daring. I had two wonderful children. The future beckoned me with promise.

EPILOGUE

Isabelle was miserable as her marriage deteriorated. Pierre grew distant and often ignored her. She speculated that he had taken a mistress. When she felt she had no marriage left, she moved out of the Auerbach mansion. With no income and few job skills, Isabelle had limited options.

She moved in with her Mother and Grandmother Camille in their tiny apartment. In fact, the apartment was so small that Isabelle shared her Mother's bed. Her children, however, stayed behind with their nanny in the mansion, since she had no means to support them, and there was no room for them at the apartment. Isabelle visited them often at the mansion.

During this time, Isabelle, took up singing in cafes in the evening, much like her student days. She had two gay friends who often went with her and taught her to play the guitar. She continued to enjoy singing and playing the guitar throughout her life.

Increasingly, Isabelle felt trapped in France. Without a university degree, and very little money, her future looked bleak. America appeared to be the option that offered hope. She first came to the United States with Pierre in 1950 on a visa to validate that she was the rightful heir to the trust fund that Granny Rose had established for her. After Isabelle and Pierre returned to France, she found a menial job and filed for divorce. Getting the divorce from Pierre was difficult, and he was given custody of Marc and Agnes. If she wanted to regain custody of her children, she needed to prove she could support them.

Isabelle emigrated to the United States in 1951 along with her Mother, Lucie. Granny Rose's trust gave her an opportunity for a new life and an education she could not have had in France.

Isabelle lived in New York and was interested in high fashion. She went to parties, where she met Merle Armitage, a well known photographer for LOOK magazine. Through Merle, she met other famous people. When he left for California, Isabelle followed. They married in 1953 and lived on a ranch in Southern California. Agnes and Marc came to the ranch in 1954, but also spent time in France. Agnes graduated from Our Lady of Peace Academy in San Diego, while Marc graduated from St. Michael's in Santa Fe.

Merle and Isabelle moved to Santa Fe for a book Merle was writing. Lucie had lived with them both in California and Santa Fe as well. Camille joined Lucie in Santa Fe. She had emigrated at the age of 90 and died in 1971. Isabelle met two priests in Santa Fe and connected to the church again. She had Agnes baptized. Marc had been baptized earlier in

France.   Isabelle obtained a Master's degree in Albuquerque, and a Doctorate in 16th century French literature from the University of Kansas.

Isabelle and Merle divorced in Santa Fe before she left for Kansas.   Once Isabelle completed her degree in Kansas, she moved to Monterey in 1978 to teach French studies at the Monterey Institute of International Studies.   Isabelle wrote many articles about French literature.   Lucie joined her in Monterey and was active in the Alliance Francaise.

Isabelle died on March 17, 2000 in Monterey. Her Grandmother and Mother had preceded her in death.   Her son, Marc, an international news photographer, was killed while on assignment in Biafra in 1967.   Her daughter, Agnes lives in France and has three daughters.   Isabelle enjoyed visits with them through the years.

Annie's Album

Rose's apartment in Budapest where she conducted her couture business and also where Annie and Vali came to live with her. The apartment is on the second floor. It is an historic building marked with a Plaque indicating that it was the site of the first Hungarian painting Academy in 1804.

1935
Some Brill family members in Guyula, Hungary. Grandma Ida is
seated in the front row. Standing from left to right: Andrew
(Moncie's son), Imre (Ida's son), unidentified man, and Moncie
(Ida's daughter). Of this family group, only Moncie survived and
returned from Auschwitz. Andrew died in Auschwitz and Imre was
shot and thrown into the Danube River.

2002
The wine cellar behind the double doors is where Annie's family hid. The house still shows the marks of shells and bullets in this recent picture. Annie and her sister Vali are in the lower left of the picture.

1999
Lily Kriszhaber, Annie's family benefactor, in Budapest at the age of 89.

1930
Annie's Grandma, Ida Brill, with her two
grandsons. On the left, Tomas Szecsi, who
later was executed at a forced labor camp in
Russia. On the right, Gabor Brill, who later
died at Auschwitz.

2001
Ann, Rachel and Rebecca in front and Julia in the back.
Annie's granddaughters

1935
Lazlo Brill's engagement. Lazlo, Annie's uncle, is on the right.
His fiancé is between him and her brother. Lazlo was also killed
at a forced labor camp in Russia by a cruel method. He was hung
by his wrists, hosed with cold water, and left to freeze to death.

1957
Rose, Annie's mother, at age 50, one year after she emigrated from Hungary to the U.S.

Isabelle's Album

Isabelle and daughter, Agnes, on a beach in Southern California after she had divorced Pierre and moved to the States.

Pierre on the beach in Southern
California when he and Isabelle come to
the States in 1950 to claim her Trust.

Isabel in New York,
after her divorce. She
had a fashion business
and lived the part. Her
children remained in
France. This was a
transformation of the
earlier Isabel, pictured at
right.

Isabelle outside of her Condo in Monterey, California in the later years of her life.

Above: Isabelle received a Masters Degree in
Albuquerque and later a Doctorate in Kansas.

Below: The author and her husband in 2002 in front of
the gates to the Farm where the Cell operated outside of
Chaponost, France.

Ene's Album

Paul and Joa on their wedding day.

The Baptism of Ene.
Front Row: Jack and Mari, Joa holding Ene, and Juuli and Josep.
Back Row: Oskar & godmothers, Helmi and Ida.

1930's: Ene's with her favorite dog, Tiki.

Ene's Kindergarten class in the camp. Ene is sitting to the right of the teacher.

Paul, Joa and the Family at the embarkation center leaving for the US.

Joa and Ene on the Boat for their new home in the US.

PROLOGUE: JOA AND ENE

When I was first asked about telling my story, I was reluctant. Our flight from Estonia occurred long ago when I was just a child. The more I thought about it, however,the more I realized that my memories, the stories my parents had told me over the years, and the diaries my mother had kept for me would not only tell the story of her life, but also that of many women of her generation. These young women's lives were changed forever by Communist Russia's take-over of the Baltic States during World War II.

My mother's and my story is one of escape from our homeland and the fears and struggles we experienced in Germany and Czechoslovakia as refugees during the War. We were like gypsies in displaced persons' camps after the war until we finally emigrated to the United States. Here we started new lives at mid-life for my parents and for me at age ten. The year was 1950, the middle of the 20th century.

I was amazed as I relived the terrible fear we felt of the Russians, yet we were also deeply touched by the often unexpected care from the Germans. Most of all, I was grateful to finally be in America with a loving family and friends who taught me English. My journey back to that time has filled me with a profound sense of gratitude.

Ene Bonnyay

Ene's mother's diary and her Uncle Oskar's memories have added dimension to this tale of a refugee journey. Who knew what was happening to the refugees from the Baltic States, or that so many were wandering about Germany? Hers is a well told story which I had never known before. I am proud to call Ene my friend and grateful that she would entrust me with her story.

Betty J. Iverson

I. MOTHER

ONE: Joa's Marriage. Ene's Birth

My mother, Joa, shared many stories with me, when she tucked me into bed at night in the camps. Because of my circumstances I grew up like a little adult and was always part of my parents' conversations. Mother told me many things about herself and our town in Estonia in order for me to know what life was like there. I was only five when we fled as refugees. She had also salvaged many photos, and through these, she brought the past to life for me. She wanted me to know about my country, my heritage. Besides telling me how the war had come to our town, she kept a journal of our refugee experience to help me remember. This is my mother's story of Valga:

The small town of Valga with its population of 17,500 people was surrounded by forests and lay on the Latvian border. Most of the streets were paved, but there were dirt roads in the outlying areas, which spread out over a vast plain. Most houses were simple wooden structures, and even the town hall and churches were made of wood. The church steeples could be seen for miles. Stucco buildings were relatively rare. Across the border from Valga was the Latvian city of Valka. Despite the similarity of names, the cities had little in common, because our languages were different. Estonian is related to the Finnish and Hungarian tongues.

Joa's parents struggled to raise their family. They were poor like everyone else in the village with no running water and only a wood burning stove for heat. The house was a humble, wooden duplex with a kitchen and two bedrooms on each side and it felt very small and cramped to Joa. They had a small eating area adjacent to the kitchen. Her parents slept in one bedroom, and she and her brother, Oskar, shared the other, sleeping on straw mattresses which they pushed against the walls during the day. They hung curtains on a wire for privacy.

Her father, Jaak Magraken, who worked for the railroad, had been injured when he fell off a train car. He was no longer able to work and now walked with a pronounced limp. Joa's life changed drastically when her mother, Mari, delivered twins, a boy and a girl. After that, Mari was never strong again. Her father would tell people that his wife had "taken to the bed." Joa was not sure what he meant by that, except that her mother was like an invalid. She complained of feeling weak and the slightest task left her breathless.

Joa was ten when the twins, Hilja and Ilmar, were born. Somehow she reared them and managed the household, while also attending school. The twins shared the bedroom with Joa and Oskar. Although Oskar was only two years younger than Joa, he was not about to be bossed around by his older sister. He looked for every opportunity to tease her and question her authority.

Their house was on a large acreage which included a potato field with bushes of red and yellow raspberries encircling it. The family had a root cellar made of cement and stone, where they kept fruit, vegetables, potatoes and onions. Pickles and sauerkraut were stored there in the winter. Fruit and nut trees were in abundance and Joa especially liked the crunchy sweet apples. Scattered among the trees were several outbuildings, one of which was their bathroom. With no bathroom indoors, bathing was a complicated weekly ritual of boiling water on the stove and filling a large portable tin tub. Once a week they went to the sauna for railroad employees where they could bathe in the hot water there. When the twins were small, Joa bathed them in a tin tub, where they giggled and splashed until she was as wet as they were.

When it became time for Joa to begin high school, she hesitated because her mother was still frail. Her father, however, insisted that she must continue her education.

"I want my daughter to have a chance in this world," he said. Joa went to the town's free high school. Her father looked after the twins. Although he walked with a limp, he managed to keep up with them, even little Ilmar, who loved to climb trees. Before long, the twins were in school too.

The boys and girls in the town went to separate high schools, but they got acquainted at organized gatherings. At one of these events, Joa noticed a tall, slim, handsome man with light brown hair. Although Joa was friendly and at times, was rather forward, this man, named Paul, seemed quiet and shy around her, a man of few words. Sometimes at gatherings Paul told jokes and was often the center of attention. Joa was puzzled by this complicated behavior.

Joa always made it a point to talk to him, and seized any opportunity to greet him when their paths crossed. Fortunately, there were many of these. She liked watching him as he marched by with the local band in a parade or played the drums at a concert in Sade, the town park. She never missed a parade or a concert.

One day, when she studied her reflection in a mirror, Joa realized that her girlish face had changed into that of a woman. Was she attractive? Her hair was thick, dark brown and glossy. Her eyes were a pretty blue. Joa speculated about Paul. Did Paul think she was pretty? He was always polite whenever she chatted with him, and sometimes his keen sense of humor seeped through. She had become convinced that he had a girl friend, because he never appeared particularly interested in her.

Joa knew all about Paul and knew that his family was not too well off either. His mother Juuli came from a well known, educated and artistic family. Everyone was surprised when she chose to marry Joosep Toime, a humble shoemaker, a tradesman. The Toimes lived behind the shop in a small wooden house at the end of an alley. Paul was very smart. As tough as it was, his parents sent him to the university where he earned a degree in economics. Now he worked in the local bank and was soon promoted to an officer position.

After Joa graduated from high school, she was fortunate to get a job as a clerk at the town hall, a prestigious place to work. She enjoyed the status that came with this job and felt important when she met the town officials.

As her 25th birthday approached, her brother Oskar teased her that no one would bother with her birthday. Then strangely, Paul called to say he was coming over to congratulate her. She was very surprised, because she was still convinced that he had a girl friend. Why would he bother with her? Was he teasing her like Oskar did? "Well, if that's the case," she said to herself. "I'll make sure I'm not here when he comes." She called her friend, Ida, and the two of them went to the forest with a picnic lunch and spent the entire day there.

When she arrived home that evening, Oskar met her, his eyes blazing with anger. "You stupid girl," he said. "How could you do that to Paul?"

"Do what to Paul?" she asked.

"He told you he was coming by. Then you weren't here when he came. He was loaded with gifts for your birthday. He had brought flowers, a cake and even a present. But you were gone. I felt so sorry for him. You should be ashamed."

Joa was ashamed and devastated that she'd missed Paul. She tore the wrappings off the present and found tucked inside a carved, ivory elephant. Only then did she realize that her jealousy had been for nothing. Oskar was right. She had been a stupid girl.

She didn't know how to apologize to Paul. She had been so foolish. As her words tumbled out, Paul accepted her apology gracefully. After that Joa and Paul spent many wonderful evenings together. They planned a bright future together despite their humble circumstances and the uncertainties of the thirties.

Russia had always loomed as a threatening presence in the Baltic States, as had Germany. Between 1918 and 1920, these two countries tried constantly to take control of Estonia. After the Bolshevik revolution of 1917, Estonia declared its independence in February 1918. Most western European nations acknowledged that independence, but they weren't sure how long it would continue. During these independence years, Estonians enjoyed a classless society, except for the wandering Gypsies who showed up now and then. Everyone looked down on that nomadic group.

Paul was very serious the night he proposed. "You're the only woman I have ever loved or ever will love." For once in her life she was speechless. Joa was radiant with joy as she accepted the gold ring he placed on the finger of her left hand, the traditional engagement symbol. (After they were married, she would move the ring to her right hand.) Joa could not stop beaming happily.

"Oh Paul, we will be so happy," she finally managed. Then she became practical and they discussed their wedding plans. They agreed that since they knew so many people, they would have to invite them all. They soon realized that they couldn't afford a large wedding, nor could their parents.

"Well, Joa," Paul said, "I think the only solution is for us to elope. Then we won't have to worry about leaving anyone out or hurting their feelings." And so they did. Very quietly one Saturday morning, they went to a neighboring village for the church ceremony which they had arranged earlier. They were dressed in wedding finery: Joa in a lace trimmed white wedding dress and Paul in a new black tuxedo.   After   the   ceremony,   a   professional photographer took their pictures. They were 28 years old. Marrying in the late twenties was customary for most Estonians.

After their wedding, they quickly resumed their lives as usual. In fact, each of them went to work on Monday. They rented a small apartment in a fairly new building on a main street, Kungla Street #25. Joa thought their two bedroom apartment was quite nice. When she discovered she was pregnant a few months later, Joa and Paul enjoyed gathering all they needed to set up a nursery in the small bedroom. Paul bought a crib, while Joa bought sheets for the crib and arm loads of diapers and baby clothes.

One sunny afternoon, Joa felt hard abdominal contractions, the beginning of her labor. Hand in hand, Joa and Paul walked to the hospital just a block away from their apartment. He went back home to get some personal items for her, assuming she would have a long labor. When he returned, the nurse greeted him with, "Congratulations, you are the father of a beautiful daughter." Paul and Joa quickly chose the name, "Ene" for their tiny daughter, who was born on May 7, 1939.

Not one to be idle, Joa went back to work in a couple of months and hired a Nanny to take care of her precious Ene. She and Paul arranged for the christening of their new daughter in July at their apartment by their pastor, Arnold Tammik, of St. Peter's Lutheran church. Joa had lovingly stitched a lace trimmed white dress for Ene's baptism. Their apartment was filled with family and friends for the special occasion. Joa's two best friends, Helmi Kull and Ida Luik were the god-mothers, and her brother, Oskar, was the god-father. According to Estonian custom, girls have two god-mothers and boys have two god-fathers. Joa's table was very festive with candles, her best white table cloth and many special food dishes.

Ene shrieked the entire time. No matter what Joa or Paul did, Ene would not be consoled. Joa wondered if she was crying because of the water sprayed on her forehead, the loud booming voice of the pastor or simply because she was beginning to exhibit some of the "jonn" or stubbornness trait that is a source of pride for Estonians.

TWO: Occupation by the Russians

Joa and Paul celebrated Ene's first birthday in a free Estonia. She was walking quite well by then. They knew that it was only a matter of time before the Russians would move into the Baltic states. In late 1939, President Pats signed an agreement with Russia, who wanted to place more bases in Estonia. The Russian soldiers were to stay on these bases, but within six months the Russians were everywhere. When President Pats objected, he and other government officials were taken away and jailed in Russia. In June 1940, the USSR issued an ultimatum that a new government be appointed. The Estonian army was swallowed up by the Russian army. The men now wore Red army uniforms. While Joa was fearful, she wasn't aware of any fighting, raping or killing in her town.

Paul and Joa noticed that many of the Baltic Germans they knew had left for Germany. By July, Russia had absorbed Lithuania, Latvia and Estonia with Germany's approval under the Nazi-Soviet Pact. All the industry, banks and land were nationalized.

Estonia's economy became dependent on Moscow. All the decisions were made there too. Now Joa waited in long lines for everything, even the shoddy products made in Russia. She felt as if her society was controlled by Moscow. Her country was now known as the Estonian Soviet Socialist Republic.

Joa found her job at the Town Hall precarious after the Russian take-over. "The Communists have come out of the woodwork since the Russians came in," she lamented to Paul one evening. "I expect them to take over the Town Hall any day now. They're in control of our town. All the community organizations have been disbanded. They've even prohibited the press. Sometimes I feel as if I'm in danger. There is not anything specific; with the Russians, I feel an uncertainty. If they suspect you are against them, they will send you to a camp in Siberia. I am very careful about what I say to my friends at the Town Hall. We all worry that hearsay could incriminate us. Perhaps a co-worker, who sympathizes with the Russians, will turn us in. I 'm growing uneasy, Paul."

Paul listened thoughtfully and advised her to continue to be vigilant. "The Russian soldiers are all over the town now. They come into the bank, too. I say only what I have to, when I deal with them. I've noticed some people disappearing, who were anti-Communist, or patriots. While others were pro-free Estonia. Anyone who is politically questionable has been sent to a labor camp in Siberia."

One morning, a Russian soldier came to their door and said to Paul, "You must leave. We need your apartment. You have two days to pack your things and move out." He left quickly as if his announcement had been routine, not one that would drastically affect them.

Paul and Joa looked at each other in shock. They had not expected to be forced out of their home. They scurried about, quickly packing all the essentials. They stored what furniture they could. Then they packed their valuable items of silver and china. They took these things to relatives in the country to bury. They did not have any gold.

They moved in with Joa's parents, Jaak and Mari at #5 Peetri St. Joa continued to work; she could no longer keep the nanny, however, since they had no room for her. Her father became Ene's nanny and the child adored him. Joa's younger sister, Hilja, who worked as a secretary, occupied the other side of the duplex.

Joa seldom saw her brother, Ilmar, who lived in an apartment in town. She never knew where he was or what he was doing. She did know that he was a policeman and an instructor for the Young Eagles, the youngest members of the Home Guard. Quite unexpectedly he stopped in one evening.

"This is a time of Red Terror, Joa," he told her. "The Russians know that the Germans are about to invade, so they are deporting more people than ever to Siberia. The Estonian Communists are knocking on doors at night and taking men, even women and children. They are then marched at gun point by Russian soldiers to waiting trains and sent to Siberian labor camps." Joa asked who they were after.

Ilmar was quick to reply, "Basically, I think they're after the less important political leaders, who still have some influence or government jobs. Sometimes, they take just anyone. You can tell who has been taken away by the empty places at work in the morning."

She felt awful about what was happening in her town. Joa was even more concerned about Ilmar, who appeared very upset. She knew her younger brother was not the type who would stand idly by while terrible things were happening.

"What do you plan to do?" she asked.

"Joa, my friends and I are going to join the Forest Brotherhood," he said. "I know some who are already in the forest, because they did not want to be conscripted into the Russian army. They chose the woods over deportation to Siberia. I haven't told anyone else what I plan to do except Oskar. I wanted you to know my plans, in case I suddenly disappear."

Joa knew very little about the Forest Brotherhood, so she asked him who they were. "The brotherhood is a bunch of young men who choose to live in the forest. Some consider themselves freedom fighters. All of us consider Russia the common enemy. As for me, I feel like I'm doing something for my country."

Joa was alarmed. She hated the idea of her brother in combat. She asked him whether the Forest Brotherhood planned to fight the Russians. Ilmar reassured her that they didn't plan any fighting now. He said that armed with only a few guns and raw courage, they were not strong enough to take on the Red troops who were numerous and everywhere.

"Oh Ilmar, I hope this will be over soon. I don't like living in fear. I'm glad you told me where you were going." Joa looked intently at her brother, who had always been so carefree. Now at 21, he looked very serious. He left quickly after she hugged him good-bye.

When Oskar came by later in the evening, he confirmed what Ilmar had told her. Oskar worked for the railroad and was an engineer on the fast train. He said that he had been asked to drive a train to Tallinn. This was not the usual run for him. "On the way back, I saw in the Tapa station a train with cars full of Estonians, among them many of my colleagues at the railroad. I'm sure that train was headed for Siberia. There was not one of them, who was involved in the government. I've heard that the Russians have already sent nearly 10,000 people to prison camps. Don't you think that's a mass deportation?"

Oskar's words alarmed Joa. "Are you worried? Do you think you'll have any problems?"

"Don't you worry about me," Oskar said confidently. "I can talk my way around those Russians." Oskar had a good sense of humor, yet he was always very direct, and one knew where he stood on any issue. When he told Joa he could talk his way around the Russians, she felt confident that he would.

THREE: Occupation by the Germans

The presence of more Russian troops in Valga signaled that a battle would not be long in coming. They could soon have a different master. On July 5, 1941, the German forces crossed the Estonian border and swept them up as they headed for Russia. There was much turmoil as these two forces fought. Joa and Paul were caught in the middle of a full scale war. Joa took Ene and fled to the country with Paul's parents, where they stayed in a small summer cottage, owned by Juuli's family. They often spent the nights in the forest, when the fighting was fierce, coming out after one side retreated, and the other took over.

Paul stayed in Valga and continued to work at the bank. For weeks at a time, Joa didn't know whether he was dead or alive, or if the houses were still standing. He came to the country on weekends, but only if he felt it was safe. Paul was a pacifist and did not believe in guns. Despite that, he purchased one anyway, and began to carry it. As he and Joa sat in the forest one night, he cradled Ene tenderly in his arms.

Then he said to Joa, "If those Russians come back, I don't want to be here. I will shoot you and Ene, and then I will kill myself."

Joa was shocked. This was so unlike her kind and gentle husband. "Paul, you can't mean that."

"I do, Joa. I love you both more than anything in this world. We would have a terrible life under the Russians. I would rather be dead." Joa felt a sense of dread she had never known before. The war was deeply invading her life.

A few days later, Paul came to them in the country with good news. "The Russians are gone and the Germans have taken over." Although the takeover had been quick, it had seemed like an eternity to them. By September 1941, Estonia was fully occupied by the Germans.

Some Estonians had chosen to leave with the Russians, while others had been drafted into the Red army. Amnesty was given to all those remaining who had served the Russians. All remaining soldiers now became German soldiers, although they were in an Estonian unit within the German army. The Germans were greeted happily by the people in Valga because they were against the Russian Communists. Their town, and their country had been run by the Russians and Estonian Communists, whom many people hated. At the same time, they realized that the Russians and the Americans were allies.

Many Estonians spoke German and were sympathetic to the Germans. The Estonians had a long history with the German people. During the feudal era, German knights and bishops had divided their country, and they became the barons and large landowners. The Estonians were the peasants and serfs who lived under harsh conditions and worked the land. To this day, they love the land.

The Germans had lived among them and seemed familiar, but the Russians were viewed as conquerors. Thus it was not surprising that many Estonian men willingly joined the German army because they saw it as their opportunity to fight against the Russians and free Estonia. Since these soldiers were branded with an "S.S." tatoo on their arms, they were later viewed as Nazis, as were the men who had involuntarily been conscripted.

Joa brought Ene into town and moved back with her parents. Germans and Estonians together now governed her country, but Nationalized property was not returned. Oskar continued to work for the railroad which was now run by both German and Estonian executives. Joa was glad that Ilmar had returned from the forest, where he had stayed during the worst of the fighting. He was back on the police force and instructing the Young Eagles.

Joa was relieved to see that Ene was happy to be with her grandparents again. The first day back, Ene ran among all the fruit trees, chasing the little dog, Tuki, while Joa went back to work at the Town Hall. Joa enjoyed watching her little two year old play with the chickens. Her father let Ene help him feed them. He built a small sandbox at the side of the house, and Ene and the chickens sat there contentedly for hours.

Ene adored her Vanaisa's (grandfather's) little dog, Tuki, whom she considered hers. She followed her grandfather around, calling out "Vanaisa." When Tuki sat on the top of the root cellar, Ene sat there, too.

Joa always knew where to find her daughter when she arrived home from work. If she wasn't atop the root cellar sitting with Tuki, she would be at the raspberry fence, picking some of those yellow raspberries with her Vanaisa. "They're so sweet," she'd say, the juice dribbling off her chin. Joa would hug her before she picked a few berries for herself.

Joa's parents adored Ene, and they were not strict with their only grandchild. Vanaisa might look at Ene with a frown. When he took off his belt, as if he was going to strike her, Ene knew it was an empty threat. He threatened her one evening when she hung on a swinging yard gate screaming because Joa and Paul were going out. They stood there and watched Ene having a temper tantrum. Vanaisa walked toward her with an upraised hand and a menacing look but still he did not hit her. She eventually gave up her tantrum.

Vanaisa often fixed Ene her most favorite meal of all. He lit a fire in the out-door oven and threw some potatoes and onions in the fire. She'd always tell Joa about her special meal when she got home from work. "Oh mommy, Vanaisa made my special meal for me today," she'd say, munching on some browned potatoes and onions. Joa was grateful that her father loved his granddaughter so much. This made Joa's life easier.

The Germans were not cruel, and life seemed almost normal again. However, the idea that the

Germans would fulfill the Estonians' hope and restore the Republic of Estonia was soon dashed when they became part of the Ostland province of the Third Reich. Paul was disappointed, but he observed that on the other hand, people were no longer being sent to Siberia at the slightest provocation. There were rumors that some of the few Jews in Valga who tended to side with the Communists or the Russians, had been sent to Germany. Joa wondered about their fate there. Most people in her area were not too concerned about the Jews, because, like Joa, they had never really known many Jews.

Paul and Joa soon felt secure enough to move to another apartment. They furnished it with whatever items they could reclaim. The air of uncertainty returned in 1944, as the Russian front moved closer. By January 1944, the Russian offensive had cleared the German troops away from Leningrad and the Baltic front. Forty thousand Estonians had joined with the German forces and stopped the Red Army at Narva in the northeast. Novgorod was recaptured on the 20th and by March 1st, the Russians were on the border of Latvia. The news filtered to them in pieces. "I think it is only a matter of time before we will be swallowed up by the Russians again," Joa observed to Paul one evening.

"The Soviets are definitely a threat. I do not want us to fall into Russian hands," Paul said and he brought out his gun. Joa was alarmed and Ene began to cry when she saw the gun in her father's hand. She was scared. Ene remembered seeing her isa (father) with a gun, that one time in the forest. Joa wondered if

Ene thought they were going back into the forest. She hugged her daughter tightly.

Paul and Joa decided to have a big celebration for Ene's fifth birthday. Celebrations had always been a big part of their lives, but lately there were few. Their last celebration had been at Oskar's wedding two years ago, when he married Salme, who was one of ten children. They had met at a wedding. Oskar told Joa he fell in love at the first sight of Salme. The festive wedding had been held in the rural area where Salme's family lived. Joa had never seen Oskar so happy.

Joa stitched a lovely Estonian costume for Ene. She invited a lot of the family to celebrate her birthday with them. Ene was so excited that she danced about as both sets of grandparents arrived. Soon the aunts and uncles came. Joa had an premonition that this would be their last celebration in Estonia for a long time. They enjoyed a beautiful occasion with much singing and dancing.

FOUR: The Russians Return

On August 13, 1944, they were ordered to evacuate the town by both the German and the Estonian authorities. The Red army had reached the capital, Tallinn. Soon they invaded southern Estonia. The Germans retreated. Ilmar came by and told Joa that he was going into the woods again with the Forest Brotherhood until he was able to escape from the country. Tears slid down Joa's cheeks as she told him good bye. "This is not a usual good bye. I don't know when I'll see you again. Perhaps in a free Estonia," she said hopefully. "You must take care."

"A free Estonia is what we're all hoping for. Wherever you go, I will find you. I'm not sure where I'll end up, but I hope I will be here in Valga." Ilmar turned quickly and left.

Joa and Paul next said their good byes to their parents. Paul's parents were going to head to the country again. Tears rolled down Joa's cheeks as she watched them bid Ene good-bye. They clearly adored their only grandchild. Josep with his curled, waxed mustache was a gentle unassuming man. Paul's mother, Juuli was a sweet woman with a round smiling face. They would never leave Estonia, they asserted. They expected that their son Paul and his family would return, and Paul and Joa firmly believed this, too. "I hope we'll be gone just a short while. This is not a final good bye," said Paul. Joa nodded in agreement.

Joa's parents, Jaak and Mari, planned to stay in their home. They said over and over that it would only be a matter of weeks or months before everyone would be together again in Valga. Ene looked puzzled, as if she didn't understand what all the good-byes were about. Hilja came in just then. She announced that she, too, would be leaving the country.

That evening, Paul and Joa talked until very late, deciding what to do. They could wander about the country and keep moving further south, staying ahead of the Russians. That was a temporary solution at best. "Everyone is heading to the harbor where they can board ships. If we're lucky, we will get on a ship for Sweden," Paul suggested.

"How will we get there? We don't have a car. Perhaps we can go by train," Joa said. But Paul observed that the trains were packed. Oskar had told him that the Germans had blown up all the bridges on the route to the harbor of Parnu to stop the advancing Russians. He and Salme had been lucky and gotten on the last train out of Valga to Riga, Latvia. Paul added that Oskar planned to look for them in Germany.

They sat there dejectedly until Paul suddenly said, "I have a solution. One of the men at the bank is a volunteer fireman and he's going to get an old fire engine and head to the harbor to catch a boat."

Joa quickly nodded. They packed only what they could carry. Paul also packed a briefcase with silver pieces to sell: glasses, spoons, cigarette cases. Joa packed a few items of clothing for each of them. Ene had a fit about her little teddy bear, the one she'd given quite a hair cut one day at her grandfather's home. Now the little teddy was a homely hairless bear. Joa tossed the bear aside, but Paul said, "Let her take it. Perhaps the bear will give her comfort." Joa packed it. They also took a small metal milk can hoping that they could get milk for Ene from farmers in the countryside, wherever they would be.

The next morning, they found the fire engine, motor running and ready to go. Paul and Joa sat up front with Ene on Paul's lap. An assorted group of friends and relatives rode out of town on that fire engine, with people getting on and off at every turn. Along the way they picked up Hilja, who told them that she, too, had seen Ilmar before he fled to the forest. Joa was overjoyed that her sister had decided to come with them. Ene was the only child on the fire engine. She was quite excited and asked often when they'd make the siren noise. All the passengers shared the common hope that they would return after the Germans came back to Estonia and had routed the Russians.

When Joa and Paul arrived at the harbor at Parnu, they found that the boats were full. So many people were eager to go to Sweden that the boats were unable to hold more. Everyone wanted to go there because it was closer, and they could more easily return home after the war. Thousands of people had taken every space. Adding to the dire situation, the Russians were bombing the rescue ships in the harbor.

Joa and Paul found a place to stay. Paul checked every day, and finally after three nights, they were able to leave. On the fourth morning, there was only one ship left, a small German vessel, the Sonnenfelder. Since this was their only choice, Paul decided that they must board that ship. There were German soldiers on the ship, standing at alert with somber expressions and guns in their hands. Ene looked up and began screaming. Joa picked her up, but Ene could not be comforted.

Joa looked at Paul and said, "I think she has a premonition that the ship will sink. We should not go."

"Joa, leaving on this ship is our only chance. If we stay, we'll be in Russian hands very soon," Paul insisted.

Joa hugged Ene, and continued trying to soothe her. When she brought out the little teddy bear, Ene's sobs changed to whimpers. They walked up the gang plank onto the ship. They boarded that ship on September 22,[nd] along with Hilja, while Russian planes flew all around them. (Later they heard the news that the Russians had reached the Gulf of Riga on the 23rd and by the 26th had fully occupied Estonia. They lost all contact with their parents from that time on.)

As the ship pulled away from the dock, Joa gazed sadly at the shore and hoped that this would not be her last glimpse of her homeland. Ene's whimpers interrupted her reverie.

II. DAUGHTER

FIVE: Passage to Germany

I was a child of five when we boarded the Sonnenfelder. I left my country and the only home I'd ever known. I could not have comprehended then, how many places I would go, always yearning for a home. I wanted an end to the constant walking.

There were 400-500 passengers on that tiny ship. We lived crammed together on the open deck for three days and nights. I finally stopped screaming, but I was still very scared. The Russian planes flew all around and continued to drop bombs, which caused our ship to rock with the waves. The fierce looking soldiers, of whom I was so afraid, were actually nice to me. My ema (mother) had convinced me that this ship journey was an adventure. We would be back home in a short time. Then mother and I became very ill and started throwing up. We had never been on a large ship before. The rolling waves made us sea sick. The sailors took us to a cabin next to the crew's living quarters, where we could lay down in small beds. I heard my ema thank them for such special treatment.

In spite of lying in bed, Ema and I were still so sick, we didn't care if we lived or died, or where we were going. The German sailors who came to our cabin were kind, and they offered us bread and water. Although this was our main diet, I couldn't eat anything. I didn't want to keep throwing up every time I sat up.

My isa (father) came to our cabin with news. "The Russian planes are still flying around. They have sunk more ships full of refugees; so far, we've escaped that fate. I hear we're heading for Danzig. I'm glad to see the two of you feeling better. We're almost there. The German sailors told me that they were sent to rescue us from the Russians."

We arrived at Danzig in the morning on September 25[t.h.] Soon a long line of German army trucks pulled up to the dock, and we climbed in. My parents did not know where we were going, and neither did Aunt Hilja. No one else seemed to know either. Finally, we heard that we were going to a processing camp. I didn't know what a processing camp was.

There were many trucks lined up to take all 400-500 of us to the Gotenhafen processing camp. I thought that we must have looked like a long green snake on the road. By now, I was very hungry, but again we were offered only bread and water. I wondered if this was all that German people ate. I remembered those roasted potatoes and onions, that Vanaisa threw into the fire. I wanted some of those crunchy potatoes and onions very much.

At the Gotenhafen camp, Ema, Aunt Hilja and I were forced to strip naked and then soak in a disinfectant solution to kill the lice, while our clothes were steam cleaned. Ema told me that this was not because we were dirty, but because this was the treatment for all refugees who came by boat. Surprisingly, she was not insulted by this. She insisted the treatment killed lice and germs. "Now, Ene," she told me, "this is a good bath for us. Remember how filthy we felt on the boat? Now we'll be clean, and we won't have to worry about bugs."

I didn't mind so much, but I held my nose, because I thought the solution smelled awful. I just wanted to get my clothes back on, and go out and explore the camp. We had no chance to settle in. The very next morning, we were sent to another camp.

There was a lot of confusion when we left Gotenhafen. Some people headed off on their own. They told my isa they were heading south to avoid the Russians. Ema told me that it was a problem for the Germans to feed so many people. The next day, we were again loaded into trucks and taken to Wilhelmshafen, a camp near Berlin. My parents hoped that at this camp they would be able to find jobs in the nearby towns.

After only a week, we were on the move again. This time we were with a group of fourteen people sent to work in southern Germany. My parents were told that they had to find their own housing. There was no truck to take us, so we set out on foot. I soon grew tired of walking so much.

Our first stop was in the little town of Butstadt in Thuringia. The mayor in this town did not want us, my isa told me, and threw us out of town. My parents were upset and exhausted. I was crying and scared because we left in the dark. I felt tired and hungry and clutched my teddy tightly. Isa picked me up. He told me we were headed for Weimar, a larger town where the people were nicer. Once in awhile a plane flew over and dropped bombs. Whenever that happened, my parents grabbed me and ran. They took me into a dark basement, which they said was an air raid shelter. These shelters were always dark and crowded with people. Somehow we always managed to find a spot.

We joined a group of Estonians, who were also looking for work. There were lots of refugees wandering around, some were Lithuanians and Latvians. Ema and Aunt Hilja said they were more comfortable with people who spoke our language, so we did not join the other groups. At last we got on the train to Weimar. We spent two days and two nights in the railway station there, sleeping on the benches. Some people had to sleep on the floor. I was very hungry, and my isa used some of his silver pieces to buy food for us.

SIX: On the Move in Germany

My parents told me they were discouraged. I heard Ema say she just wanted to give up. "But how can I do that? I don't know what to do or where to go." My pretty Ema looked so sad.

Just when there seemed to be no hope, a nice group of Germans told Ema and Isa that they should go to the town of Aussig in Sudentenland. (This was in western Czechoslovakia.) I wanted so badly to stay somewhere and stop walking all the time. My days had become a blur of trucks, walking, trains and sleeping on floors or in orchards.

We were still given bread and water most of the time. Sometimes we were fed soup after we stood in a long line at a camp. My isa often gave me his own share of food when my tummy hurt, because I was so hungry. He looked for apples to pick, when we walked through the countryside. While the apples were good, I remembered with longing those sweet yellow raspberries I had picked with Vanaisa in Valga. At least, my little milk can was usually full since the

Germans in the countryside were sympathetic to a little girl like me.

My ema's calendar read October 10, 1944, when we finally arrived in Aussig. My isa was happy, that he was given a job. Then a group of local Germans helped my parents and the other Estonians set up a shelter at a closed summer resort in Kummer, a nearby village. These nice people got bunk beds and set them up on a large glass enclosed veranda of the summer restaurant. My ema explained to me that this would now be our home. Each family was assigned one bed and the area around that bed for their living space. Since Aunt Hilja was alone, she and I slept together next to my parents. The only heat for this veranda was a small iron stove. My isa often got up at night to take his turn with the other men stoking the stove with wood to keep the fire going, so we wouldn't freeze at night.

Isa, the other men and the women without children walked six kilometers every day to their jobs at a veneer factory. I was happy that my ema could stay with me. Isa worked, until he became ill with the flu. Then he was excused. I was very upset to see my isa ill, but he told me not to worry. "You'll see, I'll be well very soon."

Then a terrible thing happened. A measles epidemic struck the children in our little community on the veranda. The children became ill one by one. Each day another child was stricken with a high fever. I often heard them crying at night. My ema was relieved that I didn't get the measles. From the day we moved onto the veranda, she had fussed about the poor hygiene and the scarcity of food. Sometimes the food smelled terrible. Ema told me it was spoiled. She kept me away from the sick children, and I spent my days on my bed drawing pictures.

Some children died of complications from the measles and other diseases. My ema tried to explain all this to me. I had never known anyone who had died. I was upset and felt sorry for the parents who were sad and crying.

Then one day I had a very high fever, too. I hoped I would not die. My parents looked very worried and tired. My fever lasted several days and nights. Nothing ema did would break the fever. I felt miserable. They were so concerned that they took me to the Reichenberg City Hospital fifty kilometers away. Apparently, the doctor there told them that I had pneumonia. My ema told me I had an infection in my lungs, and I could not go back to the glass veranda. The doctor said I would have to stay at the hospital a few more days.

I was very upset when my parents left. The nuns took care of me. They were very nice, but they only spoke German and I only spoke Estonian. They couldn't tell me what was going to happen, or when my parents were coming back. That first night was terrible. I cried all night for my ema. I thought perhaps she didn't want me anymore and had left me there to get rid of me.

The next morning, I heard a soft footstep in the hall. I peered through the glass door of my room and suddenly saw my ema's reflection. She was standing there with her knitted cap on her head. When she walked into my room I was so happy to see her that I squealed. She hugged me and told me that after my isa had gone to work that morning, she had walked five kilometers through a forest. Next, she rode fifty kilometers on the train to get to the hospital. I asked her, if I was going to die. She reassured me that I certainly wasn't. She held me tightly and told me that I was in the hospital because of my fever. "We'll bring you home as soon as the doctor lets us," she said. "That will only be a few more days."

I was calmer after that and felt better. When the nuns said I was well, my parents came for me. The doctors told my parents that the communal veranda would not be a good place for me to recover, so my isa rented a small room. He said it cost a lot of money. He had to sell quite a few of the silver items, but I was worth it. I got well very quickly in that small room. I was so happy to be with my isa and ema again.

I felt better every day. Then, the most exciting thing happened. My Uncle Oskar and Aunt Salme showed up on December 5, 1944. What a party we had. Aunt Hilja came, too. I sat on ema's lap and listened to Uncle Oskar explain how he had found us. "Salme and I took the last train out of Valga to Riga, Latvia. We spent a few nights there at a home for railroad workers. Then the Germans put us on another train to Gotenhafen."

"Did you have to take those flea baths, too?" I asked. "Didn't they smell terrible?"

"Oh yes, we did. That solution did smell awful, but we sure felt clean," he said. "Then we were on the move again. This time they put us on a train to

Linz, Austria. That was not a good place to be, because there are tank factories there. The Americans were bombing the city. Then Salme and I heard that there were some Estonians in Berlin. I guess we are young and foolish. We headed north to Berlin, thinking we might find you, but, of course, we did not. We happened to run into someone from Valga while walking down the street, and he told us that you were last seen in Kummer in the Sudetenland. We took a train immediately and here we are."

Ema kept saying over and over again, how happy she was to have her family with us. Then she asked, if Oskar had heard anything about Ilmar. Oskar nodded. "You know, I'm amazed at how news travels in this country. If you run into an Estonian anywhere in Germany, he can tell you about your family. I ran into another fellow in Berlin, and he told me that Ilmar was also somewhere in Germany."

Ema and Aunt Hilja cried and hugged each other. I didn't know if they were happy or sad. Ema explained to me that they were glad to know Ilmar was safe. They wanted so much to hear from him.

We celebrated that Christmas, our first in exile, in our little room. In addition to my parents and me, Aunt Hilja, Uncle Oskar and Aunt Salme, and Jon Ratnik, a friend from Valga, were with us. I didn't feel like it was Christmas, though, because everyone was so sad. We didn't have any presents or a tree. My ema bought some candles somewhere, and as soon as she lit them, the room immediately looked festive. I missed the special food my ema always fixed. Isa had traded some more of his silver pieces for bread and sweets and Uncle Oskar brought cakes. We shared the food we had, and it seemed like a feast.

Then the adults sat around with long faces, and kept repeating that next year we would celebrate Christmas in Estonia. I sat on the floor and listened to them. I remembered Vanaisa's home and my dog, Tuki. Was he all right? Did he miss me as much as I missed him? I missed Vanaema, too. When we sang our favorite Christmas carols, the German ones like "Silent Night" and "O Tannenbaum," I knew it really was Christmas, although we were in a strange country. Once they started singing, the adults didn't stop for a long time. I heard some of my favorite songs, songs about the beauty of Estonia, the birch forests, the North Sea, the waves of grain. I could almost see the birch forests, so yellow in the fall. Our evening ended on a joyful note after all.

By early February 1945, the front was drawing closer. My parents decided that we should leave Kummer, because they heard that the Russians were in Czechoslovakia now. They told me they planned to move further west. We left quietly one morning and boarded a train packed with refugees. There were a lot of us, including Oskar, Salme and Hilja. I was so tired and exhausted, I didn't want to travel again, even with the Russians coming. When I complained to ema, she told me that I probably had not fully recovered from the pneumonia. She and isa had a whispered chat. Then she told me that they had decided we should stay in Karlsbad for a few days, so I could get better. Oskar, Salme and Hilja continued on the train heading south, and ema told them we'd find them soon.

To their dismay, my parents learned that refugees were not given residence permits in Karlsbad. My isa did not know what to do until he met the Rudolf Kivimagi family, old friends from Valga. They helped us find a place to stay in the village of Krohndorf-Warta, just 27 kilometers away. We stayed there with Anna Kilian, a kind woman, who lived in a tiny house at the foot of the Erz Mountains. Anna had suffered a lot too, so I guess that she felt sorry for us. I liked her right away. She had a warm smile and a kind face. I hoped we could stay with her a long time.

Anna said she was worried because I was so thin. She bought goat's milk for me to drink to gain weight and cure the whooping cough I now had. Anna generously shared with us the small amount of food she had. I still felt weak and listless from all that coughing. I lay in her small bed with the feather comforter and hugged my teddy bear. One day Anna looked closely at my bear and asked, "Why has your little bear lost all his hair? However did that happen?"

I giggled and confessed, "I gave him a hair cut when I was still in Valga at my Vanaisa's house. I just got a scissors and hid under the bed and cut it all off. I thought he'd like that, and then his hair would grow back. Don't you think he looks nice?"

"Oh yes," Anna agreed, "but perhaps we should find a nice jacket for him to wear when he gets cold. Would you like that?"

"Oh yes, I would. That would be ever so nice." I said. Anna was like a vanaema to me. I missed my vanaemas in Valga, and wondered if I'd see them again.

We celebrated my sixth birthday in that small cottage. Spring was just arriving. Anna and my ema picked globeflowers and lilacs. The perfume of these flowers wafted through the house. I heard my ema tell Anna, that it was incredible to think about what we'd been through since my fifth birthday in Estonia. Then I heard ema laugh, as she said, "Ene loves that homely hairless bear so much, that we could not leave without it. Now we have a homely, hairless, homeless bear. Don't you think that's rather ironic?" Soon I heard Anna chuckle, too.

"You are so good to us, Anna." I said. "I feel better just looking at those flowers. You are making my sixth birthday very special." I was grateful to be in her little house.

"I'm glad to see you looking better, Ene. I'm sure it's that goat's milk," Anna said. "To celebrate your birthday, we will go to an inn in the village this evening." Then she put a little package in my lap and said, "Here's a little something for you that I made."

I tore off the wrappings and found inside a little gray jacket that just fit my teddy. "Oh I love it. I know Teddy will too. Thank you, thank you." I adored the little jacket with three brass buttons down the front. I quickly put the jacket on my teddy, and he looked so handsome. "You may be hairless and homeless, but you are not homely," I told my teddy.

Anna watched as I dressed the teddy. She beamed and said, "I always wondered what I could do with that little piece of gray flannel I had."

That evening, we went to a small inn. I loved the spinach porridge and potato dumplings. Anna and my parents drank wine and toasted to peace and the end of the war. Then later, they looked solemn as Anna began to speak of the war developments.

I hear that the front is getting closer, and the Germans have surrendered. Perhaps you should move farther west." She shrugged, "For me, this is my home. I'll stay here and take my chances with the Russians." I felt so sad listening to them talk about leaving. I did not want to go, but I did not say anything. I didn't want to upset Ema.

My parents packed quickly in the morning, putting just a few necessities in their backpacks. Ema gave a few of the silver pieces to Anna in gratitude for her kindness to us. We left very early and walked toward Karlsbad. I was sleepy and tired as we walked along. I asked, "Do we really have to go?" Isa simply shook his head. I thought again how much I wanted to have a home somewhere. I knew how much I would miss Anna.

My isa found a small inn and we spent the night in Karlsbad. He went out to look about the town in the morning, but came back quickly. He said, "The city is full of Russian soldiers and there are Communist Germans on the streets waving banners and welcoming their comrades into the city. We've got to leave here, immediately."

My ema got up and prepared to go right away. She dressed me in my warmest clothes: my knitted cap, wool stockings and an extra sweater. We were on the road once more.

Betty J. Iverson

SEVEN: The Russians Come

My parents discussed what to do to avoid looking like refugees. They decided to leave their knapsacks behind, and ema stuffed as much as she could in isa's briefcase. Then we sauntered nonchalantly out of the city, searching for the most likely escape route. I had not completely recovered from the whooping cough so our journey on foot was a tough slow one. We trudged along with a lot of other families who were fleeing Karlsbad, too. Sometimes, ema and I would get a ride for a few kilometers in the carts of escaping German soldiers.

We knocked on a few doors. Finally some friendly people in a farm house welcomed us inside. I wondered, if they found a little girl like me hard to refuse. They told us that they were sympathetic to our flight from the Russians. They were fearful too, but said they had to stay on their farm. We left there in the early morning and walked until we reached Saxony. Then my isa led us into the forest to continue our escape toward an American checkpoint. I didn't know what a checkpoint was, but it sounded safe. He said there was a lot of confusion now with both Russian and American soldiers in the area. Ema looked afraid when he said that.

Once we were back on the road, we became part of an ever expanding group of refugees. Some American soldiers appeared and gathered all of us into a group. They brought trucks and told us they were taking us to a school building. My parents said the Americans didn't know what to do with us. We were quite a lot of people to feed.

We stayed in that building for over a week. There were lots of people, and everything was makeshift. Most of us slept on the floor. I was so afraid and hungry that I was glad when they set up a soup line to feed us. My ema said she didn't want to go back to the Russians. Finally an official looking American soldier came. He said that we would all be placed with German families.

We were taken to a house and the people there took us in. The Americans also placed the other refugees with families. While our family fed us, ema whispered to me that she felt they were feeding us against their will. She told me to be nice and always say thanks. We stayed with this family for only a few days. My isa and some of the other refugees scouted the countryside. One afternoon when isa returned, he was very excited. "Joa, there is a refugee camp nearby," he said. "I think we should go there."

Ema told me to be quiet as we left early the next morning for the camp isa had found. As we walked along, many other refugees joined us. One of the families was the Veldis from Valga. Ema told me that their son had been in the Forest Brotherhood with Ilmar. When ema asked them about their son they told her they had no idea where he was. We arrived late in the afternoon at Oelsnizi, near Plauen. Ema told me that we were like pilgrims, searching for a safe place. Maybe we would find one this time.

Sadly, this camp was the first of many temporary stops. Still ema was happy that she could wash our clothes, and we were being fed. My longing for a place to stay for awhile was not satisfied here. I heard my parents talking. Isa said he had been told that when this little town was handed over to the Russians, we would be taken away first because we were refugees. I began to think that it was a bad thing to be a refugee.

Soon we were walking on the road again. I remember going here and there without any clear direction, except to keep ahead of the Russians. Ema told me that everything was in chaos and confusion because this area would soon to be turned over to the Russians. Some of the Germans were helpful, the way Anna had been, and gave me apples. Others were nasty and ignored me. I felt the Germans in the countryside were nice, because they shared food with us and let us sleep in their orchards. My isa was relieved that we hadn't seen any Nazis. I wasn't sure who Nazis were or what they looked like, but I felt they must be bad people.

We stayed in one camp after another. Soon the camps became a blur to me, except for the one at Coburg. I had to go pee pee in the middle of the night. I got up to go outside and stepped over all the sleeping bodies. I tripped and fell flat on my face on the cement floor. I cut my face, and my cheek became swollen and infected. My ema took me to a German doctor nearby, and he lanced my cheek, which really hurt me. I wasn't sure what lanced meant except I felt pain when he stuck my cheek with a needle and lots of yellow stuff rolled down my face. I had a big pink scar across my cheek for a very long time. I was convinced that I was ugly, but my isa kissed that scar. He told me I was still his favorite pretty little girl.

The next stop was Landsburg. From there, we were taken in American army trucks to Bavaria, which was in the American sector in the west. We must have finally reached that American checkpoint my isa was looking for. Our new camp was a muddy tent camp at the town of Rosenheim near Ingolstadt. I sat with my mom one night as she was talking with other women, all Estonians like us. They said that Germany had been divided. The eastern part was under the Russians, and the western part was under the Americans and the Allies. "Can we stay here for awhile?" I asked hopefully.

"I surely hope so," said ema. The other women around the circle nodded in agreement. I got the impression they were relieved they did not have to worry about the Russians any more. "Let's hope we can stay here until the war ends and then go back to Estonia, when the Russians leave," said another woman.

We arrived at this camp on July 5, 1945 and lived in a tent with one hundred people of various nationalities. Inside the tent were bunk beds on a mud floor, and our living space was the area around our bed. I was glad it was summer, because we lived outside in this tent for over a month.

We were delighted to connect with Uncle Oskar and Aunt Salme again. Uncle Oskar was the Estonian head of this camp. He told us that they had been here for quite awhile. He took my hand and led me to the office. "See who's here?" he said. I looked around and saw my Aunt Hilja, who was doing office work at the camp. I was so happy to see her that I hugged her tightly until she begged me to stop. Aunt Hilja was a happy person to be around. She said that I could come to visit her at the office anytime.

I didn't have much to do at first. Then a wonderful woman, Heljo Rasman, set up a kindergarten for all of us young children. I was happy to go to school. I called Heljo my kindergarten aunt. She was so loving and kind. Most of all, I liked being in her class along with other girls like me. Sometimes I felt lonely, being an only child.

Betty J. Iverson

EIGHT: Estonian Camps

A month later, the American army trucks came to move us again, this time to the town of Dettendorf near Rosenheim. Ema told me she was puzzled that we were moved again. None of the Americans explained why we were being moved. I was amazed at the new camp which was very large and in the forest. My isa told me this camp had been an army barracks. Now we lived like one large Estonian family. I went to an Estonian school and sang in the chorus. I was glad to have friends to play with.

My isa and the other men did not have jobs. The UNRRA (United Nations' Refugee Relief Association) ran these camps and supplied all our food. We stood in soup lines again. The UNRRA even sent clothes and blankets to the camp. My Uncle Oskar was the Estonian head of this camp, too.

My ema was happy to receive a supply of wool so she could begin knitting again. Ema loved to knit. I often fell asleep listening to the sound of those needles clicking. She knitted all our caps, mittens, sweaters and scarves. She made me stockings, which were like panties with legs. She knitted for isa too, usually socks and vests.

The CARE packages gave us a lot more food to eat including some things that I had never tried before. There were the usual powdered eggs, milk, flour and sugar. This time, there was something new: peanut butter. I had never eaten peanut butter before, but I liked it a lot. I began to feel like my life was almost normal again. I had friends to play with, and my mother was busy knitting.

Since we children went to school for only a half day, we had lots of time to play. Our favorite place was the "Lumber Place." This was a huge pile of boards which had been thrown into a heap in the middle of the camp. We played all sorts of games here, like hide and seek or capture the fort. I couldn't wait for school to end so I could go to the Lumber Place and play with my friends. There were about thirty of us. The Lumber Place was a perfect fort for all of our battles. I spent most of my days there. This memory always made me laugh, and was the most fun I had in any of the camps.

One evening ema was teasing Aunt Hilja about her new boy friend, Joki. My ears perked up. Aunt Hilja had always had a lot of boy friends. Ema often said she was "a flirt." I wasn't sure what that meant, but I guessed she meant friendly. Aunt Hilja's cheeks turned red and she looked embarrassed. Then she said, "I think we're going to get married. Joki has found a minister here in the camp."

My mother became very excited. "We'll make your wedding a grand celebration," she promised. And what a celebration it was. Somehow, ema had found an Estonian national costume for Aunt Hilja to wear. She prepared a festive meal and baked a special cake. Aunt Hilja looked so pretty with a wreath of flowers in her light brown hair. Joki was nervous. I was happy that my Aunt Hilja had married such a handsome and nice man. He always joked with me, and I liked being around him. He was funny. I wished he didn't smoke so much.

This was not our only party. We had masked balls, which I thought were very grand. The adults dressed in costumes and danced, while I sat with the other children and watched. My isa who was known as "Stoneface," could actually be very funny and told jokes. I was proud of him because all the people in the camp loved him. Like so many times in the past, he was the clown of the party at the masked balls.

The men had distilled some vodka. This strong drink made them all happy, or so it seemed to me. I knew that we children couldn't have any. I especially loved all the music and singing. One man played an accordion, while another played a mouth harmonica. Then the grown ups danced. Everyone was cheerful during these parties and talked a lot about the happy day when we would be back in Estonia. I liked the adults in this camp, who could make any occasion a party.

Once in awhile I thought of my dog, Tuki. Was he was all right? Sometimes at night I would dream about him. Then I thought about my vanaema and wondered if her back hurt. When I lived with her, I would give her a massage by walking on her back as she lay on the floor. I held onto the table and walked gently back and forth over her back. We both enjoyed this. She always told me how good her back felt afterwards. I worried that she had not had a treatment since I left.

My parents had begun to receive letters from Estonia, and ema received a letter from a cousin who told us all about vanaema Magraken, my ema's mother. She wrote that my vanaisa had died a year ago and now vanaema was in an old age home. I was sad to hear that my vanaisa had died. He had been so good to me. I remember the little sand box he made for me, where I would sit with the chickens. Ema and Uncle Oskar were sad to hear about their father, but glad that their mother was being taken care of. In fact, she was now 80 years old. My ema told me this was quite a long time to live. I worried about Tuki. Ema told me she was sure that Tuki had a new home with a nice family. I hoped the people were taking good care of my vanaema and giving her massages.

On November 15, 1946, the Dettendorf camp was disbanded and we were taken by American army trucks to Deshing near Ingolstadt. This time we lived in a secluded housing development. We continued our Estonian way of life, and I went to the elementary school. Isa worked for an American work company in Frankfurt. Since he was one of the few who knew some English, he had gotten a good job as a translator for the Americans. He and the other men were gone Monday through Friday and stayed in barracks at the American army camp. My Uncle Oskar also found a job working for the Americans.

I was awed by my father's black uniform. I looked forward to his visits on the week ends, and he always brought me goodies. Since the men were paid on Friday, they often bought produce from the countryside: potatoes, salted meats and even fancy birthday cakes. Sometimes, Ema and I would visit father at the American camp. I was intrigued by his barracks, a large, arched metal building, which he told me was a Quonset hut.

Sometimes the soldiers would drive us around. Some of them were black, and I had never seen black people before. In fact, none of us Estonians had. I was frightened by these American G.I.'s, because I had listened to the scarey stories the other children told about them. Once we children got to know them, we really liked them. They were friendly, and I especially liked the candy and gum they gave us.

Deshing was a special place to me because I was given a little cousin here. Salme had a baby boy, whom Uncle Oskar named Jaak after his father. He was born on December 29, 1946. I hurried tome from school to play with Jaak, my new little cousin.

After our happy stay at Deshing, we were on the move again. This time to Aschaffenburg near Ulm in Bavaria. Here we lived in a former army Kaserne, (Military barracks). We shared our large room with the Veldi family. My mom hung blankets on clotheslines for wall dividers. We slept on cots and were given a table and chairs in our section. The toilets and showers were in large rooms. Ema called them communal. I figured out that she meant big rooms for everyone to share.

Here at the Kaserne, my ema met some people who had news about Ilmar. They told her that Ilmar had left Germany and gone to England. They also heard that he had married an Estonian woman in England. My ema was so happy to hear such good news about Ilmar.

Once again, we were in a totally Estonian camp, so I continued going to school and even joined a Brownie troop. I wanted to learn to play the piano, although we didn't have one. Someone gave me a painted keyboard. I spent hours pretending to play the piano. There was also an Estonian church here. We began to have our traditional birthday celebrations with flowers and kringel, our Estonian birthday cake.

I looked forward to my occasional trips to Frankfurt on the weekends. My isa still worked at the American camp. When he didn't come home on the weekend, ema and I went to Frankfurt. I was fascinated by the guard houses at the gates of the camp. The soldiers were always friendly when they checked us in. Most of the time, they gave me some candy.

We were only at this camp a week when we received a shaky handwritten letter from Vanaema Juulia, Isa's mother. Isa looked so sad as he read the letter. He took me on his lap and told me that my Vanaisa Joosep had died. Vanaema Juulia said in her letter that "Father's illness was terribly hard. He had bone cancer. The cancer had started in his big toe. By the time he died there was nothing left of his leg but black bones." I shivered as father read that. Isa explained that Vanaisa became ill in December and died the following August. Now both my vanaisas were gone.

Vanaema Juulia wrote that the doctors wanted to amputate his leg but decided he wouldn't survive surgery. The next lines broke my heart. "Once in a while he called for Ene. I can't describe how difficult it all was." I realized how much I had missed him, too. He was always so loving to me. I began to cry. By now, my isa was weeping, too. He handed the letter to ema. "Then the night he died, he gave his hand to me and said, "Let's say good-bye now." He fell asleep, and then he was gone," Vanaema wrote.

She wrote more news about Vanaisa's funeral. I left and went out to play. I was still a child. I did not want to think about death, even though I was aware of it from the bombings that killed people and the children who had died of illnesses in the camp in Kummer.

Ema told me later that Vanaema had signed her letter wishing us much health and happiness in the new year. For Ene, many thanks and many, many kisses. Her letter had sharpened many of my memories of them and my home. Yet with each passing day I felt that my dream of going home again and seeing my dog, Tuki was not going to happen.

To supplement the boring rations of the soup kitchen, the men decided to raise pigs. By the time the pigs were ready to be killed, the weather had turned cold. The men slaughtered the pigs and salted them in the basement of the Kaserne. I thought the whole thing was horrible and had nightmares for weeks afterward. The slaughter took place in the shower room. It was a terrible mess and very noisy with all those pigs squealing. For some reason, ema thought the pig squealing was very funny.

Just after the pig slaughter, the camp inspector came by to check the showers. Fortunately the mess had been cleaned up by then. The men were hosing the last of the blood down the drain. The men knew that it was illegal to have meat. The carcasses of the pigs were still lying about on the floor. Some of the women scurried down to the basement, sat on chairs and spread their skirts over the dead pigs. The inspector left without a word.

Try as I might to remember other adventures, what always comes to my mind are the endless food lines, camp duties, and sorting through the CARE packages for clothes and blankets. I was grateful that so many people were helping us. I knew that everyone still longed for Estonia; however, I was happy to be in a camp where I had a roof over my head, food every day and children to play with. I didn't even mind that my sweet ema had become a strict disciplinarian, who made sure that I did my share of camp duties every day.

My isa explained to me that the Americans had allowed all of us ethnic peoples to set up separate camps with our common language. That way, we wouldn't have conflicts and could enjoy entertainment. Most of us refugees wandering about Germany were from the Baltic States and Poland. All of us wanted to be in the American sector. There was total chaos until the sectors were in place. Sadly, most of the Czech refugees ended up in the Russian sector.

I was thrilled when Aunt Hilja had a baby girl, whom she named Kersti on December 12, 1947. She and Uncle Joki were very proud at Kersti's christening by Pastor Juul in the camp's church. A few days later, as the women sat chatting, I was suddenly troubled. There were more and more babies being born, but none to my ema. I was now a girl of eight and I wondered why I didn't have a little brother or sister. After the chatter had quieted down, I whispered to mother, "Why don't we have a baby? I love my little cousins, but I'd like to have my own baby. Can't we, please."

Ema looked very sad. She said she'd share a story with me privately. Later, she said, "You know when the Russians were coming back, we were very afraid of the future. We knew we had to leave Estonia. Isa and I had no idea where we'd be going or what our life would be like. Then I learned I was pregnant. We felt it would be foolish to have a baby when our life would surely be difficult, if not dangerous." Tears began to flow down her cheeks, as she whispered, "I had the babies taken away."

I began to cry, too. I didn't know what she meant. How could a woman have her baby taken away? And then I realized that she had said "babies." "I don't understand what happened," I said. "You said babies. Was there more than one?"

"Oh Ene, I can't really explain it all to you, you're so young. I went to a doctor in the next village. He took them away. Twins. I didn't think it was fair to bring children into such a world. Just look at all the places we've been. Would little babies have survived that?"

271

Even though I was just a girl, I understood my mother's pain. I felt a terrible loss, too. Yet, I remembered so many places that were miserable, the times I was sick and also the little babies who had died on that veranda, and others who died as we traveled along. I trusted and loved my mother. I hugged her and said, "Well you have me and I have you and Isa." (I did not understand until I was much older, that my mother had had an abortion. Then I felt sad all over again: for my mother who had lost a set of twins, and for me who would have had a brother or sister. War often causes us to do regrettable things.)

NINE: The Final Odyssey

After two years (1949), we had to leave the Kaserne. We became displaced people on the road again. This time the Americans took us to the town of Geislingen. We lived in a section of the town known as Schlosshalde. The Americans forced the German families who lived there to give up their homes to us. Several Estonian families occupied a house. Each family was given a bedroom as their private space. All of us shared the living room and kitchen.

I liked this town and thought it was a nice place to live. I even had a bicycle, which I shared with another girl. I was back in an Estonian school again. Since we had an old piano in our room, I took lessons. I found a real piano more fun to play than a painted keyboard. That Christmas I received a piece of sheet music, and I thought this was the best Christmas present I had ever received. We celebrated my tenth birthday in this house. I felt very grown up.

Isa told me that we would be leaving Germany soon as the Americans were disbanding all the refugee camps. I began thinking about what life might be like elsewhere. I had heard America was the land of plenty. You could eat anything you wanted. Most people had cars. I even dreamed that my father had a car and I came back to the camps in that car to impress my friends. Then too, I liked all those soldiers I had met. I was sure that all Americans would be that nice.

I asked my isa where we would go. Everyone had talked about returning to Estonia in the beginning, but not anymore. By now, we knew that the Russians still occupied Estonia and all the Baltic countries. They even refused to leave their sphere of influence and remained in eastern Germany.

"Ene, we have four options, but we cannot go home. We will go where I can get a job. Our choices are: America, Australia, Canada, or Belgium, where I would work in the coal mines." I knew the choice was my father's, but I wanted to go to America. I was very happy when Isa told me, that he felt America was certainly the best option.

We chose America. I couldn't wait to leave. Then my ema fell and injured her leg. This delayed our departure because she had to be perfectly healthy and her leg completely healed before she could emigrate. When we were close to our time to leave, we went to the Ludwigsburg processing camp in March 1950. Through the years we had received some CARE packages of clothes and food from the Lutheran World Federation, so we were happy that our sponsor was the Lutheran Church.

We finally left the processing camp on March 27th to board the ship, General Haan, an old army transport vessel. When I got on that ship in Germany,

I thought back to the time when we had left Estonia on the Sonnenfelder. I remembered the soldiers with guns, the bombs dropping all around. I was terrified. This time, there were no soldiers or bombs dropping. I didn't feel afraid, only anxious. Would we have a room to sleep in or would we live on the open deck? Isa had told me the trip would take thirteen days, since we had a big ocean to cross. Our last trip had taken only half that long.

The sailors checked our names off the list. We were given bunk beds in the hold. We lived crowded together in that hold, a large area in the bottom of the ship. We were all seasick the first few days, since the ship rolled a lot. Then the weather cleared, and the sea became calm. We could then leave the hold during the day and sit on the deck in the sun. I met some other children on the ship and we spent our time dreaming about things we would like to eat. Jello and grapefruit were fed to us on a regular basis, but these were totally foreign foods to us Estonians. My friends and I were hungry for black bread with mustard and raw onion slices.

We were all excited about going to America and New York. Would everyone be as friendly as the American soldiers? Would they dunk us in that smelly flea bath again? Would we be put in a camp again? Isa reassured me that we would be staying with a family. I remembered how many times we did that in Germany and I never liked it, except for Anna. She was so kind.

Many days, I just stood at the rail and looked out at the ocean. I had never seen so much water.

Occasionally, I saw a big fish jump out of the water. We were now a very long way from Estonia, and I knew in my heart that we would never go back there. America would be a new country. I resolved to make it my home.

We sailed into the New York harbor on April 6th. When we saw the Statue of Liberty, everyone cheered and clapped, jumped up and down and hugged each other. My parents, however, were strangely quiet. When I hugged my dad, he said, "This will be our new home."

There was a lot of confusion when the boat docked. We all disembarked, some were searching for family members in the crowd. Soon greeters from the Lutheran World Federation met us and took us to the train station. So far, no flea baths. I giggled to myself. When ema asked me what was so funny, I told her, and she laughed, too. We left that evening by train for New Haven, Connecticut. There our friends, the Laans, who had emigrated earlier, met us. My parents were happy to see them. They talked rapidly, telling us the many things we would need to do. Then they took us to meet their sponsor family, Gordon and Elizabeth Clark, who lived on a large estate in Woodbridge, Connecticut. The Laans lived in an apartment above the garage, which they generously offered to share with us, because we did not have a sponsoring family yet.

I was eleven years old now and spoke not one word of English. I suspected that our sponsoring family would not speak any Estonian, either. Would they like us? If they didn't, would we have to leave?

My ema was concerned that we were very crowded in the Laan's apartment and anxious that we not be a bother. We met the Clarks, the Laan's sponsors. Isa spoke with Mrs. Clark, and she suggested that perhaps her parents, Milton and Gladys Mapes could be our sponsors since they wanted to sponsor a family. They had a big house and Mrs. Mapes's father lived with them. They would like to have a family in the house with him as they were often gone. Mrs. Mapes was a busy volunteer, and Mr. Mapes played golf.

The next morning, Mr. and Mrs. Mapes came to meet us. My ema made sure I was dressed in my best dress. The Mapes's quickly decided that they would like to sponsor us so the meeting took only a few moments and warm handshakes all around. Before I had grasped it all, we had gathered our meager belongings and were on our way to the Mapes's house in their big black Cadillac.

The Mapes's drove slowly down a quiet street with large trees on either side. I asked about the small concrete strip on each side of the street. Mr. Mapes laughed as he explained to my isa, that this strip was a sidewalk where people walked. After Isa translated for me, I laughed, too. How odd, a little street just for people. I had never seen anything like that before, not even in the countryside of Germany. I was used to walking on the sides of dirt roads.

Soon Mr. Mapes slowed and stopped in front of a huge gray house. We got out and stood uncertainly in front of the house. There appeared to be three floors. I had never seen a house so grand. My jaw dropped in awe.

Mrs. Mapes smiled warmly and her eyes twinkled as she said, 'Come on in. Here we are."

"This is wonderful," my father said. I was proud of my father that he could speak English so well. Since he had been working for the American army, his English had improved. He quickly translated for Ema and me. Mrs. Mapes led us to the dining room, where she offered us some food. She said she knew we'd be tired and hungry. From that day on, she was like my second mother.

Mrs. Mapes led us upstairs to the third floor of her large house. "This area will be your home," she told us. "We want you to be comfortable here." I stared at all that space with beds and couches. I felt I had never seen anything so grand. I went to sleep that night on a soft bed with a down pillow. For the first time in years, I didn't wonder when I would find a home.

My ema, however, cried and cried that first day. When Isa asked her what was wrong, she pointed to the garage in the back of the house. She asked, "Why couldn't they put us in that little house by ourselves, instead of this big fancy house?" Then he told her that the little house was actually a garage for cars and not a house for people.

The Mapes family instantly took us into their hearts. They were such loving people, they included us in all meals and family celebrations. We soon met Mrs. Mapes's father, Grandpa Blakesley, a man of 91 who appeared very sharp and active. We were all surprised that he still played golf every week. The

Mapes's children were all grown up and had moved away, but they often came for celebrations.

Mrs. Mapes took me to the neighborhood school, the very next day. My ema had carefully dressed me in my finest dress and my knitted wool stockings. The next day, Mrs. Mapes told my mother that she shouldn't send me to school in those heavy woolen stockings. I was relieved to shed those heavy itchy stockings.

I was placed in the fifth grade, where everyone was nice to me. Since I did not know English, they assigned a buddy to sit with me. Before long I was invited to sleep overs and birthday parties. By September, I spoke English fluently. I had an easier time with English than my parents did, despite the fact that they both knew some English.

Mr. Mapes took my father to meet his friends in the banking business, but had no success in landing him a job. My dad told me later, that as Grandpa watched his son-in-law march him from one bank to another, Grandpa became annoyed and muttered, "This is ridiculous."

I vividly remember the morning he took my father by the elbow and said, "You could be an accountant. Let's go get a job." He then took my father to a friend of his who owned an accounting firm. Father told me later, that he had a job in fifteen minutes. My mother was employed as a clerk by the seed company owned by the Clark family.

The funniest incident I remember during those wonderful three years that we lived with the Mapes concerned Grandpa. Milton Mapes collected clocks, and they were his pride and joy. His most prized clock was the tall Grandfather clock that rested on the landing of the stairs.

Grandpa sometimes wandered at night. On this particular night, he headed down the stairs. Suddenly he stumbled and stood tottering on the landing, where he grabbed the clock to steady himself. He hugged the clock and he and the clock took off, tumbling down the stairs together. There was such a racket that we were all awakened. I ran to the stairs just in time to watch this strange sight of Grandpa and the clock rolling down the stairs. Grandpa got up without a scratch. His son-in-law hurried down, and quickly looked over the clock. He was obviously more worried about his pride and joy, than Grandpa. He never asked Grandpa how he was. Fortunately, the clock was fine, too.

I learned to play softball and jump rope. While she approved of my sports activities, Mrs. Mapes also pushed me to read. I have fond memories of that first summer, lying on my stomach on the screened porch reading scores of library books.

I thought we became Americans very quickly. After three years with the Mapes, we rented an apartment. Years later, something happened that was beyond my wildest dreams. I went to Vassar college, and I owe it all to Mrs. Mapes. She had brainwashed my parents from the day we arrived that education was important. She wanted me to work toward a top notch college.

After all those years of Gypsy existence roaming around Europe with no home, no security and little food, I was now given this opportunity to begin a new life. I loved my home, my new country. I knew that whatever journeys I might take, I would always come back to my home, America.

EPILOGUE

My father bought his first car, a light blue Mercury, which he drove only on Sundays to the Estonian church. Both my parents worked downtown, so they took the bus to work during the week. The car was a significant purchase for our family.

My father worked at the accounting firm where Mr. Blakesly had gotten him the job until he died in 1963 of a heart attack. My mother retired many years later. They lived in an apartment and later bought a small home in Hamden, Connecticut in 1957, the first home of their own.

Mrs. Mapes continued to encourage me to go to college. I was accepted at Vassar, and went to Germany for my junior year. There I met Lazlo who became my husband. He refers to himself as a G. I. Bridegroom. He also had a journey of his own from Hungary during the uprising there in 1956. We live in California. Our two children and a grandson live on the East Coast.

I visited Valga with my mother in 1991. I was saddened to see our town so dilapidated after the years of Russian occupation. At the same time, I found it interesting that besides the aesthetics, nothing had changed. Everything looked physically as I remembered or had seen in photographs for the past 47 years. I took a second trip back to Estonia and Valga in 2001, where I found the same story. I even went inside my grandfather's home and the place appeared just as I remembered it.

We have kept in touch with the Mapes family, or at least with some of their children, as Mr. and Mrs. Milton Mapes, our benefactors, died many years ago.

My mother is still alive at 91, but unfortunately remembers nothing about her journey to America, since she has Alzheimers disease. Her sister, Hilja, ten years younger, is also institutionalized with Alzheimers in Chicago. Hilja and Joki emigrated to Chicago after the war along with a group of Estonians. They eventually had two boys to join their daughter, Kerstie.

My Uncle Oskar and Salme left before us from Ludwigsburg and entered America at New Orleans. Their little son, Jaak, was ill with measles on the boat and taken from their ship in the harbor to a hospital. Oskar and Salme were frantic, until they finally found him in a hospital two weeks later. When he was well, they took a train to Memphis to meet their sponsor.

In Memphis, Oskar and Salme met their sponsor, a lady from Barkins, Arkansas. She and her husband owned a cotton farm and a mill. Salme was their housekeeper and Oskar their handyman. Life was hard. Oskar and Salme felt they were little more than servants.

When they heard from Hilja about the plentiful jobs and the large Estonian community in Chicago, they headed there. In Chicago, Oskar worked at Sunbeam all his life. Salme became a nutritionist at Western Electric. They eventually bought a home in Berwyn where they still live in retirement.

Ilmar left Germany in 1947 for England where he married an Estonian woman. They live in Adelaide, Australia and have no children. Ilmar raises orchids and enjoys curling. Apparently he is interested in the new free Estonia and visits there occasionally. I and my cousins keep in touch, even though we are scattered throughout the states.

The Forest Brotherhood remained active into the 1950's and 60's, since the Baltic Nationals loathed the absorption of their republics into the Soviet Union. They were supported by the emigre communities overseas, especially in the United States.

A retired German and history teacher, as well as an occasional university administrator, I enjoy photography and have published three books about the areas where I lived: one about Westport, Connecticut, the second about my present town across the bay from San Francisco, California, and more recently, a book about Nantucket.

I still have my homely, hairless Teddy and some of my father's silver pieces. (Brandy glasses) Life has been good to me.

Ene Bonnyay

PROLOGUE: MARGRET

Margret was initially hesitant to tell her story. Given time to think the matter over, she decided she would like to talk about her journey because she felt it was important for people to know what it was like to wander homeless and have nothing, yet manage to survive. Margret agreed to share her story on one condition: that she could tell it anonymously. She did not want any reprisals against herself and her family.

Margret is a woman who has known much fear in her life. Even now she has fears. She overcame her reservations and told her story, in spite of the fact that remembering her journey meant she would be reliving some difficult times. In the process, however, she remembered the kindness of people who were total strangers, yet took her and her son into their homes and fed them. People willingly shared what little they had. This was a positive experience for her.

Most important of all, in the telling of her journey, she discovered within herself a profound courage.

ONE: Fleeing Romania

My life changed forever that day in October 1944 when I heard the town reporter play his drums and shout, "The Germans have been driven back. Everyone must get ready to leave." His words frightened me. I had never lived anywhere but this village. Where would I go? I listened to the crack of rifles in the street and heard the cannons booming outside the village during the night. Were the Russians defeating the Romanian army and the Germans who had come to fight alongside them? I was scared by these armies fighting over my village.

I was home alone with my six- month-old son, Kurt. My husband, Michael, had been drafted into the Romanian army in 1942, as had all the young men in the village. When we were married, he knew he'd be called to serve soon and so he was. Barely a year after our wedding, he was sent to Transylvania. I had not seen him for a long time. In fact, he had not seen our precious son, Kurt. I glanced down at my son's smiling face and big blue eyes, and I knew Michael would be proud of him. We had not been able to have a place of our own, but lived with my parents. While I had no home to leave, my parents would be leaving everything they had worked for all their lives. Now, there were only elderly men or young boys left in the village. Most of them were in the fields this day tending the crops, as was my father.

My family and I lived in the small farming village of Deutsch Sankt Michael "German Saint Michael." Our village had been shifted back and forth between Hungary and Romania through the years and was one of the smaller Danube Swabian villages in the province of Banat. While the villages were populated mostly with Danube Swabians, they also included some Hungarians and Romanians, who worked as farm laborers.

We were proud of our heritage as descendants of the Danube Swabians, who came to colonize the frontier lands over 250 years ago after the defeat of the Turks. The first wave of Germans, invited by Charles VI, came to the area bordered by the Danube, Tisza and Maros Rivers, and the Carpathian Mountains. Waves of settlers continued to come in the 18th century during the reign of Empress Maria Theresa. These pioneers on barges from Swabia in southern Germany became known as Danube Swabians because they settled near the Danube River.

Our industrious ancestors established a Christian civilization and made our area so fruitful that the southeastern part of Europe became known as the Breadbasket of Europe. By 1900 the total population of our villages had grown to over one million.

After World War I when the Austro-Hungarian Empire was dissolved, and the various territories of the German settlers were parceled out to Romania, Hungary and Yugoslavia, my village had been absorbed into Romania. Deutsch Sankt Michael, like so many others, was weakened by this change. To the Romanians, we were now an ethnic minority and we felt animosity from the majority who had different customs and a different language.

When World War II began, the difficulties of our life increased. With Hitler marching his armies and invading countries, all of us Danube Swabians who remained in our villages began to experience hatred from the people around us who disliked anything German. The Communists in particular distrusted us. As the war ground on, we Germans fought with the Romanians against the Russians. Early in the war, however, Romania had chosen to be a neutral country.

After the drummer finished his drum roll and left, I cradled my son and fought back my anxieties. I didn't want to believe what he had said. I couldn't imagine that I would have to leave my village. This was the only place I had ever lived and all my relatives were here. This was my home. I was terrified at the thought of leaving.

I suddenly thought of Michael. How could he find me if I was sent away? I loved him so much. I had known him ever since we were children. I couldn't imagine life without him. I thought back to my wedding day. He had looked so handsome. We had a simple wedding with only our families present:

our parents, Michael's brother Heinrich, my sister Elisabeth and her fiancee Hans. I did not have a wedding dress, and instead wore my favorite navy blue dress. We did not have enough money for an elaborate celebration. After the ceremony at the church, my mother served a festive meal to everyone. I was so happy on my wedding day and looked forward to our life together.

I pulled out a trunk and began to pack sacks of clothes and small packets of grain to take along in case the drummer's dire prediction came true. I also felt that if we were bombed, the trunk would protect our provisions. The drummer had said that the Russians were defeating the Romanians and advancing toward Deutsch Sankt Michael. I wondered where my mother was. When I looked out the window, I saw a small crowd of people running toward a large house at the end of the village. There appeared to be chaos and confusion. What was happening? Our village was so small that I could easily see from one end of town to the other. There were only two main streets intersected by three smaller streets.

I stood at the window, not sure what to do next. When I looked out again, I saw an army marching in the middle of the road. Were they Russians? Romanians? Germans? Then I saw more people running after the army had passed. I decided to follow the crowd to the large house where people had gathered. Once inside this house, I was greeted by Michael's teenage brother, Heinrich. When I told him about the army marching by, Heinrich went outside and listened to the soldiers. When he came back in, he told me that they were speaking German. I was relieved. The Russians hadn't come; at least not yet.

The next morning, I met with my parents and sister, Elisabeth, and we decided that there was no choice but to leave, if we did not want to live under the Russians. We left in such a hurry that we had no time to dress in layers of clothes. We simply wore what we had dressed in that morning. My father got out his wagon, hitched up the horses and threw in our trunks. He told us that we would head for the Yugoslavian border. Quickly my mother and I climbed aboard and I held Kurt. My sister, Elisabeth, climbed in and sat beside me. Next Michael's parents got into the wagon. Finally my father let some neighbors get aboard who begged to go along.

Heinrich was sent home to set the cows and pigs free so they could forage for food. He told his parents that he would go back to Freidorf where he was a blacksmith's apprentice. When I gave him a final hug good bye, he told me not to worry. He could take care of himself. He promised he would leave before the Russians arrived. I had a soft spot in my heart for my young brother-in-law and was sorry to leave him all alone.

Once our wagon full of refugees reached a village on the border, a German soldier stopped us and announced that everyone must get out and board trains. The soldier proudly announced the trains were run by the Germans and assured us that we would be taken to safety.

My heart sank as I looked at the long line of freight cars and the scores of people climbing inside.

When my trunk was thrown into one, I fought the crush of people so I could get inside with my stuff. I was followed quickly by Elisabeth, my parents and my in-laws. Soon other people got in, until we were crammed so tightly together that we couldn't sit down. I looked around and counted about forty people in our car.

Suddenly the door clanged shut. We were in total darkness, and I was freezing cold. Kurt began to cry and I tried to comfort him, but I was too scared to even croon a lullaby. I began to cry, too. My thoughts returned to Michael and how he would find us. I didn't know where I was going. The soldier had only told us, "To safety."

I am a timid woman, who has always been taken care of by someone. My parents took care of me and after I was married, I had Michael. I could always depend on him. Would I now be able to meet the challenge of taking care of myself and my son? Even though my parents were with me, I felt they would have enough to do to survive themselves in these dire circumstances. I was cold, exhausted and now very hungry. The train started up with a jerk and I hung on to my baby tightly in the darkness. Some children in the car began to cry and soon Kurt whimpered more loudly. Elisabeth came to my side and made a space for me to sit down. I began to nurse my baby. How long will I have milk to feed my son if I don't eat, I thought. I heard other mothers in the car say that they were worried because they had no milk for their children.

The train stopped at stations along the way and the freight cars were pushed aside and left on a side track for a few hours. People climbed out and relieved themselves in the fields. (There was no room for even a bucket in the freight cars.) The mothers scurried about looking for milk. One baby died because his mother had no milk. I looked through my trunk and picked out some clothes I could trade for food or milk.

I glanced at the long line of nearly eighty cars and pondered the many lives that were so suddenly interrupted. All the older folks, including my and Michael's parents, had left everything they had worked for their whole lives. I chatted with some of the others and realized that not only had our town been evacuated, but the neighboring villages as well. Everyone wanted to leave before the Russians arrived.

Whenever the train stopped, I got out quickly and rinsed Kurt's flannel diapers in cold water. My mother and mother-in-law then laid the diapers on their ample chests to dry them. The weather was turning colder and my mother-in-law bargained for a blanket and told me we'd use the blanket to make an outfit for Kurt. At one stop, the two mothers went off in search of milk and, to my horror, were left behind when the train pulled out! I was very upset when I realized they weren't with us. What should I do? My father was surprisingly calm and said he was sure they'd catch up to us. And so they did.

As soon as our train was parked on a side track at the next station, I climbed out. Suddenly, I saw two women running toward me. As they drew closer, I recognized my mother and mother-in-law. "Look,

look, we got some milk," my mother cried. The women didn't seem worried at all. "I knew we'd catch up," my mother said confidently. "We just hitched a ride with the next train going through. When we got here, we looked around until we recognized our train. The one we were on was not so long as ours." The women seemed none the worse for their adventure, and were proud of the fact that they had found some milk for Kurt. I was relieved to have it, because I no longer had milk to nurse my baby. I quickly fed him. I planned to carefully parcel out each day any food or milk I had for Kurt. That way, I reasoned the food would last until I could bargain for more.

After a week of travel, our train crossed the Hungarian border. A German soldier told us that we were being taken to a "Safe Town." The safe town apparently was Bisbegnadas on the Hungarian Austrian border. The soldier assured us that the people living there would take care of us. I had my doubts about how willing the people were, since the soldiers were forcing the residents to take us in.

Kurt and I were placed with a family in a large farmhouse, and they treated us well. The Frau let me use her sewing machine to make Kurt a warm jacket and pants out of the blanket my mother-in-law had gotten. The cold winds left no doubt that winter had come.

I wasn't the only wife who didn't know where her husband was. None of the women whose husbands were in the army knew where their men were. I was grateful that at least I had not been separated from my family on that freight train. Elisabeth, my parents and in-laws were also placed with families.

We were in this town for two weeks, which was long enough for me to become accustomed to standing in line for my food at a soup kitchen. While this was not pleasant, I was grateful to be fed. I could usually pick out small pieces of soft food for Kurt to chew. Sometimes I was given milk for him.

TWO: Into Germany

I was awakened one morning by the sound of shots. I rose quickly and looked out the window, but saw nothing. At the soup kitchen, we were told by the town leaders that we must leave because the Russians were getting close. This was an announcement I had heard before, only now there was no drummer. People sitting nearby grumbled and asked, "Why did we leave Deutsch Sankt Michael if the Russians are here, too?" I shrugged my shoulders as I looked about for my family. I hurried to the railway station carrying my trunk and Kurt in my arms. Amazingly, I found all of them in the midst of a crowd waiting to board a train.

Once more, we were herded onto a train, only this time into passenger cars. We could sit in seats. As usual, we were not told where we were going. Since there was not enough room for luggage, a German soldier snatched my trunk away, and promised me that I'd get it back later. Gone were all those precious things I had packed for Kurt. I worried most about that. How could I keep him warm and dry? Elisabeth and my mother moved over to me in the passenger car. We hugged each other to keep warm. "Where do you think they're taking us this time?" I asked. Mother threw up her hands and said she didn't feel it really made much difference. Austria? Germany? The war was everywhere. She just hoped the Russians wouldn't be where they were taking us.

The journey seemed long. We were fed soup occasionally when we were parked on a side track at a station along the way. The train proceeded to Thuringia in central Germany. After a few days journey, we were unloaded at the small village of Hainsdorf. Once again, the soldiers forced the residents of a village to take us in.

Kurt and I were placed with an elderly couple, the Eberhardts, who lived in a small house by the railway station. I had been with them only a few days when my trunk arrived. My parents and Elisabeth were placed with a family just three houses away. Michael's parents were just outside the village on a farm with the Horstman family.

There were no soup lines here in spite of the fact that more refugees kept coming to the village from Poland, Estonia and Lithuania. The Burgermeister gave out food stamps to all the families. The Eberhardts' stamps included my and Kurt's rations. The food stamps were only a small measure of relief since there was very little food on the shelves of the village stores. I felt blessed whenever I found a loaf of bread. I appreciated how well the Eberhardts treated Kurt and me, and I did all I could to help them. I not only went shopping for food but helped with the cooking, taking care of their garden and the animals, a pig and a cow.

I was surprised one day to hear the strains of a Christmas carol drifting from a church as I walked by. Only then did I realize that Christmas was near. The many days on the train and my vagabond life had erased normal life and things like holidays. Yet, Christ's birthday would come as always. I was grateful that my son and I were safe, and I had been able to provide for him. Kurt seemed to be thriving in spite of the circumstances. I hoped we would now be settled for awhile. Maybe then Michael could find us.

While Kurt had some clothes, he was a growing boy and kept needing more. My parents had brought along a small ham and a slab of bacon from home to eat or to be used for bartering. When my mother told the Frau in the house where they were staying that her grandson needed some clothes, the Frau said she had a relative who owned a little clothing store in the city. Since she knew mother had some meat with her, she mentioned that perhaps her sister would trade some baby clothes for a little bacon. Mother told me later that she did not hesitate, but traded her bacon for baby clothes for Kurt. I was so excited to have some new clothes for Kurt that fit him.

"Those people in the city were down to nothing, too, Margret," mother said when she handed the clothes to me. I nodded. I had noticed that everyone had very little food, not enough for a full meal, just enough to stay alive. Like the Eberhardts, most people had a garden. I appreciated all the more the generosity of this older couple who shared so willingly with me and Kurt. Mrs. Eberhardt even baked some cookies for Christmas and asked if she could give a cookie to Kurt. I nodded and enjoyed watching my son munch on a cookie. Kurt's eyes grew large as he ate that cookie, the first he'd ever tasted.

I never gave up hope of reuniting with Michael. I sent him letters every day. Even though I never heard from him, I continued to write. This was the only way he could know where I was. I walked with Kurt in my arms to the railway station every day. There were several trains coming through town in the afternoon. I made this a game for Kurt. "Let's look for papa," I'd say. "Maybe today he'll be on the train."

One afternoon Kurt and I were standing at the railway station. A train pulled in and I walked alongside. As usual, I scanned each car intently, hoping that this time I would see Michael. My hopes had begun to dwindle. I almost skipped the last car, I was so discouraged, but something urged me on. When I reached the very last car, I glanced up and suddenly saw a familiar face peering over the window. Could that really be Michael? I hadn't seen him for so long I wondered if I'd recognize him when I saw him. I pointed to Michael and said to Kurt, "Look up there. He's your papa." Kurt squealed with excitement even though he had never seen his papa. I was so happy I cried. "How did you find us, Michael?" I asked.

"Margret, it was your letters. I got them all," Michael told me. He was choked up seeing me again after a year and a half, and his son for the first time. "I tell you, the Romanian and German armies are protective of their soldiers," he asserted. In minutes, Michael had climbed down and enveloped Kurt and me in a big bear hug. I wanted to ask him so many questions, but he told me clearly that he could not discuss anything about the army or where he'd been. That was fine with me, because I didn't want to know anyway.

I took Michael to the small house where we had been staying. I told him about the kindness of the Eberhardts. When I introduced him to them, Herr Eberhardt shook Michael's hand politely and apologized for his small home. He mentioned that the tiny bedroom upstairs where Kurt and I had been staying would not be big enough for Michael as well. He told us that we could all sleep in the living room. Michael slept on the couch, while I slept with Kurt in his crib.

Before I could ask, Michael answered the question foremost in my mind. "I only have a week here with you, Margret. Let's make the most of it." And so we did. After he had some time to get acquainted with his son, I took Michael to see my parents and Elisabeth, who were only three doors away. Then we went to see his parents, who were overjoyed to see him. Soon, too soon, the time came for him to leave and rejoin the army. Of course, I did not know where he was going. I only knew he would be off fighting somewhere. But I was happy to have seen him alive and well and feel his arms around me. My deep longing inside was satisfied until I bid him a tearful good-bye.

One day, Ebert, the Burgemeister, announced that his people did not have the room to continue to keep all the refugees with them. He added that the food supplies in the town were dwindling. He told all of us that we must move to other buildings. I bid the Eberhardts a sad "Auf Wiedersehen." Of course, my parents were moved too. They were placed in a wing of a school building in a tiny room next to the laundry. There was only enough space for one bed and a crib. An ancient iron stove occupied one wall. The Burgemeister had decided that my parents and Kurt could stay there. He then arranged for a room at the Gaststube (rooming house) across the street for Elisabeth and me. We spent our days with our parents and Kurt in that tiny room, and our nights at the Gaststube. Michael's parents were allowed to remain at the Horstman's farm.

This room next to a laundry room was in the wing opposite the class rooms. The teacher, his wife and their two-year-old son, Otto, also lived in an apartment at the school. They were a pleasant family. Otto was a lively boy who loved to run down the hall calling out, "Alle Mann zum Keller," ("everyone go to basement") whenever he heard the shrill sound of sirens. The basement was actually quite tiny. When we did go down, there was not enough room for anyone to sit.

Unfortunately, the sirens sounded frequently since there were air raids nearly every night. Schmalkalden, the larger town nearby, was bombed often while Hainsdorf, a small farming town, was spared. Still the bombing raids over Shmalkalden shook the buildings in Hainsdorf. I was frightened by the air raids since there were few air raid shelters. When the siren sounded in the middle of the night, Elisabeth and I would just lie in our beds with our blankets pulled over our heads, waiting for the siren to stop and the ground to stop shaking.

Kurt learned to walk in the tiny room by toddling from his crib to the window holding on with both hands. Then he'd go from the stove to the door. Unfortunately one morning the stove was hot. Kurt screamed when his tiny hands grabbed the hot stove. His hands swelled with blisters. I actually felt pain seeing my little son's blistered hands. Even though Kurt cried with pain, he was soon toddling about again on his chubby bowed legs. I proudly watched these first steps and wished that Michael was here to share the moment with me.

I found clever ways to find food for my family. I struck up an acquaintance with the woman who owned a small grocery store next to the Gaststube. This kind woman would often save vegetables for me, usually potatoes. *I* never ceased to be amazed by the fact that while no one had enough food, people shared generously.

THREE: The Americans Come

The war ended like a whisper in May of 1945. The news came slowly to us in Hainsdorf. I had little knowledge of what was happening in the outside world. One morning, American soldiers drove into the village in jeeps. The American commander announced an 8:00 p.m. curfew.

As soon as it was dusk, Elisabeth and I ran across the street to reach the Gaststube before curfew. We were careful to wait until a jeep full of American soldiers had passed. We chose to go up a back stairway at the Gaststube to reach our room and avoid the stairs by the bar. By now, the bar was packed with noisy soldiers. Once upstairs, I heard laughter, shouts and occasional screams from the bar below. Suddenly I heard a woman wailing, "My child, my child." As the noises from the bar grew louder and louder, my chest tightened with fear. I didn't know what was happening. Were Elisabeth and I in danger?

Now more scared than ever, I turned to my sister and said, "We can't just sit here. If they're looking for women, they'll come for us soon." I looked out the window and noticed a wide ledge. I called her over to look. "What do you think? Shall we go out there?" I asked. Elisabeth nodded and we climbed out the window and sat on the ledge, listening to noises below that continued unabated. "We have no choice but to jump," I told her. "When they open the door, they'll see us." Elisabeth nodded.

I looked below and saw welder's implements and tools stored in the fenced yard. Even though I felt the fall could be dangerous with all that equipment lying about, I gathered my courage and jumped. I was shocked that the fall was much farther then I had anticipated. What was I thinking? Did I want to be some kind of hero? I shook my head and then realized that this was our only chance to avoid any trouble. I landed on a tool with sharp edges, and my leg was cut.

"Margret, someone just opened the door," Elisabeth called to me. I stood still with the blood streaming down my leg. I told Elisabeth to jump and I would catch her. She did not hesitate but jumped and landed safely as I caught her by the waist and guided her away from the sharp implements. We sat huddled together in the yard. I put my coat around Elisabeth since she was shivering in her thin nightgown. Occasionally, we peeked over the high fence and saw jeeps moving slowly down the street. Then we saw men coming and going at the house next to the Gaststube where there were jeeps parked about. "The men got drunk, and that's what caused the trouble," I told Elisabeth.

We waited until daybreak and quietly opened the gate. We saw no one around and ran across the street to the school. I knocked at a window of our parents' room and awakened mother. She came quickly and asked what we were doing up at this early hour. I told her what had happened and she quickly let us in. Mother cleaned the leg wound and bound it with some strips of cloth. "The wound isn't deep," she said, "the only thing I'm concerned about are those rusty tools which cut your leg."

Elisabeth and I slept on the floor in our parents' room for the next few days until things calmed down and we felt safe again. The American Commander met with the Burgemeister and apologized for his soldiers' behavior. He reassured the townspeople that there would be no more drunkenness or attacks on women. After that, the Americans were helpful and passed out food and blankets around the village.

One day, I heard a sharp knock at the door of the school wing. I quickly answered and could hardly believe my eyes. Michael and Hans were standing there, dressed in casual pants and shirts. Gone were the uniforms. I was so happy I cried. Here were my husband and Hans. Then I noticed that Michael was walking with a limp. He explained that he'd been shot and the bullet remained in his leg. "But I'll be all right," he said. "And Hans has an infected hand and may lose a finger." They were wounded and had been in the hospital for a couple weeks prior to being discharged from the army. "We knew the Americans were occupying this area, so we rode bicycles around, asking for you and Elisabeth. Finally, we found you here at the school."

I called Elisabeth and she came running and she cried too She kept murmuring over and over, "Oh Hans, I can't believe you're here. I'd almost given up hope." She gently touched his bandaged hand. "What happened?" Hans shrugged and made light of his injury, saying his hand did not hurt so much now.

I spoke through my tears. "Now that you're here, Michael and Hans, perhaps we can go home." I didn't ask Michael about his leg wound. I didn't want to know anything about the war or any battles. I was just glad he had come back to me and Kurt.

Soon the American commander announced that they would be moving all the refugees in Hainsdorf by trucks to a displaced persons' camp near Eisenach. The commander said that the refugees would be sent home from this camp. I had many good byes to say. I went first to the teacher and his wife. Little Otto gave Kurt a big hug. Then I crossed the street to see the owners of the Gaststube, the woman grocer and the blacksmith. Later the Burgemeister came to say good bye. He was very sad and lamented that he did not know what had happened to his son, who had been drafted into the army. I also thanked him for his kindness. "Our five month stay here was very good, Michael," I said. "I've grown attached to these people."

There were many refugees like us being loaded into the army trucks. Finally my family and I climbed aboard with our meager belongings. "These trucks are better than the freight cars we had to travel in when we left our village." I said to Michael. "We're not in the dark and crammed inside, and we have benches to sit on." I hated to leave for yet another place. This time we would be in a camp and not a village. I didn't know what to expect, but at least I would be with Michael.

FOUR: Displaced Persons' Camps

Once at the camp, American soldiers directed us to a large hall. I strung blankets on wires for privacy. Michael and I slept on straw mats with Kurt sleeping between us. No sooner had Kurt laid down, then he began to cough, the loud bark of whooping cough. He coughed so much the other refugees told me that they hadn't gotten much sleep because of my son's coughing. I apologized profusely, but what could I have done?

The familiar soup lines had been set up for food. The first morning, Michael and I were suddenly enveloped in a firm hug by none other than Heinrich. He was excited to see us again, and I was elated, too. I was relieved to see him alive and well and couldn't imagine how he had found us. Michael and I watched as Heinrich found his parents in the crowd of refugees. Soon his mother was laughing and crying. She told me later that she was so thankful to see her youngest son. True to his word, Heinrich told me later that he had taken care of himself and made his way alone through Germany. He dressed like a laborer, and said that he had no trouble finding odd jobs along the way. "Now that you've found us, we'll make our way home together," I told him.

After two weeks we were moved again. This time to Jena, a city in eastern Thuringia. We had just gotten settled in the large hall there, when I noticed that many of the refugees were leaving the camp. Overnight, the number of refugees dwindled down until there were only two thousand, from the Baltic States and those of us from Deutsch Sankt Michael, left. Among these fellow townspeople were the Schillers, my cousins, a family of five. Soon I discovered why the people had left. I had heard rumors that the Americans were leaving, and the Russians would be in charge. I had doubted this rumor before, and now I knew that the hearsay was true.

After the Baltic people left, the only ones showing up at the soup line were those of us from Romania. I investigated and found that there was only three days of rations left in the kitchen. The Americans left Jena, and that same day, the Russian troops marched into town at 10:00 a.m. In a matter of hours, the Russians had herded those of us left into freight cars. They did not tell us where we were going, but within a few hours we arrived at the Bavarian border in the American sector. While I was leery of the Russians, I was upset that they would get rid of us so quickly. They mustn't want to bother with us or feed us, I thought. If we're gone, they get all that food left in the kitchen.

As soon as our train pulled into the station at the border, an American soldier walked up, shaking his head as he delivered a message from the commander. The American commander refused to let us in. I was shocked that we were turned away. Michael was furious. Next, our train was turned around, and we were told that we would be sent back to our village in Romania. Instead, our train went south toward Prague, Czechoslovakia. We arrived in Prague at 5:00 p.m. and were parked on a side track.

Michael, myself, and all our family were together in a freight car, along with the Schillers, and some others. We had no room to lie down or sleep. Civilians came to our train and offered to take us with them for a bath. But other people came quickly and warned us not to get off the train, since this was a plot to kill us. Although I was very frightened, I was determined to manage the best I could in the crowded train car. After all, I reasoned, I hadn't survived so much for so long to be killed now in Prague. Michael and I did not get off the train, and neither did anyone else. After a few hours, our train of eight cars, all full of Danube Swabians, continued on to Bratislava in Slovakia.

FIVE: Bratislava

After ten days with many stops along the way, we arrived in Bratislava, the capital of Slovakia. The train of eight cars was parked on a side track as soon as we arrived. We did not see any soldiers standing around, only an occasional local policeman walking by. We were left alone and no one came to offer us food or water. Since we had to fend for ourselves, Heinrich, Michael, and some other refugees found fields nearby and picked up the potatoes that were left after harvest. Michael made a stove of two bricks and a piece of metal, so we could cook the potatoes. We were nearly starving, but occasionally I found some milk to buy. At least we were at a station, where there was water available for us to drink. I also bathed Kurt. Sometimes Partisans came to our train, asking for women. I never left the train without either Michael or Heinrich with me.

We soon learned that this area was under Communist control. The war had officially been over for two months. It was now July 1945. I felt as if the Russians were everywhere. Michael and I discussed

317

what to do. "We're starving here—why can't we leave?" I asked. Michael agreed that we were foolish to wait around here without food and very little water. We'd probably all die.

One morning, the police ordered all of us off the train and then began to question some of the men. I watched as Michael and Hans spoke with them and I wondered what the police were telling them. There was much shaking of heads and shrugging of shoulders. Foremost in my mind was what did the police plan to do with us? There were about two hundred in our group, all from Deutsch Sankt Michael. We stood around the train uncertainly.

Michael and Hans came back, shaking their heads. "Once they found out we were Germans, they didn't offer anything, not even food," Michael told me. "They're just going to leave us in here in these freight cars on this side track"

"Don't they know we have a baby, and there are other children here, too?" I asked. "How long do they expect us to live in freight cars with no water or sanitary facilities? They're treating us like animals."

Michael shrugged. "We'll have to make the best of it until we can figure out what we can do." After a few days, Michael and Hans took matters in their own hands. They decided to go to the city hall in Bratislava to request permission to go to Austria. They had heard that many of our countrymen had gone to the city of Reid in northern Austria early in the war. I told Michael before he left that we must leave Bratislava no matter what.

Michael and Hans returned in a couple hours and described their meeting with a Dr. Vaceck to Elisabeth and me. "He appeared to be a top Communist. I explained that we were nearly starving and he seemed to understand, and gave us permission to leave," Michael said. "Hans and I then decided that we should exchange some of our clothes for hand carts to carry what is left of our belongings into Austria." I nodded, glad finally to be leaving Czechoslovakia. We passed the word along to the rest of the group, who agreed to leave, too.

We did not delay. That afternoon, Michael and I and our relatives, a group of nearly 20, left on foot. The rest, a group of about 175, decided to stay one more night. We crossed over the Danube River and into a corner of Hungary. From there, we planned to walk into the Russian sector of southern Austria. I pushed Kurt along in a baby carriage, while Michael, Hans and the other men in our group pushed the hand carts. Surprisingly, the guards at the Hungarian border were no problem and did not ask us any questions.

SIX: To Austria on Foot

A day later, the rest of the people from the train caught up with us in Hungary, about five to ten miles from Bratislava. "You were wise to leave," one woman told me. "Some of our women were raped."

As we walked along, everyone was talking about where they planned to go. The final destination was uppermost in all our minds. As I caught snatches of conversation I had the impression that most of us wanted to return to Deutsch Sankt Michael. Michael and I, at first had wanted to go home. Now we were having reservations. We knew that Romania was under Russian control. What kind of future would we have there? My parents wanted to return home. However, after they listened to my doubts, they, too, began to question what their life would be like under the Russians.

We arrived at a small town and were directed to a school house. Each family chose a section for themselves and stacked their belongings there. Those families with young girls hid them under blankets or piles of clothes. Even so, when the Russian soldiers came in, they managed to find and rape some of the girls.

The next morning, the majority of the people said they had decided to go back to Deutsch Sankt Michael. They planned to walk in the direction of Wein (Vienna) and from there they would travel back to Romania. Michael and I had talked until late in the night, and decided that the wisest thing to do would be to head toward Reid in northern Austria. We separated from this large group. Our families all agreed to go with us. Our group was now about fifteen: Michael, Kurt and me, our parents, Elisabeth and Hans, Michael's younger brother, Heinrich, and my cousins, the Schillers, a family of five.

We headed west toward upper (northern) Austria. Michael suggested that we stay off the main roads, because there were Russian troops on the highways. I pushed Kurt along in the carriage and walked with the women. I noticed that the Schiller's daughter and their two teen age sons walked along briskly, setting a pace for the rest of us. Michael and the men walked up and down the hills with their hand carts. They would pull the carts up the hills with ropes, and then use the ropes to hold the carts steady when going down hills.

Overnight, we usually rested in ditches, because we feared the Russian soldiers. Our husbands hid us under blankets because Russian patrols would search for young girls to rape. Herr Schiller and his wife kept their young daughter well hidden between them.

I often begged for food as we went along. We stopped at a house one day and a woman came to the door and said she didn't have much, but she gave me the biggest potato I had ever seen. Somehow that large potato was enough food for all of us. Fortunately we had kept those bricks and metal piece for cooking. Many people were sympathetic to our plight and shared food with us. However, the farther north we went, the fewer people would help us. I thought this was strange, because northern Austria was reputed to be the richest part of the country. We continued on foot and only once hitched a ride on a freight train.

Michael and I discussed where the safest place would be to cross from the Russian to the American sector. We knew there were Russian soldiers patrolling and had even heard stories of barbed wire. Michael drew a rough map of the area in the vicinity of Reid, and asked people along the way about the border. Many were willing to share information and give advice. No one felt too kindly toward the Russians, and some had relatives who had already crossed over. I watched as Michael studied all his findings and plotted a route. Michael and Hans decided that crossing in a rural area would be best, and they headed west for the town of Behanberg.

The Soviet zone was the largest in Austria, occupying most of the eastern half of Austria, while Britain had the southern area, the United States the west and France the southwestern finger.

As we walked along, an air of excitement built up among us when we sensed we were drawing closer to the border. I was amazed at the stamina of both our parents. They walked long distances every day without complaint. Amazingly, not one of us became sick. Since we were traveling in summer and into early autumn, the weather was pleasant, except for an occasional rain shower. We often slept in the fields or orchards along the way. A nip in the air reminded us that colder weather was coming. I was prepared and had gotten some warmer clothes for Kurt.

The closer we came to the border, the more we studied the terrain looking for just the right place to cross. Since we had decided to cross in a rural area, we hoped we would be near a small town once we had crossed over to the American sector. Michael, Hans, Heinrich and Herr Schiller held earnest discussions every evening.

SEVEN: A Dangerous Crossing

The closer we got to our crossing, the more impatient and eager I became to leave the Russian sector. I knew if we were caught crossing, we could be killed or arrested. I had heard awful stories of what happened to those caught. Apparently the Russians considered it illegal to cross from the Russian to the American sector, while the Americans did not consider it illegal to go from the American to the Russian sector. Very few people wanted to go in that direction.

Finally the men felt they had found just the right spot. We were at the stream near Behanberg, which formed the border. This stream was about 20 feet wide and flowing with a swift current. There was a small foot bridge near a farm with a large farm house on the Russian side of the stream. I looked across and saw another large farm house on the opposite shore on the top of a hill. The hill was clear of any trees or vegetation. I speculated that this could be a problem because anyone crossing the stream and going up the hill would easily be seen.

Michael told the group that this looked like a good place to cross. I pointed out the danger of the bare hill, yet he insisted that this was the best spot they had seen. A lot would depend on the farmer who lived on the Russian side of the stream.

We walked up to the farm house. The area was flat and the farmer's crops looked ready for harvesting in the adjacent fields. The farmer greeted us warmly and introduced himself as Herr Tanner. He welcomed us and offered us food and beds in his house in exchange for the men working his fields. "Besides," he pointed out, "If the Russians get used to seeing you in my fields, they will think you belong here." Although we had just met him and hadn't told him that we were planning to cross to the American sector, he appeared to know our intentions. He was very protective of us and warned us that the border was patrolled at frequent intervals by only one Russian soldier carrying a rifle on his shoulder. He added, "My sons are still away in the army, and I need help with my harvest." He appeared undaunted by the size of our group and told us he had a large house. I was relieved that he did not ask where we were from or if we were refugees. Yet I felt he surely must have guessed that.

When we walked into the yard, we were greeted by a flock of geese. Kurt had gotten down from his buggy and was toddling about. He was still unsteady because he spent so much time in the buggy. The geese were honking and flapping their wings. When they came up to Kurt, he began to scream and run away. I scooped him up in my arms. "They're only geese," I said comfortingly. "You've never seen

geese before. They just want to get to know you."
Kurt wasn't convinced and continued to cry. He
stayed in my arms until we went inside.

Herr Tanner introduced us to his wife and
explained to her about their guests. She was willing to
have us stay, but warned that we would be sharing
what little bit they had. She looked at Kurt, and
mentioned that they had a cow and plenty of milk.
Besides cows, they also had horses and pigs. "There is
room for everyone," Frau Tanner said. I offered that
we women could help in the garden or with whatever
tasks she needed help.

The house was indeed quite large, and was U-
shaped with three wings of bedrooms and, in the
center, a courtyard where the horses could enter.
Unfortunately there was an enormous manure pile by
the kitchen, and the odor often wafted inside. Michael,
Kurt and I were given a bedroom, and so was everyone
else. My cousin, Herr Schiller was given a bedroom
big enough for him and his wife, their young daughter
and two sons. I was amazed at the number of
bedrooms in the house.

Herr Tanner gave the men rakes and pitch
forks, and they quickly got busy in the fields the next
morning. I watched out a front window for the
Russian patrol and kept a record of his appearances.
Soon I concluded that he marched by about every 30
minutes, walking very slowly, carrying a rifle on his
shoulder. I kept a firm picture of this soldier in my
mind and memorized his schedule.

I told Michael that this would be our greatest
test of courage. "Thus far we have survived starvation,

fatigue from the constant walking every day and we
have avoided any major difficulty with the Russians.
We are now facing our biggest challenge."

When we had been with Herr Tanner for a
week, Michael and Hans walked across the bridge after
the patrol had passed and scouted the area where we'd
cross the border. They met later to discuss their plans
with Herr Tanner. He warned them to be careful since
people caught crossing the border were either shot or
sent to Siberia. Michael and Hans decided they would
take two days to cross. The men would go across the
bridge at night, and the women and children the next
day. They speculated about getting their belongings
across the stream. Herr Tanner took care of that detail.

Since he worked the land on both sides of the
stream, Herr Tanner could cross any time. He knew
his neighbor, Herr Kirchmayer, who lived in the house
on the hill across the stream, quite well. He said that
Herr Kirchmayer had a wagon and a team of oxen
which could carry our luggage up the hill. There was a
sturdy bridge further down the stream that could
accommodate the weight of the oxen and wagon. Herr
Tanner planned to ask Herr Kirchmayer to get our
belongings the next time he went across the stream to
his fields. He also said that the house on the hill was
as large as his. Michael told me all about this later. I
was overwhelmed by the kindness of Herr Tanner. I
felt strongly that he was putting his life in jeopardy by
helping us.

In the meantime, the men continued working in
the fields every day. Elisabeth and I tended the
garden, and the other women helped Frau Tanner in

the kitchen. Kurt enjoyed playing in the garden and gradually grew accustomed to the geese, even running about and honking with them. I enjoyed watching my young son run. I often worried that this long journey would harm him, and I wanted him to be a happy child. I prayed for this every night.

The time for our leaving was precipitated by the arrival of a Russian major and two of his soldiers. I was unnerved by the Russians' presence, and was very careful about what I said since the major spoke German. Herr Tanner put the major and his soldiers at the end of a wing, so they slept in another part of the house away from us. I observed that the Russians liked to drink vodka in the evening and sleep late in the morning.

As decided, the men left one night after the patrol had passed: Michael, Hans, our fathers, Heinrich, Herr Schiller and his two sons. Michael told me later that Herr Schiller was extremely nervous. Herr Kirchmayer came with his oxen and wagon down the hill and over the sturdy bridge. He loaded all our belongs and carts and took them across the stream and up the hill. The men would look less suspicious without carrying any belongings. Fortunately the Russians were back in their rooms by this time. The men were out of sight at the top of the hill by the time the patrol guard marched by.

That evening, I spoke with Herr Tanner and thanked him for all he'd done for us. We had been with the Tanners for three weeks. He told me that he would explain our absence to the major. "I'll tell him you were finished here and were heading on to Wien to look for work." I told him that I didn't want him to get in trouble for helping us. Herr Tanner shrugged his shoulders. "I'm not worried about those Russians. They're often not too smart. Besides the major hasn't paid too much attention to your group. I told him you were workers I had hired. I don't think he even knows how many of you are staying here.

Early the next morning, Michael and Hans returned for us women. I was ready and had told Kurt that we were going on a wonderful adventure today. We watched nervously from the front windows and, at the go ahead signal from Hans, Elisabeth and I,our mother and Michael's mother and Mrs. Schiller and her daughter carefully followed Michael across the bridge. We did not rush but attempted to appear casual as we walked up to the hill to the farm house and into the American sector into freedom. I felt my heart pounding and I squeezed Elisabeth's hand as we walked up the hill. My initial fear soon gave way to excitement. We had crossed the border.

I carried Kurt until we reached the top of the hill. I fully expected shots to ring out or soldiers to come running after us. Miraculously we reached our destination without any shots or shouts. Herr Kirchmayer greeted us and helped us unload our belongings. He kindly offered us rooms in his house. "Our house is empty now," he said. We stayed with him for two days.

On Sunday morning, he came along with us to guide us as we walked into the city of Styer, just two miles away from where we had crossed the border. We did not have to go through a check point; nor did we see any American soldiers around. We occasionally saw American soldiers riding about in jeeps. To our relief, they did not stop us or pay any attention to us.

When we started on our final leg of the journey, Michael observed that we could now walk on the main roads since there were no Russian patrols. The last 40-50 miles went by more quickly. We again slept in fields or barns along the way and washed in streams.

EIGHT: Austria to America

As we drew near the town of Wels, which was east of Reid and on our way, we noticed that the town had been heavily bombed. I asked if we could stop for a night and rest. Michael and Hans agreed, but they had other ideas. "With all these bombed out houses, we could easily get jobs in construction. Let's stay here and not go on to Reid." Elisabeth and I agreed. The rest of our group seemed happy to be stopping too.

As soon as we walked into town, we stopped at the Gemeinde Haus, the Burgemeister's office. He sent us to a school where refugees were being placed. No sooner had we gotten settled then Michael and Hans left to look for work. They found jobs with the R. Gerstl Construction Co. Skilled carpenters were in big demand, and they were assigned that day to rebuild a three story home with the front half missing.

There were a large number of refugees staying at the school. After a few days, I noticed that Kurt was scratching all the time. I looked him over and discovered that he had lice (Scabies). I told Michael that we would have to leave this place. Michael got permission, from Mr. Gerstyl and the owner of the house they were rebuilding, to stay there.

I met with the owner Rosina, an elderly widow, and told her about our family. Rosina was very gracious and invited all of us to come. She said she had plenty of room and we could all stay there while the men rebuilt the damaged sections. After we had moved in, I noticed that Rosina appeared scared and seemed to be avoiding us. After a few days, I was pleased to see that she had gotten used to us and appeared to like having us around. Rosina told me that she really had no family since her husband had died, and she had never had children. She enjoyed watching Kurt play, and often talked to him.

The house was three stories with the front half missing. My parents and in laws each had a bedroom. Hans, Elisabeth and Heinrich were given rooms on the second floor. Michael, Kurt and I slept in a large hall by a door. Rosina occupied her bedroom which amazingly had not been damaged. This house was in a beautiful section in the middle of Wels. Once we were settled in the house, no one even mentioned going on to Reid.

Heinrich helped Michael and Hans with the reconstruction of the house. After a short time, he told Michael that he was more of a mechanic than a carpenter. He looked around and soon found a job as a mechanic in a nearby garage. Before long Heinrich had a girlfriend. I laughed when he told me that he hadn't dated for so long he almost forgot how.

In the meantime, the Schillers had settled elsewhere in Wels. Herr Schiller could speak English, and he was hired immediately by the American army. Later he found a job with an architect who invited the Schillers to live with him and his family.

I thought back on our trip. We had started out in July 1945 and arrived in Wels on All Saints Day, November 1st. Our journey to Wels had taken about four months. I was grateful that we had all survived the trip. And now we even had a home to live in.

While the men worked on rebuilding the house, I took care of the cooking. The kitchen was on the ground floor. We survived on food stamps and rations. Everyone was given a ration of cigarettes, and I exchanged these for bread. Rosina gave her ration of cigarettes to the delivery people. I became acquainted with a grocer two doors away, and she saved food for us in exchange for our food stamps. Again, our mainstay was potatoes. A farmer let me glean in his fields outside of town.

I did not have to work because I had a child, while everyone else did. Elisabeth got a job in a factory. She told me that while the work was hard, everyone was nice to her. "I think the people are nice to refugees because they need workers in this town."

We had decided to keep our clothes in the attic. One day when I went up to get some pants for Kurt, I discovered that most of the clothes were gone. I was horrified at the thought that someone had stolen our things. I quickly called Michael and Elisabeth, and they agreed that this was a theft. "We really don't have a way to lock the doors right now," Michael pointed out. Elisabeth wondered if a refugee had taken them. I called the police. An officer came and looked around. He told us there wasn't much he could do, especially since the house was not completely restored yet and wasn't locked. He gave me a receipt for the missing articles so we could get more clothes.

Rosina took mother and me shopping; however, we found very little on the store shelves. The woman at the grocery store lent me her sewing machine. I was fortunate and found some material and made a few outfits for Kurt and some dresses for my mother and sister as well as for me.

As they worked on the house, Michael and Hans moved to the basement and completed the two apartments there so they were habitable again. I was glad to move down there and have some privacy. I also felt our belongings would be safer. Hans and Elisabeth moved to the other apartment.

I began to correspond with an uncle in California. When he learned of our plight he sent us boxes of clothes. My uncle also encouraged us to emigrate to America. He told me that he had heard from some other relatives who had emigrated a few years ago and were living in the Cleveland area. Soon I began receiving letters from the Cleveland relatives, who also encouraged Michael and me to come to America.

Hans and Elisabeth were married in 1946 by a priest from the small Catholic church nearby, a year after we had arrived in Wels. I saved up our food stamps and prepared a festive meal to celebrate after the simple ceremony. Their wedding reminded me of

Michael's and my wedding. Ours was also simple and in an uncertain time. I hoped they would be as happy as we had been, in spite of the war.

We also began to receive mail from Romania. Hans received a letter from his mother back in Deutsch Sankt Michael, who begged him to come home. He was her only child, she wrote. Hans said he felt compelled to go. I tried to dissuade him and encouraged him and Elisabeth to emigrate to America with us. But Hans and Elisabeth were determined to go home.

I talked with Elisabeth one day when she returned home from the factory. "You know, Elisabeth that the Russians are there now. Do you really think they'll let you alone, to live your lives in peace?"

Elisabeth looked troubled. "I've thought about nothing else since Hans made this decision to return. I don't know what our future will be like there, but he is my husband. He is determined to go back and be with his mother, to be there when she needs him. Hans told me that since our village is so small, he doesn't think the Russians will bother us." I sighed and hugged my sister and told her, that I would miss her terribly.

A few weeks later, Hans and Elisabeth began the long journey home. Michael and I were worried and anxious to hear from them, to know that they had arrived safely in the village. Instead, Hans and Elisabeth showed up back in Wels, saying they were stopped at the Hungarian border by the border police and jailed for a short time.

I felt surely that they would stay for awhile in Wels and rethink their plan. Elisabeth and Hans remained firm in their resolve to reach Deutsch Sankt Michael. They decided to try the trip a second time.

Elisabeth sent me a note later telling me that this time they had gotten through into Hungary and then into Romania. Elisabeth sent a second letter, this one addressed to our parents, and she encouraged them to come home. "Your house is empty now," she wrote.

I feared for my parents taking that long trip back to their village. I tried to persuade them to emigrate with us; however, mother insisted that they wanted to see their village again and live in their own house. My father simply said, "I'm a farmer. I don't know what I'd do in America. I want to return to my own land."

In late 1946, my parents started on that long journey back to their village. I was quite worried when we did not hear from them. Finally I received a letter from them after they had arrived in Deutsch Sankt Michael. Mother wrote that they were also stopped at the Hungarian border and put in jail. When they were released, the Hungarian border police took their shoes away, so they could not walk any further. Mother went on to say that some nice people in the border town gave them old shoes to wear so they could continue on their way. "When we finally got home," she wrote, "We found that we had come home to nothing. Our house was dilapidated and most of our furniture was gone. We will have to start over."

Life sounded very tough, and I was sorry to learn of my parents' plight. I remembered our comfortable house and the well tended fields they had left.

Although I would miss my family who were now back in the village, I was still determined to emigrate to America. Michael and I both maintained that a future in Romania was not promising. We thought especially of our son, Kurt. Michael's parents and Heinrich also decided to emigrate.

Heinrich was very excited about going to America. He told me that he felt a man could have a great future there. "I've asked my girlfriend, Anna, to come along, but her father won't let her. He told me that Anna is his only daughter, and America is too far away. Anna will go along with her father's wishes. As much as I love her, I'm not staying here. As much as I will miss her, I'm coming with you to America."

Kurt had started kindergarten in Wels at age three and loved it. He was very happy at his school and had friends. He often told me that he did not want to leave. He tried to imagine a big trip over lots of water and brought home his drawings of a big ship sailing over the ocean. I questioned how much he really understood. He gave one of his drawings to Rosina, and she looked sad. She was like part of our family and adored Kurt.

Our day of emigration drew near, thanks to relatives in the United States. An aunt and uncle had sent us the necessary papers to apply for emigration. These relatives also arranged our passage to the United States on the Queen Elizabeth in April 1950. Michael's parents would have to wait another year before their emigration papers could be processed.

For me, this would be another big journey, farther than I could imagine. I would call another country home, and learn a new language. But I knew I could do this. I had met many challenges and adjusted to many changes. I looked forward to my future with hope and confidence.

EPILOGUE

Margret and Michael emigrated to the United States in 1950 with their son, Kurt. They built their home in the Cleveland area in 1953 and still live there. Margret can look out her kitchen window and see some of the homes her husband has built.

Michael took English classes at night, while Margret worked as a cook at the school Kurt attended. When Kurt was in first grade she studied along with him and learned English. Kurt found school very difficult at first, because he didn't speak any English. Kurt eventually married and lives in the area.

Heinrich lived with Margret and Michael at first. After he married, he moved to Cleveland, and continued to work as a mechanic. Michael's parents emigrated to the United States in 1951 and are now deceased. Margret and Michael have kept in touch with the Schillers, who also emigrated to the United States in 1951.

They have visited their relatives in Romania, and found life far different than when they lived there. Many of the citizens were eventually driven out and forced to settle in an obscure, barren area of Romania. Margret's parents are deceased. Elisabeth and Hans eventually emigrated to Augsburg, Germany because of the terrible conditions in Deutsch Sankt Michael. Margret and Michael visited the people in Hainsdorf, Germany and also in Wels, Austria.

They kept in contact with those friends who had taken them into their hearts.

Margret is happy that she has friends both in her community and also in the Danube Swabian groups. She and Michael attend a monthly function of the Danube Swabians. They also contribute to the upkeep of the cemetery in Deutsch Sankt Michael, even though the village is gone.

ABOUT THE AUTHOR

Betty J. Iverson is a nurse by training, but writing is her first love. She has a Bachelor of Science degree in Health Science from California State University at Hayward. In her first book, TABEA'S STORY, her interest in World War II stories increased and she researched the history of that era. She has narrowed her writing to stories about women and has interviewed all her subjects. She has the uncanny ability to sense a story and the interviewing skills to unearth amazing events. She lives in Moraga, California with her husband, Ted. Three of their four children and two grandchildren live nearby, while one son and family live in southern California.